PRAISE FOR *WHERE WILD ROSES BLOOM*

The perfect ingredients for a sweet read: unique setting, a delicious plot, and a yummy romance.

~**Patty Stockdale**
Author of *Three Little Things*

In *Where Wild Roses* Bloom, author Angela K. Couch gives historical romance readers everything they could ask for—vibrant descriptions of the Canadian prairie, rich historical details, a heartwarming romance, and a swoon-worthy Mountie.

~**Kelly Goshorn**
Award-winning author of *A Love Restored*

Angela K. Couch has written a beautiful, emotional story of a woman wrestling with the consequences of her choices and the constable who must overcome the revelation of her secret to determine where his heart truly lies. I loved the true-to-life struggle. It is a story that will long live on in my heart. Fans of sweet historical romance won't want to miss this book!

~**Crystal Caudill**
Author of *Counterfeit Love*

Other Books by Angela K. Couch

A Rose for the Resistance, 5: Heroines of WWII (Barbour)

Heart of a Warrior (Prism Lux)

The Blacksmith Brides: 4 Historical Stories (Barbour)

Hearts at War Series (White Rose Publishing)
The Scarlet Coat
The Patriot and the Loyalist
The Tory's Daughter
The Return of the King's Ranger

The Backcountry Brides Collection (Barbour)

Dancing Up a Storm: 9 Christian Short Stories (HopeSprings Books)

Mail-Order Revenge (independently published)

I Heard the Bells (independently published)

A Bit of Christmas: 6 Christian Short Stories Celebrating the Season
(HopeSprings Books)

Out of the Storm (HopeSprings Books)

WHERE WILD
ROSES BLOOM

ANGELA K. COUCH

FICTION
An Imprint of Iron Stream Media
Birmingham, Alabama

Where Wild Roses Bloom

Iron Stream Fiction
An imprint of Iron Stream Media
100 Missionary Ridge
Birmingham, AL 35242
IronStreamMedia.com

Library of Congress Control Number: 2021949051

Scripture quotations are from The Authorized (King James) Version. Rights in the Authorized Version in the United Kingdom are vested in the Crown. Reproduced by permission of the Crown's patentee, Cambridge University Press.

ISBN: 978-1-64526-334-0 (paperback)
ISBN: 978-1-64526-335-7 (ebook)

1 2 3 4 5—25 24 23 22
MANUFACTURED IN THE UNITED STATES OF AMERICA

DEDICATION

*Dedicated to the legacy of the North-West Mounted Police
and the role they played in settling the Canadian West
I know and love.*

ACKNOWLEDGEMENTS

A huge thanks to all those who have helped bring this story to life. To Jonathan—there is no way I could write, homeschool, and keep up with five young children without an incredibly supportive husband! Thank you for giving me wings. To my kids, who play together and take care of each other while Mommy is writing. To my critique partners, beta readers, and editors for making my work shine. And to the Lord for all His tender mercies that made this possible.

CHAPTER 1

Helena, Montana–June 1910

This was all Channing's fault. And still, his words taunted.
You belong to me now.

Lenora Perry's steps faltered. What if he was right? What if leaving had been in vain?

"No." She said it aloud, needing to hear it, to feel it as strongly as when she'd snuck away from The Pot O' Gold Saloon over three weeks ago.

Deep in her handbag, the last of her funds huddled beneath her derringer. Seventeen cents remained to her name—that and her grandmother's ruby ring. Lenora pulled the small ring from its nest in a handkerchief. She would rather not part with her last family tie, but what choice did she have? Maybe she should have taken the train from Cheyenne all the way to Oregon.

Home.

And defeat.

Would Papa even let her back in the house? Surely not if he knew how far she'd fallen.

"Out of the way, miss!"

Lenora jumped aside as a large man barreled past her with a sack over his shoulder. She tucked her grandmother's ring away and straightened the hideous green skirt she'd exchanged her satin one for—the shade of sickly moss or the cud that cattle chewed. She'd rather wear a sack and ashes, but as far as penance went, this gown shrieked poetic justice.

"Now what?" she murmured under the ruckus of the jostling crowds and wagons rolling past. She'd spent weeks seeking employment and watching her resources dwindle. But always the same answer. No one had work she was suited for. She wasn't quick enough at washing dishes to please most and had never been talented enough with a needle to survive as a seamstress. The one thing she was good at was the thing she couldn't turn to. Not here, where only saloons and businesses of ill repute sought singers.

With no other direction to turn, Lenora started back toward the hotel. She could easily curl up under the bedcovers for the rest of the day. Her head hurt enough to justify lounging ... if she knew where her next meal was coming from. Never mind money for her room when payment came due in a couple of days. Perhaps it was time to look beyond Helena and try another town for employment.

A man stepped from the doors of the hotel as she reached the corner of the large brick building. He pressed his hat over sun-bleached hair while looking about.

Lenora lunged out of sight. Heart thudding against her ribs, she stole another glance at the hotel doors. A large mustache curled down around the man's mouth. Fred Anderson. Channing's lackey. She had heard he'd once worked for Pinkerton's detective agency but hadn't put much stock in the rumors. Men talked all the time, and few of their stories were true.

What now?

He'd probably already learned of her residency at the hotel. She hadn't thought to use an assumed name—had thought herself out of Channing's grasp.

You can't ever leave ...

His words sank deep and clutched her insides. She couldn't return to the hotel for her few belongings. Too risky and hardly worth it.

Unless all this was for naught.

Lenora sank against the ridged bricks and glanced heavenward. She was at the end of her means and had no prospects but to return to Channing and the stage. Perhaps she was already too lost to be saved.

It's too late to change who you are.

No, she told the whispers in her head. She dug the small ruby out of her handbag and grasped it in her palm. Her mother would prefer she sell the heirloom than herself.

Though your sins be as scarlet, they shall be as white as snow ...

She sneaked another glance at Fred as he sniffed, crinkling his beak of a nose. She'd come this far, and she'd not go back. Not now. Not ever. Deeper into the narrow passage, she hurried until she found the alley. She quickened her stride, the race of her pulse pressing her forward to the next street.

"Reckon this'll do ya?" The toothpick of a man who spoke hefted a sack of flour into the back of a chuck wagon. A table-like platform lowered like a tailgate, allowing shelves and cubbies to be loaded with supplies.

A second gent followed, an older man with a face like rawhide, toting a side of bacon and a bag of salt. "At least for a few more miles." He tucked his load under his arm and shook the hand of the first man, who looked to be the proprietor of the mercantile, apron draped to his knees.

A shuffle behind her spun Lenora to the shadows of the alley. Fred's large form appeared on the same route she had taken. Their gazes met, and his mouth curled up.

Lenora scampered to the front of the buildings and out of his view for the little good it would do. He had tracked her this far. Was there anywhere to run, to hide?

"Good doin' business with you," the mercantile owner said, shaking the other man's hand. "All the best with your travels."

Travels. Lenora skirted around the front of the wagon, seeking an entrance. The canvas cover was pulled taut, secured to the sides. The wagon shook as the men lifted the overlarge tailgate and secured it in place. Lenora hefted her hem and scrambled up onto the bench seat at the front.

"Thank you," the second man said with an easy drawl, circling toward her.

Trying not to jostle the canvas, Lenora slid over the back of the seat and onto the lumpy piles of supplies below. She wriggled into a crack and ducked her head.

The thud of footsteps at the mouth of the alley proclaimed Fred's arrival, but the driver of the chuck wagon had already mounted his seat.

Lenora clamped a hand over her mouth and tried to still her breath.

The released brake squeaked, and the wagon shifted.

"Did you see a woman come through here?" Fred's voice sifted through the thin canvas concealing her. "A pretty blonde about yea high?"

The wagon heaved forward, and Fred's voice faded.

Lenora closed her eyes, not allowing for relief. Not yet. She prayed the turning of the wheels and plotting of horses' hooves drowned out the drumming of her heart. Only as the sounds of the town grew distant did she dare fill her burning lungs.

Just when she thought things couldn't get worse. She should have realized Channing wouldn't give up so easily, but not because he loved her. Oh, no. He might spout his adoration, even pretend to care about her, but the Pot O' Gold was the only thing that mattered to him. She was nothing more than an effective tool to draw customers. A singer. Ha! New York had been her goal. Boston. Europe. Channing had never been able to bear that she wanted more than his *fine* establishment. And now he'd won.

He had destroyed her.

"You comfortable back there, or do you want to climb up on the seat now?" The wagon rocked to a stop, and the driver turned to look down at her. "We're away from town and that man looking for you."

She rose, and he offered her a hand in maneuvering to the front. Her face flamed. "I'm sorry, I …"

"No need for apologies. We're not far from town, so you'll have time to figure out what to do next on your way back."

"I can't go back." Panic spiked through her. Fred would be

watching the train station and probably have left her description with the liveries, as well. Only a matter of time before he found her again.

The man's frown deepened along with his well-set wrinkles. "You thinkin' to come along?" He looked her up and down as though assessing. "This ain't no pleasure ride, ma'am. Got near five hundred head and a passel of cowboys. No place for a lady like yourself."

He appeared a full decade older than her father, and surely, a man so anxious about her well-being would serve as a safe chaperone. "I can pay my way and help you with the cooking. At least to the next town."

A grunt offered little promise.

"Please, sir. I won't be any trouble."

With a harrumph rising from the back of his throat, he dragged a weathered hand down his whiskered chin. "I'll take you out, but you're going to need the boss' approval to continue on with us." He shook the reins over the horses' backs. "Giddyap, there."

Lenora clasped her reticule on her lap and allowed breath to seep back into her lungs. "You have a name, sir?"

"Don't everybody?" He chuckled. "Mine's Lyman McRae. I assume you have one as well."

She'd already reaped the consequences of using her real name at the hotel, a mistake she had no wish to repeat. "Lena Wells." Her mother's maiden name suited her fine.

"Pleased to make your acquaintance, Miss Wells. I hope you don't have too much trouble on your tail."

"I ..."

"No need to say anything, miss. What lays behind you ain't no one's business but your own." He kept his face forward, driving the horses on past a scattering of homes and smaller farms. They jostled over the rutted path for most of an hour before dropping into a valley where a sea of white-faced cattle grazed. The odor and din rose to meet them.

A man on horseback reined their direction, loping over the low brush. His attention riveted on her, he scowled. Not the usual reaction she garnered from men. "What is this?"

"A woman. Thought you'd recognize that easily enough." McRae didn't twitch, but she could almost hear a smile in his voice.

"What are you doing with her? We have cattle to move."

"Then I suggest you get back down there and start moving them. I'll follow along like I always do."

The man stared hard, as though daring McRae to look away and admit defeat. Minutes—or perhaps very long seconds—passed.

"Mr. McRae agreed to let me come along just as far as the next town." Lenora forced a smile. "I assure you, I'll be no trouble."

"Trouble?" The trail boss laughed. "Did he tell you where we're headed? Where the next *town* is? We're driving these cattle straight north and across the border. We probably won't be seeing more than a supply depot until we reach Canada."

Canada? She hadn't planned on going *that* far north! But what other option had she? Maybe the great white north would be far enough away from Channing Doyle that he would give up pursuit. And far enough away from the crumpled remains of her dreams that she could forget them.

"I ain't had nothing to do with that!"

"You *didn't* have anything to do with that." Edmond Bryce dropped his flat-brimmed Stetson to the desk and faced the youth who stood across the small office from him. "But Mrs. Hanover insists she saw you, and six of her hens are now missing."

Matthew Lawson stiffened his jaw, but his gaze dropped. "I was just fooling around."

"Do you still have the hens?" Edmond pressed.

The boy glanced away.

"Matt."

"I traded them."

Edmond shook his head and dropped into his chair, frustration gnawing. "You're not a child anymore, Matt. This is no longer a prank, but theft."

Matthew Lawson's eyes grew wide. "You can't lock me up, Constable. You can't. Ma needs me. She'll worry something fierce if I ain't home by supper."

Seventeen was a hard age to become the man of his family—Edmond knew that better than most—but all the more reason for the boy to learn responsibility. Edmond leaned forward and eyed Matt, gratified to see the sweat beading on his brow. "Now listen here, I—"

"Constable!"

At the shout from outside, Edmond gave Matt a look to stay put and stepped to the door.

Frank Walsh already had it half open. "Constable. The boss is having a fit. Says he'll run them off if you don't."

"Run who off?" With the ranchers in the area, it was always something.

"Whole herd of cattle tromping right over our best grazing."

"Whose cattle?"

"Don't know."

Edmond snatched his hat from his desk. He shot a look to the fidgeting boy but spoke to his friend. "How many cattle are we talking about?"

Frank was beside him like a shadow. "Few hundred of them white-faced Herefords."

Edmond took his rifle from the rack on the wall and sent another glance at Matt in his worn Levi's and shirt hanging off him, meant for a man twice his size. Probably his father's, God rest his soul. As much as Edmond wanted to let him hurry back to his family's farm, Matt had done wrong and needed to recognize the consequences of those actions. "Come on back here, son. I need to leave, but we're not done with our conversation."

"You know where to find me, Constable Bryce. I'll come back in the morning if that's what you want."

"Afraid not this time." He'd let the kid off too easy for too long.

"You're going to stay right here until I get back."

"You going to lock me up?"

The panic in his voice tugged at Edmond's resolve, but he nodded and motioned to the open cell door.

Stiff-jawed, the young man stepped inside, and Edmond locked the door. "I'm not liking this any more than you, but you've got some thinking to do. Start with your mother and siblings. They depend on you now."

Matt looked to the solid wood floor, blond hair flopping over his eyes.

Huffing out his breath, Edmond hurried to follow Frank out to where the horses were tied to the hitching pole. He slid his rifle into the scabbard and swung into his saddle. If ever there was a bane to his existence since joining the North-West Mounted Police, it was hotheaded cattlemen.

They rode hard, the horses' hooves churning up the distance between them and the extensive miles of Bar L land. Thirty years ago, the range had leased at a cent an acre. Men who'd first settled here found it easy to spread out across the prairie and foothills.

The bellow of cattle and calls of cowboys rose over a low hill before the river of deep red came into view. A dozen riders flanked the herd, pushing the cattle forward. With the foothills and Rockies rising behind them, it was a sight to behold. But he hadn't come to admire the view.

Edmond eased Ranger, his bay gelding, into a trot and reined him toward the back of the herd. Keeping the cattle moving was in everyone's best interest.

A rider from the herd met them halfway down the slope. The man looked Edmond up and down before speaking. "You're one of those Mounties I was told about. I dare say you stand out like a British flagpole."

Edmond refused the impulse to straighten his red coat, tailored after British regimentals. "I'm Constable Bryce, and this is Mr. Walsh from the Bar L Ranch. You are?"

Instead of answering, the man tugged the brim of his sweat-stained hat a fraction lower. "Are we in some sort of trouble, Constable?"

"Might say that. This is Bar L land. They're not too keen on that herd of yours trampling the grass. Where are you bound?"

"The Mackenzie ranch. According to the map Mr. Mackenzie sent, this looked to be the shortest route." His dark eyes glinted with challenge.

Frank's saddle squawked, and Edmond shot him a warning look. Frank wore a chip on his shoulder the size of the Northwest Territories when it came to Lawrence Mackenzie. Knowing his story, Edmond couldn't fault him, but he had more than a grudge to worry about right now.

"Mr. Mackenzie would have known better than to send you directions through this valley."

The trail boss' lip twitched under his thin mustache. "I didn't say that, exactly. Just said it looked to be a shorter route. I aim to get these cattle to their destination before nightfall."

Edmond gritted his teeth against the urge to tell the man what he thought of his detour and make them go back around the longer way to their destination, but that wouldn't benefit anyone. Two miles north would see the cattle off Bar L land, while any other direction would prolong the trespass.

Frank kicked his black mare, wedging himself into the middle with a string of curses. "You turn these cattle around or—"

"Or nothing," Edmond inserted. "That would do more damage, and you know it."

Frank glared at the herd, then yanked his horse around. Dirt clods flew from his animal's hooves as he tore away.

The trail boss tipped his hat and turned his horse. "Obliged, Constable." The mockery in his tone grated Edmond's nerves.

He nudged Ranger to follow. "I'll ride along a ways to make sure there's no trouble."

The man turned a glare on him. "We can take care of any trouble ourselves."

From the two revolvers holstered on his hips, Edmond could very well imagine how. "Afraid we do things a little differently up here, Mr.—?"

"Jim Greer." He yanked his horse to a full stop.

Edmond tried for a congenial smile while keeping his gaze hard. "Law and order are important to us, Mr. Greer. I'd appreciate it if you keep that in mind."

"Of course, *Constable*, of course." He raised the reins, but his hand froze mid-motion as a wagon rolled over the rise, following the herd from a comfortable distance. Its canvas cover bobbed and swayed, denoting the roughness of the trail.

"Actually, Constable, I have just the thing if you want to make yourself useful." Greer nodded toward the wagon. "Where's the closest town?"

Edmond bit back a retort on how he'd like to make himself useful. "Cayley is about five miles east of here."

"That's just fine."

Edmond eyed the wagon as it grew nearer. It had the look of a typical chuck wagon.

"She's been with us since Helena. After two weeks, I'm ready to be rid of her. Should have never let her come along."

"She?"

Sure enough, perched on the seat beside a lean fellow was a piece of calico—the ugliest green he'd ever seen. The woman wrapped up in it, though …

Greer headed in that direction, and Edmond followed. He nodded to the lady, who stared back at him with open interest and eyes a man could lose himself in. Couldn't tell the color because of the distance, but he imagined they were blue to go with the honey locks she had pulled up under a man's straw hat.

"She's all yours, Constable. I'm done keeping my men in line around her."

Even dressed as she was, Edmond could understand the distraction. The smudge of dirt on the delicate slope of her jaw and a faint scattering of freckles over the bridge of her nose only complemented her creamy complexion. "Who is she?"

"Miss Lena Wells. That's as much as she's told anyone. I'm guessing she's on the run from someone, but as far as I'm concerned, she's no longer my problem."

Which made her Edmond's.

Lena Wells. He reached into the front pocket of his coat to retrieve the shortened pencil and small notebook where he collected names, then decided against recording hers. Cayley had little to offer a single woman. Unlikely Miss Wells would be in his jurisdiction longer than a day or so.

CHAPTER 2

L enora lowered her eyes from the penetrating gaze of the uniformed man and his silent interrogation. "Who's that?"

Lyman McRae kept the wagon moving, following the herd as they had for the past weeks. "That is the sheriff, you might say. The mounted police sent out to keep peace in the west."

So very different from any lawman she'd ever seen. His scarlet coat fit to the breadth of his shoulders, adorned with brass buttons down the front. Even his dark pants wore a thin gold line on the sides. Where a US marshal or sheriff sported nothing more than a silver star to set him apart, this man's whole apparel would be visible for at least a mile.

But from that distance, one wouldn't be able to see the strong lines of his face or the depth of those brown eyes. And that would be a shame.

As they approached, she straightened and again attempted to maintain his gaze.

"Miss Wells." Greer brought his horse alongside the wagon. "Constable Bryce will escort you to the nearest settlement."

Constable. So proper a word. Stalwart and unforgiving. She could very well picture the same to describe this man in his immaculate uniform and lack of expression.

"Thank you, Constable."

He removed his flat-brimmed hat to reveal thick but trimmed locks beneath—a shade lighter than his eyes. "The train comes through Cayley regularly now. I'll see that you're set up at the boardinghouse tonight, and you can be on your way tomorrow."

Lenora managed a gracious smile, though the biscuits and beans she'd snacked on an hour ago threatened to return for an encore. What good would a train do her when she'd given her last possession of any worth to Greer for allowing her passage north?

Before she could ask what manner of town Cayley was, Constable Bryce busied himself in conversation with the trail boss. Neither man looked pleased with the other, but they kept their voices civil. She didn't care for talk of boundaries and cattle—had heard enough of the latter to keep her for a lifetime—with her future so unsure this far away from everything she knew. If only she'd listened to her father sooner, but she'd been distracted by the idea of beautiful clothes and the admiration of every man who had walked through the doors of the Pot O' Gold.

A weathered hand squeezed her shoulder, and she looked to McRae beside her on the seat. His expression held understanding. But then, he was the one she'd trusted with her story—or, at least, part of it.

"That creek marks the boundary between the Bar L and Mackenzie ranches."

Constable Bryce's comment gave Lenora a start. She looked out over the rolling green to the snaking stream ahead. Their destination. All those smelly, bawling cows would finally have a home.

What about me?

"As soon as you're across, I'll be on my way. Stay in the valley, and another three miles or so will see you to the main homestead and ranch."

"Riding along to keep us from trouble?" Greer's tone held an edge.

"Fortunately, while ranchers up here are just as ready to protect their lands, they're also generally eager to keep the peace." Bryce cut his gaze to the other man, a warning in his brown eyes. "Just see that you take the long way around on your way back."

"I'll pass the message on to the boys, but I plan on staying for a season or two. I've worked ranches from Texas to Montana and aim to stretch my horizons a bit farther."

"Then I suppose we'll meet again." The lawman seemed to try for impartialness, but the corner of his lip turned down a little.

"I'm sure we'll learn to stay out of each other's way," Greer replied with a nod and a heel to the rib of his animal. The horse lunged forward into a gallop.

Good riddance. Lenora would not miss the company of so irritable a man, and she had the feeling Constable Bryce—who withdrew a small notebook and jotted down a line or two—shared her sentiment.

"You're probably well familiar with the area." McRae spoke from beside her.

"My father was with the first North-West Mounted Police that Prime Minister MacDonald sent west in seventy-three." Constable Bryce tucked the leather-clad notebook back into his breast pocket. "I was born and raised out here. My sister and I keep our family's homestead not far from Cayley."

A look of respect smoothed McRae's wrinkles.

Lenora opened her mouth but closed it just as quick. It wasn't her place to ask what became of the rest of his family, and it didn't matter to her. He was merely another tie in the endless railway she traveled over.

Still, it was hard not to watch him as he nudged his horse to follow the herd. Probably just the scarlet uniform that drew her eye.

"You can continue on to the ranch with us if you want to," McRae told her.

Lenora jumped at his comment and dragged her attention away from Constable Bryce.

McRae pulled his hat off and fanned a fly away. "How's Greer to know that Mackenzie has no work for you?"

Lenora looked ahead at the billowing dust in the wake of so many hooves. As much as she liked the prospect of employment and staying close to McRae, she'd seen how some of the cowpokes looked at her—how most of them looked at her. On the drive, there'd never been a lack of tasks, and McRae had been almost constantly at her side. Things would be different once they reached the ranch.

Lenora shook her head. A town was a much more suitable location for a lady. "Best I go now."

"Would you prefer I drive you to town later?"

The temptation to accept his offer mounted within her, but who could say how long it would be before he'd was able to get away from the ranch? "Should I not trust the constable?" He'd not looked at her with any suggestion of lingering desire. A spark of attraction, perhaps, but respectfully.

"Seems a decent enough man."

But ...

Though he didn't say it, the sentiment lingered between them. *But* he was a man in his prime. And she would be alone with him for the duration of the ride to the settlement, however far.

"Not all men are like that." She said it out loud for her own sake and his. To remind herself that not all were like the men who had crowded into the saloon every evening to leer up at her as she took the stage. The ones whose hands tried to possess her if she stepped too near. Some men were salt of the earth like her father, God-fearing and hardworking to provide for their families. Some men were like McRae, gentle and protective. And others were stalwart and honorable. From the little she'd seen of Constable Bryce, she imagined him to be like that.

Water sprayed over the backs of the cattle as cowboys forced them through the stream.

Was her situation any different? What choice did she have but to press forward?

Any confidence she held fell away as the last cow bounded across, and the wagon drew closer to the stream that marked another ending.

Constable Bryce waited for them. "I need to head back to Cayley. You're welcome to follow, ma'am."

"On foot?"

His dark brows rose. "You have no horse?"

Lenora shook her head. Maybe she'd have to ride along as far as the ranch, after all.

"How much luggage do you have?"

She held up her reticule, heavy with her small pistol, and always kept close at hand. She'd abandoned everything else in her haste.

He eyed her in disbelief before swinging down beside the wagon. "Let me help you mount, then."

"I ..." She cast a helpless glance at McRae, removed the hat from her head, and handed it to him. "Thank you."

He nodded his reply.

Moistening her lips, Lenora slid to the edge of the seat. The constable's ready hands lowered her to the ground.

"Are you comfortable sliding behind the saddle and riding astride, or do you prefer sidesaddle?" He loomed over her, almost a head taller.

She'd never ridden sidesaddle before, but her skirts were considerably longer than the last time she'd sat a horse as a young girl. She tugged at the fabric covering her legs and grimaced at their lack of fullness. As much as she'd rather ride with her legs placed securely on either side of the horse, neither did she want her hem hugging her knees.

Lenora glanced up to see the constable frown. "You sit sideways in the saddle, and I'll ride behind. That will probably be best." He placed his hands at her waist. "Are you ready?"

A short nod from her, and he lifted her high onto the horse's back.

She grabbed the horn, but the horse shifted under her, threatening to spill her over backward.

"Easy, boy." Constable Bryce grasped the reins, then passed them to her. "Hold the horse steady while I swing up behind."

With two fingers, Lenora gripped the thin strips of leather while she continued to cling to the horn. No way she was letting go. With her luck, she'd land in one of the many rose briers sporting simple pink flowers and a bounty of thorns.

Hat tipped back, the constable stepped into the stirrup, leaned into her, and hoisted himself up in one smooth motion. His arms surrounded her, one hand taking the reins. "Comfortable?"

Not at all! But she nodded just the same. She glanced at McRae to say goodbye, but he looked steadfastly at the constable.

"You a believing man?"

The horse moved under them, and Lenora became immediately grateful for those powerful arms.

"I am," Constable Bryce replied.

"Then see that you take good care of that little girl. Both God and I will hold you accountable."

The arm behind her relaxed. "She'll have nothing to fear as long as she is in my protection, sir."

"Good." More of a grunt than a word, and he snapped the reins over the horses' backs.

As the wagon creaked forward, the horse under her turned. Lenora gasped at the motion, and Constable Bryce's arm tightened around her.

"You're all right." His voice rumbled in her ear.

"It's been a while since I've ridden. And never like this." Her face heated at how ridiculous she must appear.

"You can hook your leg over the horn if that makes you feel any more stable."

"It might … if it didn't require me to let go of the horn with my hands."

His chuckle vibrated against her back. "However you are most comfortable. It's a few miles back into town."

"Is walking on my own feet an option?"

"I'm afraid I haven't the time." Though said with no terseness, she could feel tension travel through him. "Why don't I keep my eyes on the horizon, and you swing your other leg over? My sister finds astride by far the easiest ride. I'll let you down before we reach town if you like."

"Um …" As much as she wanted to agree to his plan, she'd

witnessed the effect the sight of her legs had on men. "I'll make do as I am."

"If you're sure."

The horse picked up his pace to a trot, almost jostling Lenora from her precarious perch before smoothing into a hip-jarring lope. *Lord, please keep me on this horse.*

The plea came unwanted to her thoughts, and she quickly locked it away. Even if she desired God's intervention, she asked too late. He, like her own father, would want nothing to do with her now.

Edmond usually enjoyed racing across the prairie ... but never quite so much as right now. Though he shouldn't. The poor woman clenched the saddle horn as though her life depended on it, oblivious to the fact he would never let her fall. Hard to ignore the way she fit against him or the loose stands of corn silk escaping down her neck.

Better to consider why the young lady would travel so far on her own and under such an unusual arrangement. Jim Greer had suggested she was on the run. It wouldn't be the first time someone had come north to escape American justice—just the first lone woman Edmond was aware of. If running from the law was the case, what was she guilty of? What manner of woman hid under a dingy gown and demure looks?

"How much ... farther, Constable?"

He eased Ranger to a walk. The horse might not require a breath, but Miss Wells would no doubt appreciate one. Matt would have to wait on him a little longer.

"About three more miles."

She shifted in the saddle, a small sound breaking from her throat. "Maybe I should switch positions as you suggested."

"Whoa." He pulled Ranger to a stop and relaxed his hold.

Two narrowed eyes, as blue as he'd assumed, peered over her shoulder at him. "You promised to keep your gaze averted while I situate myself."

"And I intend to." He tipped his head to look straight up, only then feeling the kink building in his neck. A spasm of pain begged for release, but he held his position. The saddle shifted, and the horse did the same.

"Can't you hold him steady?"

"I'm doing my best, but you're bumping my arm."

"Oh." The sigh she released moments later was less than pleased. "I'm ready, but …"

"But?"

"I am trusting you to be a man of decorum, Constable. Please keep your vision on the horizon and let me down before we reach town."

"Yes, ma'am." Thankfully, she hadn't outlawed smiling. One thing was certain, even if she was running from an unfavorable past, she was a woman of virtue. He had to respect that.

They continued on their way, both of his arms now comfortably around her and resting on the pommel while she maintained a vice-like grip on the horn. Ranger pulled at the bit, eager to get home to his oats, but Edmond kept him to a walk. He might not have another opportunity to uncover the mystery surrounding this woman.

"Where are you bound for, Miss Wells?"

She tensed. "Does it matter?"

"Helps to know whether to put you on the north or southbound train."

"I … I'm not sure I wish to take the train."

He frowned. "There's not a better way out of Cayley. We're quite isolated."

"Isolation may not be so bad." Her voice hinted at sadness. And fed his curiosity.

"Why are you here, Miss Wells?"

"Am I under suspicion for an infraction of the law, Constable?"

He settled back. Suspicion, yes, but he would keep that to himself for now. "No, ma'am."

"Then I would prefer you keep your focus on reaching our

destination. You may show me the boardinghouse you mentioned and the train station if you wish, and then I shall no longer be your concern."

Except, as long as she remained in the area, she would be his concern. Seeing newcomers suitably settled was part of his job.

As promised, Edmond stopped Ranger on the western outskirts of Cayley and looked to the sky while Miss Wells disembarked. He'd offered to assist her, but she'd declined. Her sense of propriety kept him in place until her boots were the only things visible under her hem.

He joined her on the ground. "I need to pause at my office for a moment before taking you over to the boardinghouse."

"Hence your rush to return?"

He nodded. The dinner hour was spent, and he'd not had time to ask Mrs. Newton at the boardinghouse to take over something for his prisoner. Just as well. Matt had probably had enough time to think on his crimes.

"Do you always walk so quickly?"

Her terse question brought him around to where she hurried across the rutted prairie after him. Though low, the heels on her boots did her no favors.

"Usually, but I can probably make myself slow down if I try."

She huffed out a breath, already winded, as she came alongside him. "That would be appreciated."

As they entered the community, Edmond considered how Cayley must appear to a woman like Miss Wells. While her apparel did not set her apart from other frontier women, her manner and tone made him question what life she was accustomed to. Most certainly not a hamlet with hardly a main street. The stockyard and train station, almost one and the same, stood at the heart of the town with other businesses and homes spread out to the east—a questionable planning flaw seeing how often the wind blew from the west.

The small log building designated as his office and the jail waited up ahead. A woman stood from the steps and hurried toward him.

"Mrs. Lawson." Edmond straightened his hat. "I meant to send word to you as soon as I returned."

"Word already reached me, Constable Bryce." She hugged herself, the furrows on her brow deepening. Her eyes appeared more sunken than the last time he had paused at their ranch, her cheeks more hollow. The past year and a half of widowhood had transformed her. "It's true, then?"

"I'm afraid so." He tied his horse to a hitching post and started up the steps. Better they speak of her son away from the public eye.

"Who's this?"

Edmond turned back, having almost forgotten Miss Wells on his heels—though uncertain how that was possible. He motioned both women inside. "Miss Wells has been detained in town to wait for the next train." He closed the door behind them. "Now, Mrs. Lawson, I—"

"Mama?"

The call from the cell sent Grace Lawson across the room to her son.

Matt's dirty hands gripped the bars. "I'm sorry, Mama. You shouldn't have come."

"Did you do it, Matthew? Did you steal those hens from Mrs. Rundle?"

The boy opened his mouth to speak, then glanced at Edmond and dropped his head. Answer enough.

"The Rundles will have to be recompensed for their loss." Edmond sat behind his desk to record whatever agreement they came to.

"How many?"

"Six."

She winced. "I have some fine hens, good layers." Mrs. Lawson turned away from her son. "We will take them to the Rundles' homestead first thing in the morning along with our apology and promise that Matthew will not go near their property again." She shot her son a look as though daring him to argue.

He stepped back and dropped onto the narrow cot.

"It's not just the Rundles' property I am worried about. Complaints of Matt's behavior and mischief frequent my office on a weekly basis. He's no longer a child and needs to face the consequences of his actions according to the law. Another incident like this ..."

"We understand, Constable." She glared at her son. "Don't we, Matthew?"

"Yes, ma'am." He stared at the floor.

"Can you release him?"

Edmond hesitated. Then nodded. He took the key from his pocket and swung open the door.

Matt rose and moved to pass by, but Edmond gripped his sleeve. "We have laws for a reason, and they are for you and your family as well. To protect you. With your whole life ahead of you, don't make the law your enemy."

The boy pulled free and hurried out the door, leaving his mother to mumble a goodbye before following.

Edmond dropped the key on his desk and slumped into his chair. "What am I going to do with that boy?"

"I thought you handled the situation quite well."

He glanced back to find Miss Wells watching him. "I'm not so sure. His mother is the one paying the consequence. Not him."

"But if he loves his mother, he will bear the burden. I think his greatest punishment was having his mother see him behind those bars. The shame ..." Miss Wells glanced at the floor, her lips pressed thin.

"Shame can be a powerful deterrent." He folded his arms across his brass buttons while studying her. "It can also be a reason to run away." Though he hadn't fully discounted lawbreaking yet.

When she raised her eyes to his, fire ignited in their blue depths. "You said there was a boardinghouse. I'm weary and would appreciate you pointing me in the right direction rather than trying to read my soul. I have done nothing illegal in this country of yours, so please rest any concerns you may have on that point."

She started for the door, but he caught her arm before she could step into the waiting sunshine. He'd done the same not two minutes earlier with someone trying to leave his office, but this didn't feel at all similar. His pulse kicked up its rhythm when she looked up at him, sparks in her glare. Another kind of spark concerned him more.

Edmond cleared his throat. "But you don't deny breaking the law before you came across our borders?"

"Someone may harbor a difference of opinion on the matter, but as far as I'm concerned, I've done nothing wrong." She tugged away. "So, unless you intend to lock me behind those bars of yours, let me go."

He held up his hands, not sure if he should continue his questioning or apologize. Probably the latter, so he straightened his coat and pulled the door closed behind them.

CHAPTER 3

Lenora let the constable take the lead, glad to be the one to watch him for a change. This lawman in red saw through her too easily.

"After you, ma'am."

Constable Bryce stood at the front of a two-story home bathed in white, door open.

Maintaining some distance, she stepped past him and was met by raucous laughter. Men's laughter. All too familiar. She backed out until a hand pressed against her spine.

"It's all right. Sounds like you aren't the only boarder Charlie has."

"Charlie?"

"Yes. Charles Newton is the proprietor. He's a good man."

But a man. A boardinghouse run by a male and filled with others of his gender.

"Ah, good evening, Constable Bryce!" A bear of a man with a beard to match thumped down the stairs leading from the second floor. "Who's this you're bringing me?"

The constable stepped around her to greet Newton with a handshake. "This is Miss Wells. She needs a room for the night." He glanced back and gave half a smile, a charming gesture if she wasn't so uncertain about the situation. "Also, a hearty meal would probably do her a world of good."

"Of course. One of my best rooms just opened up. I pulled the stew off the fire but won't take a minute to have 'er warm again."

Another burst of laughter from a back room made Lenora flinch.

"Aw, don't mind them, ma'am." The burly man swatted at the

air as though dismissing the sound. "Got a few boys who will be headed out to the Bar L first thing tomorrow. They're just enjoying a relaxing evening in there with some cards."

The deep red of Bryce's coat tightened across his shoulders. "Should I be poking my head in there, Charlie?"

"Naw, they're behaving themselves. I'll make sure they don't give the lady any trouble."

"That won't be necessary, sir." Lenora drew herself up to her full five feet, eight inches. "I won't be staying. Thank you for your trouble." She spun and plunged out the door before either man could protest.

The constable caught up with her far too quickly. "Why won't you stay? You heard Charlie say he'll make sure you don't have any trouble. We have no fancy hotel here. There's nowhere else for you to go tonight."

"You expect me to remain in a house full of *men*?" She kept walking. "I'd rather sleep in that jail of yours."

"Wait? Is that the problem?" He caught her arm and pulled her around. "Charlie has a wife. She was probably busy in the kitchen or upstairs making up beds."

That information may have appeased her a few minutes ago, but there was no way her pride would let her return now. Lenora withdrew her arm from his hold and dusted her skirts. "I assure you, Constable, the cot in your jail will be comfortable enough for me tonight." So long as she didn't consider who else may have slept there—or the possibility of fleas and bedbugs. It would be for no more than one night. Tomorrow she'd figure out her next steps.

"You rode hundreds of miles with a passel of cowboys but won't stay in a boardinghouse because a few men are there?"

She leveled a glare at him. Only a man wouldn't understand the difference. "Out on the trail, they were always together, night and day. And Mr. McRae—I trusted him."

"But you don't trust me?"

Lenora lifted a shoulder. She wasn't ready to make a final verdict on that yet. "Why would I suggest you allow me to stay in your jail?"

Not the most desirable accommodations but better than backing down from her stance. She was too tired to do that. Once her course was set, it was easier to close her eyes and push forward. She had nothing left but stubbornness.

"You are not spending the night in the jail, and that's final."

"How can it be final? What if I were to break a law? Would it not be your duty to lock me up?"

His closely shaven jaw slackened, then stiffened, as though he had let himself in on a joke. "Which law are you considering breaking?"

Hands on hips, she took in the small settlement. A mercantile and other small shops. Livery. The boardinghouse. And homes. "What if I were to poach a chicken like that boy you locked up earlier?" She cocked her brow at him and received the desired result.

The corners of his mouth turned up. "You'd have to catch one first."

"You think me incapable?"

"Don't take that as a challenge to prove your abilities as a chicken wrestler." He held a hand up in defeat. "You win. Let's get you settled for the night." He moved to the door of the jail, but instead of opening it, he shoved a key into the lock and gave a quick turn. Then moved toward his horse.

"Where are you going?" She hurried after him, not braced for the panic clutching her chest. Did he plan on deserting her to fend for herself? With no funds and nowhere to spend the night? The mercantile and other shops appeared to be closed for the evening, so it was too late to ask about employment, never mind room and board. Why hadn't she listened to McRae and continued on to the Mackenzie ranch?

"*We're* going home." Constable Bryce motioned her forward.

"Home?" With him?

"Home." He boosted her into the saddle before swinging on behind. "My sister will probably appreciate the surprise."

Home. The word, and the gentle way he said it, settled into her heart, opening it and making it bleed. And sisters. She missed hers and wondered if they ever thought of her. Saddle horn gripped, she turned her face away enough to cover any emotion she was incapable of hiding in her exhaustion. She closed her eyes and pictured Mama, soft but sturdy Mama. In her blue gown and with golden waves down her back, she looked every bit like an angel. A lump expanded in Lenora's throat. What a blessed little girl she had been. How had Papa ever convinced Mama to leave Ohio for the frontier where work wore fingers raw and the sun turned fair skin to leather?

Oh, Papa. As much as she complained about her father, she did love him. Had thought to make him proud, make him see she could be everything he told her she couldn't. She'd go east and prove him wrong.

But he'd been right, and she'd only made it a short distance from home.

Until now.

Yet she was further from her dream than ever.

The sun skimmed the peaks of the Canadian Rockies, and the eastern sky darkened. A chill moved down her spine. She rode away from the only settlement for miles with a lone man dressed in a red coat and a flat-brimmed Stetson. She had learned through experience that most men were not to be trusted. Other than the uniform, was this one any different?

It wasn't long before darkness stole in around them, leaving no sign of the trail. If there was one. The stars appeared in patches, most blotted out by clouds. Lenora locked her jaw against a yawn, but it still watered her eyes. She had to stay awake, couldn't trust this stranger enough to fall asleep in his arms. How far had they come? Or, more importantly, how much longer before they reached their destination? She glanced over her shoulder, hardly able to make out the constable's face though only inches away.

"What's wrong?"

She settled back into the saddle. "Nothing."

"We've not much farther to go."

He sounded confident enough. Much more so than she this far

from anything resembling civilization. A safe place to lay down was all she asked for, to close her eyes.

"Look straight out in front. That flicker of light."

"I don't see anything." She shook her head, impatience spurred by an overwhelming ache for sleep. "There is no shame in admitting you're lost."

"I have no problem admitting when I'm lost." His voice held a chuckle. "But I have nothing to admit tonight."

"I don't believe you."

"You think we're lost?"

"No." She sighed. "You probably know the area well enough. But I do think you would have difficulty admitting to being lost even if you were."

"You are such a good judge of character? You know me so well after only a few hours?"

Far too many hours ago, in her opinion, seeing that most of their acquaintance they'd spent on the back of this horse. "I know how men are."

"And how are men?" The flatness of his tone warned her to bite her tongue, but she was past heeding and couldn't push aside the heat rising through her with thorns that scratched from the inside. Channing's fingers had left bruises on her arms more than once.

"Egotistical. Bullish." *Pigs.* "Men don't admit when they are wrong …" *or when they are in the wrong. They take what they want.*

A tear rolled free, making her very grateful for the dark. She was too exhausted to hold her emotions at bay. They swelled within her, demanding release.

The constable remained silent, making it even harder to conceal the cry welling within her. She bit her lip hard, focusing on that pain so she didn't have to confront the guilt tearing at her heart. Much easier to pretend it didn't exist, to blame Channing.

Constable Bryce shifted behind her. "Please don't judge all of my gender by your previous acquaintances."

Though spoken quietly, the chastisement rang through her.

His arm pressed against her, reining the horse to the left, toward a lantern hanging from a hook on a covered porch. The home was fully visible and so close. And yet she'd not seen it until now.

An excited yapping welcomed them, and a collie burst from the house as soon as the door swung wide. A woman followed, donning a shawl. "Edmond?"

Bryce swung from behind Lenora and led the horse the last few feet.

A grin spread across the young woman's face. "Now this is a sight I feared I'd never see."

"Quiet," he growled. "Miss Wells needs a place to stay for the night. Please show her into the house while I unsaddle Ranger and put him up."

As soon as he had set Lenora's feet on the ground, he paused to address her. "This is my sister, Melina. Let her know anything you need." Without so much as a nod, he started to the barn with the horse.

His sister snatched the lantern from its hook and hurried after him. Winged insects were quick to follow with an incessant buzz as they danced off the glass. "You'll probably need this, Edmond."

He took the lamp and continued on his way, the light glowing off the red of his coat.

Melina turned back, her smile only slightly subdued. "What has him so grumpy?" She raised a brow and then took Lenora's arm. "Well, never mind him. I'm starved for company and conversation. Come inside and tell me about yourself. How did you meet my brother? Or need I ask? I suppose he came along in the line of duty, eager to the rescue."

"I suppose you can say that."

Melina closed the door behind them and hurried to the fireplace to position another log over the low-burning embers. "The nights still get cool. Why don't you sit down nice and close, and I'll bring you some tea and supper from the kitchen?" She motioned to an open doorway flanked with portraits on either side—one of a man in uniform and the other a woman closely resembling Melina, though older. "The kitchen's through there. Our parents' bedroom is there beside the stairs, but they are no longer with us, so Edmond insisted I stay closer to the fire. You look exhausted and are probably ready for a nice warm bed. I'll fetch your supper, and then you can retire if you wish."

"Thank you." A meager offering, but the best Lenora could manage. The sitting room was welcoming with cream walls, two stuffed chairs, and a wood rocker. A small table against one wall held an intricately woven doily and several books, including what appeared to be a family Bible. A painting of the Rockies hung nearby. Comfortable for such a rustic location.

Instead of sitting by the fire, Lenora moved to follow the chipper girl, probably no more than a couple years her junior, but paused at the chessboard set up on a low crate beside a chair. She paused and lifted one of the knights. Smooth, stained wood carved with skill. Much nicer but similar to Papa's set.

A pang of regret stole into her heart. She returned the piece to the board and continued into the modest but homey kitchen. Red and blue fabric formed a beautiful array across the table. It was thicker than any tablecloth she'd ever seen. She fingered the flowered pattern stitched over its entirety.

"Oh, let me get that out of the way." Melina hurried to fold the large quilt. "I lay my quilts over the table while I stitch the edges. I hadn't planned on company tonight and can never be sure when Edmond is coming home or staying in town."

"It's beautiful."

A blush crept into Melina's cheeks. "It gives me something to do with my evenings when I'm alone. Porter, my dog, is nice to have around but isn't much on conversation. At least, not much more than he welcomed you with."

"I understand." Not that there had ever been a lack of people in her life, but Lenora was well acquainted with loneliness. Even in a room of little sisters or loud cowboys.

Melina set the quilt on one of the five chairs and hurried to the cast-iron stove hosting a Dutch oven. "I always keep something warm until I go to bed in case my brother does come home. There's not much, but some bread will stretch it enough for the two of you."

Lenora was about to sit when the front door opened. The black-and-brown collie bounded into the room, panting hard but more from excitement than fatigue. From the way the dog's back end wagged with its tail, she doubted the animal ever tired.

Slower and much heavier footsteps followed.

Lenora straightened and backed away. "Leave the food for your brother. I'm too weary to eat a bite." Or to sit across a table from Constable Bryce after the end of their last conversation. "If you have a glass of water I can beg and will show me where I can sleep, I'll say goodnight."

"Of course."

Lenora stole a glance at the constable. *Edmond Bryce.* Tall and stalwart and far too handsome in that scarlet coat of his. "Excuse me." She was forced to brush past him to exit the kitchen. His disapproving glower followed her. But of course, a man like him would object to a woman like her.

The bedroom door closed, and Edmond sighed. Though not looking forward to more conversation with Miss Wells tonight, neither did he wish her to go hungry on his account. As soon as he'd stepped into the kitchen, her spine had stiffened, and she'd begun her retreat. Maybe he should have lingered a while longer in the barn as he'd had a mind to.

Minutes passed, and no one returned, so he washed his hands and dished up half of the soup from the pot on the stove. He'd intended to sit down with a loaf of bread to tame the hunger he'd been hosting since midday, but his desire was premature.

Offering in hand, he moved to the bedroom and rapped on the stained cedar. Womanly mumbles rose and died before the door opened a crack. Melina poked her head out, mouth already open with something to say.

"Oh." She took the bowl and smiled at him like a little imp, brown eyes twinkling. "I'm impressed."

Knowing exactly what the little matchmaker was thinking, Edmond shook his head and retreated to the kitchen. Now he could eat without guilt encouraging indigestion. Peace of mind was not so readily available.

I know how men are.

Miss Wells' words pestered him, as did her anger. No, not anger. Something deeper, a self-protectiveness. He'd seen enough wounds to recognize one festering. He'd also been around his sister long enough to recognize the tremble in the woman's shoulders and the slight sniffle Miss Wells attempted to conceal.

"She's settled for the night." Melina swept into the kitchen and plunked down on the chair across from him. "I'll make up a pallet on the floor by the fireplace for as long as she's here."

He swallowed his spoonful of potato and onion. "Just for tonight. And you'll sleep upstairs. I'm used to roughing it."

"Exactly. I need more adventure in my life, so I'll take the floor." Her smile dared him to continue the argument.

"Either way, the train is due tomorrow afternoon. I'll let you take her into town and see her off. I'm behind on my rounds."

"I don't mind." She leaned her elbows on the table, resting her chin on her hands. "Just sad to see her go so soon."

The thick cream clung to the back of his throat, and he shoved away from the table for a drink of water. Melina had been the one to insist on returning to live with him, but he'd never felt comfortable about the arrangement. It was a lonely life on the prairie with a Mountie as your only company. He'd seen Mother face that seclusion, but she had thrown her energies into raising three children while Father was on duty or away. Melina just had the farm.

At least, someday she would marry—probably one of the many young ranchers or hands who slowed to look twice when they passed her in town or at church—and have someone besides a uniform to build her life around.

As for him, he'd do his duty as his father had. His country and maintaining the law came before taking a wife and starting a family. Maybe someday he'd find a wholesome, hardworking woman who would stand by him the same way his mother stood by the Mountie she had given her heart to more than thirty years earlier, but he was in no hurry. And he certainly wasn't settling for a woman on the run.

CHAPTER 4

Cigarette smoke and the perfume of whiskey hung on the air like the embrace of success ... but Channing Doyle knew better. Less than half the tables held occupants when the room should be filled. The pathetic wailing of the brunette perched on the stage scratched his nerves and gave answer for the lack of patrons. Not that her voice was horrid, but she was hardly the *Lovely Lenora*. Channing drew deep on his cigar before grinding off the glowing ash clinging to the end. Lenora's disappearing act would be his ruination.

Your own fault.

He doused the voice in his head with the last of his brandy and pushed from the corner table—his favorite haunt for keeping his finger on the pulse of his establishment. A weakening pulse.

Ye are no better. Ye'll fail. Ye'll not ever amount to anything more.

Gruff and thick with an Irish brogue, his father's voice taunted, prophesying his demise. His fate.

"No," Channing growled. He clenched his teeth and forced a smile at the several regulars sitting near enough to hear his protest. "Evening."

He skirted the table, pushed through the curtain to his office, and hit the equivalent of a brick wall. Fred Anderson scooted out of the way.

"I've been waiting for you, Mr. Doyle."

A surge of hope died with a quick glance around the room. No Lenora. "I wasn't told you were here." He sat behind the large oak desk littered with order forms and notices of payments due. "I thought I told you not to return without her. What happened?"

"Gone without a trace."

Channing slammed his palm onto the desk, ignoring the sting spiking through his hand. "Unacceptable!" A sensation akin to panic rose in his chest and clamped his throat as though Da's hands clutched him again.

"Then I don't know what you expect."

"I expect you to bring her back here. She stole from me." Though the jewels that he had bought for her use were the least of his worries. As was the debt she owed for every extravagant frill she had left behind in her room. He'd been on the brink of failure before she'd arrived and was quickly plummeting again. The one thing he despised more than his dependency on her was proving Da correct.

He needed her.

In more ways than he cared to admit.

"You have to find her."

"There is only one direction I can think she went, and it's not likely."

Channing grasped what remained of hope. "What? Where?"

"I did hear about a large cattle drive passing through the area the same time she disappeared. A lady claimed she saw a girl with similar coloring to Miss Perry near a chuck wagon just before it rolled out."

Channing pushed upright. "And you didn't follow her?"

Fred shifted the bulk of his weight to his other foot. "They were long gone by the time I talked to the woman. And the chance of her—"

"Go after her."

"All the way to *Canada*? I need more funds."

A curse formed on Channing's tongue, but he fished into his vest pocket for the key to his safe. He'd have Lenora back. Mistakes were made, but he'd set them right. Just as soon as he found her.

Anderson left the room with a month's worth of wages and more for travel, and Channing sank into his chair. He'd invested a fortune in Lenora Perry. Probably much more than she was worth.

He laughed out loud, but bitterness only penetrated deeper. The Lovely Lenora had always considered herself better than him, always wanted more than he could give. She'd come with eyes bright and focused eastward. The Pot O' Gold, though one of the finest saloons in Wyoming, had never been enough for her.

He'd never been enough.

Channing swept his hands over the desk, and a flurry of papers scattered over the Persian rug, covering the ornate design of crimson and blue. "I'll find her." And if his business failed, in the meanwhile, she would reap the reward.

CHAPTER 5

Blackness. Lenora opened her eyes to the shadows of night, but the oppressive darkness stretched deeper, sinking through her. Flitting memories of her dream—or rather, nightmare—lingered just beyond her grasp. She blinked, confirming her eyes were open as she reached for the derringer beneath her pillow. Springs squeaked under her. A mattress. Not the hard floor of McRae's chuck wagon.

Of course not. She closed her eyes and allowed her breathing to steady. The red-coated lawman. The home of a Mountie. Safety. More than she'd felt in a month—in years, really. Last night, she'd kept her small gun close, only out of habit. She'd learned to take comfort in the smooth handle and the cool curve of the trigger.

Lenora sat and felt for the lamp Melina had placed on the bedside table. Her fingers brushed something hard. It toppled, and glass shattered on the floor. Her gasp merged with a curse, but there was nothing she could do about her blunder in the dark. Yet another mistake. At least, she couldn't smell spilled oil, so hopefully, only the chimney had shattered. Impossible to know for sure until morning.

Lenora flopped back onto the mattress and pushed the disaster from her mind. Other images quickly took its place. Last night's awkward maneuvering to avoid Constable Bryce. *Edmond* Bryce. His sister's chipper conversation and eagerness to make Lenora as comfortable as possible. Melina even lent a nightgown and laid out a dark-blue skirt with a cream blouse for morning so Lenora could launder her single dress and unmentionables.

Lenora stretched her arms over her head. Was it wrong to anticipate the stalwart Mountie seeing her in something more attractive than green rags? She could finally wash her hair and pin it properly. Though maybe she would leave some waves on her shoulders. Men liked that. She'd not brought any makeup, but perhaps Melina had a little color to add to her lips and some powder for her face. The last two weeks in the sun had ruined her complexion.

What are you doing?

As much as she didn't want to acknowledge the thought, it remained. She'd sworn to leave that life behind her, but, deep inside, she couldn't set aside the desire to be beautiful. She missed the attentions of men. Their praise.

Look what vanity got you.

Nothing but emptiness and an oppressive sickness that resided in her center. Was it possible for a heart to fall ill?

Better to listen to her parents' advice, though belated.

Sleep distant, Lenora scanned the room. Despite the hint of moonlight in the single window, all remained in shadow.

Oppressive darkness matched the torments of her own mind as it wandered, against her will, to the last few weeks at the Pot O' Gold. Thoughts of Channing. His kisses. His hands …

She jerked back into a sitting position and swallowed against the sourness clinging to the back of her tongue. Her stomach rolled. Nausea climbed.

Water. And maybe a pot or a bush.

Pain sliced through her bare foot, spasming up her leg before she'd realized what she'd done. She yelped and threw herself back onto the bed, which sang along with her cry.

Idiot. Idiot!

She pulled her foot upward and gingerly felt for the wound. A shard of thin glass protruded from her arch, and wet warmth flowed over her fingers.

What now? Cry for help or find a solution to her own stupidity? Again.

Teeth clamped, she sniffed hard. The pulsating pain in her foot did nothing for the churning in her stomach.

Footsteps pounded down the stairs before hesitating at the door. Relief sank through her, and warm moisture tickled her cheek.

"Miss Wells?" Sleep clung to Edmond's voice, making it gravelly. "Are you all right?"

She swatted at an unwanted tear. "There's glass."

The door opened slowly, and Melina pushed in front of her brother with a candle. "What happened?"

"Glass ... on the floor."

Edmond took the candle from his sister and motioned her out. "Fetch a lamp. I need more light." He needed his boots too. His feet were bare, but at least he moved carefully, candle low to shine a light on the fragments of curved glass beside the bed. He made a wide circle, hooking his holster on a wall peg as he passed. "What happened?"

"I bumped the lamp in the dark." She turned to accommodate his approach from the foot of the bed.

"Hold this." He passed her the candle, eyeing the sizable shard embedded in the sole of her foot. There was no way to know how deep the puncture. "Do you always sleep with your gun?"

"What?" Lenora followed his gaze to the derringer beside the pillow.

"Did you feel unsafe?" He slipped his hand around her ankle.

She nodded toward where his own revolver dangled from the peg. "Did you?"

"You screamed." A lock of hair fell over his brow as he leaned to examine her foot. "I like to be prepared."

She winced at his gentle prodding. "As do I."

Edmond raised a brow, an all too attractive look on the man with his hair messed from sleep and undershirt hugging his solid chest. It appeared all he'd taken time to don was his pants, the suspenders still hooped at his thighs.

The room lightened as Melina stepped inside.

Edmond glanced at his sister. "I need a basin of water from the kettle and some cloths. A cloth first."

Melina slipped away but returned in a moment and tossed a small towel at him before disappearing again.

"I'm going to pull the shard so we can see how deep this cut is." Edmond met Lenora's gaze and gave a commiserating smile. "Can you hold that light a little higher?"

She leaned back, bracing on her elbow while raising the other hand with the candle—trying her best to hold steady so the wax wouldn't spill beyond the small holder's tray. Blood dripped from her foot and had stained the intricate design of the blue and cream quilt. One of Melina's masterpieces, no doubt. She'd ruined it. Just as she had ruined their lamp and their sleep. And so much else.

"I'm—"

A jolt of pain stabbed through her foot and stole her apology. Edmond tossed the bloodied shard on the floor with the rest of the glass. He pressed the towel over the deep gash to stanch the flow, but the damage was already done.

Black spots blipped in her vision, and the light wavered in her hand.

"Careful with that." He took the candle while maintaining pressure over the wound. "Lay back."

She gave no complaint, biting down on her lower lip to keep from crying out as she dropped her head onto the pillow.

"We'll wash the wound well, bandage it, and then you can go back to sleep. Maybe Mel can make some tea to settle your nerves."

A laugh broke from her throat and then a moan. "Water is fine. I just wanted a drink of water."

"I'll fetch that next," Melina answered as she entered the room. She brought the basin to the foot of the bed along with some clean rags and then shifted the bedside table closer and set the lamp on it. Even with shoes on her feet, she carefully chose her steps. "I'll also fetch the broom."

"And a needle with thread."

Lenora jerked upright. "A what?"

Edmond lowered the candle to examine the gash before setting it aside. But not quickly enough to hide his face's lack of color. "Just one or two stitches." Why did he sound as though trying to convince himself?

"Have you … have you done this before?"

Done this before? At her words, Edmond was twelve again, watching his four-year-old brother's blood stain the jagged rocks Auguste had fallen to. His screams pummeled Edmond with renewed force. He swallowed hard … and pressed the memory back.

"Yes." He tried to say it in the most reassuring way possible. Auguste wasn't present to share his opinion of Edmond's abilities or show the jagged scar that remained down his shin and across his palm. Edmond had gained more training since then, but the prospect still brought moisture to the back of his neck.

Miss Wells didn't appear at all reassured. She clutched the pillow across her chest as she lowered back down onto the bed.

"Do you want a swallow of whiskey to help with the pain? We have some on hand for cleaning wounds, but no one will think poorly of you for needing some."

She shook her head, and his respect for her grew.

Melina returned with everything he'd requested, including the small bottle of alcohol. With the whiskey trade one of the main reasons for the formation of the North-West Mounted Police and one of their greatest banes in the early years, Father had never condoned drinking—especially by his sons. Edmond had yet to taste the stuff but kept a ready supply for medicinal purposes. Their community was lucky enough to have an experienced midwife nearby, but the closest doctor resided in Calgary—a full day's ride north. The train had shortened the distance substantially but not enough. People often called upon the closest mounted police, which was him, for most of a twenty-mile radius.

Needle threaded and dipped, Edmond instructed Melina to hold the lamp close. He held the bottle over the finely shaped foot and glanced at its owner.

"Are you ready?"

A single nod.

He poured the whiskey directly into the wound, but despite the flinch of her foot, she made no more than a slight hissing sound. That was the easy part. He took up the needle and rinsed it again. "Try not to move, or I'll need to have Mel sit on you."

Edmond had meant it in jest, but the thin glower she leveled at him suggested she didn't appreciate his humor.

"I am not a child, Constable," Miss Wells said through gritted teeth. "I would appreciate it if you'd get on with it."

"Yes, ma'am." He would have smiled if not for the task before him. Maybe he should have pressured her into accepting some whiskey to numb the pain. She looked far too frail and—dare he admit it—pretty. He'd rather jab this needle in his own foot.

Her sudden intake of breath at the first poke did nothing for the steadiness of his hands. "Easy," he said, more for his own sake than hers. He'd done this dozens of times on busted-up cowboys, a couple of cows, and even an old dog. But never a woman.

He wanted to leave it at one stitch, but the gash gaped on one side.

"Almost done."

Her eyes remained closed, and he really didn't like her sudden paleness. Almost ghostly in the lamplight.

Edmond forced himself to complete the last stitch and tied it off. Melina had the bandage ready with a generous glob of salve in the center. He pressed the bandage over the wound and wrapped it in place. Then covered the foot with a clean stocking Melina supplied.

"I suggest we all go back to bed." Edmond stood, his arms and legs weighted by the need for more sleep. He rotated his shoulders to loosen the taut muscles. The hour was probably close to two or three in the morning. Dawn would arrive far too soon.

Melina swept up the last of the glass and slipped from the room, leaving Edmond alone with the lady. Under other circumstances, he'd never have stepped foot inside a lady's room, and it would be best if he hastened his departure. He took the pillow from Miss Wells' hand and slid it under her head. Her tangled waves spread over the pristine white reminded him of a wheat field ready for harvest. Almost enough to undo a man. He drew the quilt over her, mindful of her injured foot.

"Are you comfortable?"

Lashes fluttered as she focused on him. "Yes. Thank you, Constable."

Edmond. He almost corrected her, wanting to hear his name slip from those lips more than he should. "Rest. And don't plan on going anywhere tomorrow. Not until your foot heals a little."

The relief in her expression made him want to suggest she stay on as long as she wanted, but instead, he bent over her for the small pistol at her side. "Will you need this again tonight?"

"I'm not sure. Will I?" Her lips curved up.

"I don't imagine so." He set it on the bedside table and backed a step toward the door. "I'll send Mel in to get you anything else you want."

He turned, almost colliding with his sister propped in the open door looking far too pleased.

Escaping required an awkward *dos-à-dos.* Edmond climbed the stairs, the creaks of boards muffling the feminine chatter behind him. He dropped onto his bed, very aware of his bare feet and the rolled sleeves of his undershirt. Not his usual attire for calling on a lady.

Edmond swallowed a laugh. When was the last time he had even let a pretty face turn his head? He hid behind that uniform and his responsibilities—he had enough of those without adding more.

Like a wife. Or children.

He would do better to look at Miss Wells the same way he looked at everything else. What was the lady running from that made her reach for a gun in the middle of the night—that made her keep the derringer always within reach?

A man, perhaps? That would explain her vehemence against

males in general. A suitor who had not taken kindly to rejection? A husband?

The air seeped from Edmond's lungs. Lena Wells would not be the first woman to run from an abusive spouse. He'd dealt with his share of violent men. But the thought of her married sat heavier in the pit of his stomach than Mel's pound cake. The woman had secrets, and he needed to keep his distance until she boarded that train.

CHAPTER 6

The sun peeked around every corner of the curtain, filling the room with mid-morning light, but Lenora had no desire to move from the blissful mattress beneath her. Even her throbbing foot couldn't detract from her revelry. Too many nights, she had tossed and turned with attempts to find a reasonably comfortable position in the narrow space McRae had made for her on his wagon. With little success. Even if the floor had been comfortable, she wouldn't have slept well with men so near. She'd never slept well above the saloon, either, for the one week she had relented to stay there before insisting on a room at the boardinghouse. She was a singer, not a …

A shudder moved through her, and she pulled the quilt to her chin.

If only she could pull it over her head and hide from the memories. Or pretend she was home—had never left in search of recognition and wealth.

Eyes closed, Lenora pictured the cabin where she'd been raised. Mama and Papa. Little sisters who always watched her with such wonder, who she'd sung to sleep thousands of times. How selfish she had been to leave them. Patricia cried when Lenora packed her carpetbag. At eight, Pattie hadn't understood how suffocating life on the farm had grown. How important it had been for Lenora to find her own way.

Now she would give almost anything to go back. And couldn't.

She could never go home.

Not after …

"I can't wait any longer." Edmond's voice came from outside the door. "I have rounds to make, and the morning's half spent."

"Fine, but let me slip in," his sister answered. Lighter footsteps drew near. "She had a terrible night and was already exhausted."

"She's not the only one," the constable grumbled. Lenora could very well imagine him standing there in his red coat, tugging his flat-brimmed Stetson into place.

A tiny knock tapped on the door.

"Come in." Lenora sat up and pushed her hair behind her shoulders, hoping Edmond wasn't close enough to see into the room. Not that he hadn't already seen her in less than flattering situations ... In fact, he had yet to see her in any way that could be considered flattering.

Not that it mattered. She didn't want a man, any man, to look at her with the hunger she had seen in so many eyes. In Channing's eyes.

Why didn't I listen?

Lenora needn't have worried about the door. Melina slipped into the room and eased it closed behind her. "Sorry to bother you so early, but Edmond forgot his holster in here last night. For as much as he claims to never need it, he sure seemed uncomfortable without his gun this morning." She smiled and lifted the holster from where he had left it hanging on the wall, then slipped away as easily as she'd come.

Lenora settled back into the down pillow and wrapped her arms around her, blanket held in place. The resumed voices in the front room kept her attention. The noble constable thanked his sister, and the steady thud of his boots led toward the front door. Melina's chatter followed him, fussing over where he'd eat lunch and if he had any concerns about his plans today. They sounded more like a longtime married couple than siblings.

Lenora smiled, warming even more to the young woman who looked after her strapping brother—though he seemed more than capable of caring for himself as well as the town.

She hugged herself tighter. Hard to remember what it was like to be cared for, taken care of. Distant memories of warm embraces and soft kisses on her forehead expanded the ache within.

Another rapping sounded against the door.

She sighed and pushed upright again. "Yes?" It was past time she dressed and began planning her future. Maybe she'd run far enough. Even Fred Anderson wouldn't be able to follow her here.

"I'm sorry for bothering you again, but since you were awake, I wondered if you were hungry."

The mere mention of food awakened her stomach to its hollow state. Her insides both pinched and rolled. "I'm starved. Let me dress, and I'll come lend a hand." Something to help her earn her keep. She was in no hurry to wear out her welcome.

Melina waved her back down. "Nonsense. You need to stay off that foot. And there is no hurry to dress. My brother is riding out to check on a new family that arrived in the area last week."

"He keeps pretty close tabs on newcomers, doesn't he?"

She laughed. "He's what you might call our local welcoming committee."

"I've noticed."

Melina leaned into the door frame, one side of her mouth creeping upward much like her brothers did. "Did he make you feel very welcome?"

"I …" Lenora wasn't quite sure how to answer—not when the girl seemed to be asking a very different question. "Not as welcome as his sister has made me feel. For which I am so very grateful." Redirection seemed in order. "I can't thank you enough for taking me into your home."

"Nonsense. It's what anyone would do. Besides, your coming is more of a favor to me. I decided to stay on here, but some days get mighty lonesome with Edmond always off seeing to everyone's needs. I don't know how Mother survived so long without Father around."

"He was a Mountie too?"

"Yes. As is my younger brother, Auguste. He's away in Regina training." She dusted her hands on her skirt and crossed the floor to a trunk. "I have a robe you can wear and save the hassle of a gown for today."

Lenora grimaced. "I'm sorry for prying you about your family."

Melina drew a bright yellow robe hemmed with white lace from the trunk and laid it across the foot of the bed. "I didn't consider that prying. You're more than welcome to ask about my family."

"It's not painful to speak of them? Of your parents?"

"I miss them, but I think they are happy where they are. That's what matters."

"I'm glad you've found comfort." Lenora had avoided thoughts of the afterlife the past few years but envied the peace it would offer someone with faith.

"Comfort?" She gave Lenora a curious look. "I suppose so. Mostly, I'm happy for my mother as she will have much more time with Father now that he's a superintendent and not off chasing whiskey traders or pacifying the local tribes."

Lenora was aware of her gaping mouth, but she couldn't seem to command her jaw. "I'm so sorry. I thought …"

"You thought my parents had passed on? No. They are in excellent health. Quite alive."

"I somehow assumed when your brother said that only you and he shared the family homestead …"

Melina dropped onto the foot of the bed with her laughter. "My father received a promotion and a transfer north. My mother and I went with him, but I missed home too much. Also, at twenty-one, a woman no longer wishes to be underfoot. It's been fun running my own house and ordering my brother about." She winked and gathered Lenora's hideous green gown from where it draped over the lone chair in the corner. "But tell me about your family. You must be a long way from them."

"Yes." Mindful of her bandaged foot, Lenora draped her legs over the side of the bed. "I grew up in Oregon. My father is a pastor there."

A smile bloomed on Melina's face. "A pastor? How wonderful. And I hear Oregon is stunning."

As soon as Lenora heard the appreciation at the mention of her father's profession, she regretted saying anything. How much greater Melina's expectations would be for her now. "It is beautiful, but not so different from here. At least, where we lived."

"But warmer?"

Lenora felt a chuckle of her own. "I have yet to experience your winters, but I imagine so."

Eyes overflowing with warmth, Melina focused on her. "Edmond said your name is Lena. Do you mind if I call you that?"

"Of course not, only …" She was in a different country now. Surely, she wouldn't be followed so far. She craved this blooming friendship so badly. "Lenora is what I usually go by."

"Lenora Wells. You have a beautiful name."

Lenora held her smile despite wanting to grimace. Though too late to correct her surname, it was probably safer this way. "Thank you."

"Do you have many siblings?"

"Six. All girls. I'm the eldest."

Melina's eyes grew wide. "Sisters! I envy you. I only had brothers."

"I never did want one of those."

"Why is that?"

Lenora pushed to her good foot, keeping pressure from the other, and ignored the throb. She couldn't tell her how much Papa wanted one. Or her fear of being loved less if he had his son. The younger girls had drawn away enough of the attention as it was. "You know how boys are." She'd leave it at that.

The sun rose with strength in the day, as did the wind. It whipped across the prairie with dry heat, as though attempting to push Edmond back the way he had come. A place he wasn't ready to return. Miss Wells had stirred something in him he was not comfortable with. Any attraction to her was imprudent.

The sea of grass whipped over the rolling hills, swirling around his horse's legs as they loped across the plains. Hard not to remember yesterday's extra burden snug against him and the feelings she stirred. The longing for something more than a hard saddle and endless miles of patrols.

He pushed Ranger harder.

At the quicker pace, little time passed before Edmond sighted a wagon with its canvas billowing in the wind, despite the low valley the newcomers had chosen for their homestead. Few trees blocked his view of Mosquito Creek or gave timber for the start of a house. A woman stood over a basin with a line of clothes strung up between two willows. Two children, not more than waist high, chased each other past her. They were the first to see him.

"Papa!"

A large man charged from around the side of the wagon, rifle coming to his shoulder, and Edmond raised his hand in greeting. The gun lowered, but not as quickly as he would have liked. Nor was it set aside.

"Good day." Edmond smiled and pulled his horse up.

The man's scowl remained in place. "What do you want with us?"

His wife and children moved to join him, eyes wide. The little boy, not more than two, stretched his arms out to his mother. The girl, a few years older, snuggled her father's leg.

"Only here to introduce myself, sir. And to welcome you and your family to the area." Edmond swung down and approached on foot, noticing the horse hobbled near the stream. A fine-looking mare as black as coal, making it hard to focus on the task at hand. "I am Constable Bryce, and if you have any concerns or questions, I am at your disposal."

The man's eyes narrowed even more. "Is that so?"

"Yes." Edmond tilted his chin toward the rifle. "Why don't you go ahead, set that down, and we can talk?"

"With all due respect, *Constable*, I'm more comfortable as I am."

"Where are you from?"

Hesitation showed in the man's eyes. "What does that matter?" The defense in his tone was enough to make note of. Only people hiding something would take offense at the question.

"We're from North Dakota most recently." The woman stepped to her husband and set a hand on his arm.

Edmond nodded in acknowledgment, but still, what had brought them north? "Well, you'll find we run things a little differently, Mr...?"

"Cornwell," came the blunt reply.

"As I was saying, Mr. Cornwell, we don't take well to violence up here. If you have a concern, you come to me. If you have a disagreement with your neighbor and can't work it out peaceably, you come to me. We have agreements with our Indians, and they've been pretty good at minding their own business as we hope you will yours. What I'm saying, Mr. Cornwell, is that if you plan to settle here, you're going to have to get used to asking questions before you start shooting. For all concerned, unless you are hunting or running off a coyote, it would be best if you leave your gun at home. You're Canadian now."

The man's frown was still etched deep, but his wife looked pleased. She added a jostle to the child on her hip. "Thank you, Constable ... Bryce, was it?"

Edmond nodded.

"My name's Cassandra Cornwell, and this here is Lindon." She boosted the boy higher. "And Heather."

The little girl, hair in blonde braids, grinned up at him. "And I'm six."

Impossible not to return the smile. "Are you now?"

"Lindy's only a baby, so I have to keep a close eye on him."

"I'm sure you take good care of your brother."

She stepped closer, expression matter-of-fact. "Lindy's my cousin, though he's like a brother since Mama went back to heaven."

Mrs. Cornwell set her hand on the girl's shoulder. "My sister passed a year ago, leaving Heather to our care." She glanced sideways at her husband and cleared her throat. "George and I are grateful you took the time to come welcome us. We look forward to getting to know others of our neighbors as well. Was that a church I saw near town?"

"Yes, ma'am. We meet every Sunday at ten. My sister and I attend as well, and Melina will be very excited to see these two little ones. We don't have a school yet, but maybe we will by the time they are old enough to attend."

Mrs. Cornwell looked at her husband, who appeared only slightly deflated. "Won't that be nice, George?" She smiled at Edmond, swatting a loose strand of honey-brown hair from her face before tucking it up under her bonnet. "I was a schoolteacher before I married my husband, so I hadn't worried much about our children's education, but it would be nice for them to be around other children their ages, won't it, George?"

Edmond couldn't help but smile at the pleasure she seemed to derive from her husband's discomfiture.

"We appreciate you stopping by, Constable Bryce."

"Of course. If there is anything you need, any questions about the town or the area, you have but to ask."

"I heard tell ranchers have lost a lot of cattle past winters." George Cornwell didn't set down the gun, but his knuckles no longer showed white.

"Ranchers have found some winters too harsh not to have hay put up. If the snow gets too deep, cattle can't forage on their own. Also, best to keep cattle close and in low areas with some shelter. Our west winds can melt two feet of snow in a day, but a north wind will drop the temperatures and bring in a blizzard with another two feet of snow in a matter of hours."

George looked to the mountains looming in the west. "Sounds like we have a lot of work ahead of us."

"Anything worthwhile requires work," his wife said, slipping her hand into his. Their gazes met, and something passed between them—a dedication, a love—that was hard not to envy.

What would it be like to have a woman working at his side?

Edmond mentally shook his head. He was a Mountie, not a rancher or farmer. Even if he married, his wife wouldn't be at his side. She'd be at home waiting for him as Melina did. Alone.

"If there's nothing else, I should be on my way." Edmond stepped back and mounted. "But I do wish you the best and hope to see you at church this Sabbath."

"We'll be there," Mrs. Cornwell answered before her husband had a chance to voice the decline plainly written on his face.

Edmond touched the brim of his hat and rode away. He could only hope George Cornwell took his speech to heart and left his gun at home. Once out of sight, Edmond paused long enough to scribble each of their names into the small pocket notebook he kept for the sake of his memory.

Since the farm wasn't far out of his way, Edmond dropped in on the Widow Bagley next, an older lady who lost her husband almost a decade ago. The couple had been among the earliest settlers in the area, so the farm was well set up, but with their daughters grown and gone, Edmond liked to look in on the widow regularly. She greeted him with a hug and a plateful of warm scones. It didn't seem to matter when he came—she was always ready with something sweet and eager for conversation.

"Sit yourself down, Edmond, and stop fussing over my woodpile. It'll hold for another week." She pushed him toward the lone chair and handed him the platter before sitting across from him on the porch rail, arms crossed.

He'd learned long ago not to argue, so he smiled his compliance and took a big bite of the offering. Soft enough to dissolve on his tongue, and the honey drizzle burst upon his senses, inspiring a soft moan of pleasure.

The skin around her amber eyes wrinkled as she began plying him with questions about his family's health and the happenings in town. For the next while, he tried not to think of everything he needed to accomplish today and enjoyed laughing and visiting with the silver-haired frontierswoman who had become as dear as a grandparent to him over the years. He'd not known his own, Father's parents offering no more than a yearly letter from their home in Toronto until Grandmother's passing a decade earlier. Edmond had a few memories of his *pépère*, but the weathered fur trader had been laid to rest before Auguste's birth. Mother was pregnant with him when she'd traveled to Medicine Hat to settle Pépère's affairs after his death.

After their visit, and when Edmond was too full to take another bite, he hugged her goodbye and promised he'd be back soon to see about that woodpile. Following the river provided some protection from the wind as Edmond meandered toward town. He had a few more visits to make, some errands in Cayley, and a report to file, but after the craziness of yesterday, it felt good to slow up a little.

The crack of a rifle's discharge cut through the wind's howl.

Edmond jerked Ranger to stop, but it was useless trying to pinpoint the shot's origin. A rancher shooting at prairie dogs or a coyote, most likely. The hair on the back of his neck disagreed with his logic, however, rising along with pinpricks down his back. He swung out of the saddle and looked toward the river.

A bullet kicked up dirt inches from his boots, and the boom of the gun split the air. With no other cover, Edmond lunged behind his horse. Ranger sidestepped, but Edmond maintained his grip on the reins while drawing his revolver. A few more paces put a half-dead willow between him and whoever was taking shots at him. He released his horse as a third bullet planted itself in the old wood.

CHAPTER 7

"Checkmate."

Lenora flicked the white king with her finger and sent him toppling. Maybe she should have given him a fighting chance, but after an hour of battling herself, she was ready for one side to forfeit the game. Hence the problem with playing against oneself—no matter how good or inept a player, you were always evenly matched.

At the approach of footsteps outside the door, Lenora set the king back in his proper place alongside his ever-devoted queen.

Melina swept into the house with a pail of young vegetables and a huge smile. And men's pants, though they seemed to fit her well enough. "You are up. If I'd known, I'd not have gone on such a long ride. How are you feeling?"

Besides her roiling stomach or throbbing foot? Restless. Weary. Foggy-headed from lying in bed too long. "I'm fine." Lenora pushed to her good foot, steadying herself with a hand on the back of the chair. "Is there anything I can do to help?" The less of a burden she was, the longer they would likely allow her to stay. Just a few more days to catch her breath and make a plan.

"I need to change and fix dinner, but you'd better rest."

"I've been resting all morning." She hadn't changed from Melina's bright yellow robe, and neither did she have a desire to. Much too comfortable.

"Miss Wells, plea—"

"Please call me Lenora. Helping you is hardly a footrace. I'm sure there is something I can do sitting down, even if it is just to keep you company."

"Company is certainly something I would enjoy. I must admit, I could probably get used to having someone around."

A glimmer of hope infiltrated Lenora's defenses as the younger woman assisted her to a chair at the kitchen table. She slid a second one close enough for Lenora to set her foot on.

Melina hurried to wash her hands. "Why don't I set what you need on the table, and you can mix up some cornbread?" She hefted the sack of cornmeal into place before gathering the smaller canisters of salt and baking soda. "What else do you need?"

"I … um …" Lenora hadn't baked cornbread—or anything, really—since she'd left home. That had been the point, to live without the need to lower herself to the menial daily tasks that plagued women on the frontier. "Do you have a recipe you like?"

"I'm not choosy."

"Neither am I. And I enjoy growing my repertoire. From what I've tasted of your cooking, I'm sure your family has a simply wonderful recipe." She smiled to add to her act of normalcy. As though baking an everyday dish didn't fill her with dread.

"Of course." Melina took a thick book from the shelf. "This is the book I learned to cook from." She set it in Lenora's hands. "Page twenty-three has a couple recipes to choose from. Either is fine."

Lenora ducked her head with the pretense of flipping through the loose, stained, and tagged pages. Melina likely saw right through her. Thankfully, she said nothing as she set a bowl and pitcher on the table for Lenora's use.

It's not as though I've never done this before. She'd simply never enjoyed it and had done her best to avoid kitchens for most of her life. Her mother hadn't seemed to mind, sending her to tend the younger girls instead. That was a job she could do if anyone this far west wanted a nanny. Or a music tutor.

If she could find someone to hire her. Not the most common of jobs this far west.

Then why not go east?

Lack of funds for even the shortest train ride kept her bound in place for the time being.

Lenora studied the stained page briefly, memorizing what she could so she didn't appear too dependent on the recipe. Even still, she stole a glance between every ingredient while trying to recall all Mama had taught her about baking. Little came to mind.

"I never asked what brought you north." Though Melina's question held no guile, the intensity of her curiosity pressed against the walls.

The truth mounted Lenora's tongue, but she swallowed it back. Neither Melina nor her brother seemed the type to wish an association with a singer from a saloon. Or any performer, for that matter. Perhaps if she had made it as far as a New York stage, her presence would be an honor … but then she wouldn't be here up to her elbows in batter.

"Edmond told me about the cattle drive from Montana."

The only way out of town when she'd needed one. But the other woman wanted more than some trite remark. She wanted Lenora's motivation for taking such a risk. "My father always said I had too much of a hankering for adventure."

"I wish I could say the same for myself." Melina's hands were busy washing half-grown potatoes, the largest no bigger than a silver dollar. "So what adventure awaits you next?"

Please, no more adventures! "I … I think I am good for now. I will need to find work somewhere, but the constable—I mean, your brother—informed me there's not much for a woman in the area. Having seen the town, I can't argue with him."

Melina dropped a handful of scrubbed potatoes into a pot of clean water. "You would find more opportunity in Calgary. It's quite the big city now."

"So the constable said." Lenora's tone rang with more weariness than she'd intended.

"There's no hurry." Melina's smile stretched across her face. "Give your foot time to heal, and rest from your last venture. You're welcome here as long as you like."

As long as she liked? With how Lenora felt right now, she might never leave. The thought of facing the world again … Lenora sucked a breath and straightened her shoulders. She was a capable woman and fared well enough on her own until now. She just needed a little time.

"Are you not feeling well?" Melina looked on, the downturn of her mouth showing concern.

"I'm fine. And I appreciate your offer." Lenora put her energies into mixing the pale-yellow batter until it ran smooth. Her thoughts, however, strayed to Melina's brother, the intrepid Constable Bryce. She had doubts that he would be as generous with an invitation to stay.

Ducked low, Edmond wrestled out of his red coat. No more shots echoed through the river valley, but a murmur of voices had risen briefly above the wind and river. He shouted out his warning, but it wasn't as though they could mistake their target for anyone other than a Mountie. What was it Greer had said, he stood out like the Union Jack?

With his coat hooked on a low branch so it was partly visible, Edmond crawled through the high brush and long grasses that grew under the willows. He moved slowly as the wind would carry any sound he made. A few groupings of saskatoon bushes allowed him to rise up enough to increase his speed and spare his knees without revealing his location, but by the time he reached the river, the outlaws had gone. Nothing remained of them but the indention of horses' hooves in the soft earth. One animal wore shoes, but with an average size and no defining markings except a small notch on the left front shoe. The barefoot indentions gave more clues. While trimmed, the hooves were smaller, and one was slightly splayed, the crack extending almost a quarter inch.

With the head start they'd gotten, there was little point in trying to run them down until he figured out what they had been doing here. The horses had been tied. One of the animals appeared to have taken a liking to the willow bark and had gnawed off a large strip. A tuft of black hair on the tip of a broken branch suggested the horse's color. Boot prints led farther upstream where a large bough hung in an arch, a butchered cow dangling off the ground, much of the meat cut off the bone.

From the feel of the carcass, someone slaughtered it the night before. A Hereford, but with the brand removed along with most of the hindquarters. Only the shots fired at him implied illegal activity.

After cutting down the carcass, he fetched his horse and coat. Ranger didn't much like passing near the butchered cow, but Edmond wanted to examine the site one last time. The tracks led in an easy trail until they entered the river. Edmond scanned the banks on either side for the next two miles or so, but there was no sign of where they left the water. Unless they had gone west instead of east. Back onto Cornwell land.

Edmond slowed Ranger, looking upstream. Could George Cornwell have anything to do with this? Edmond had left their place almost two hours ago—plenty of time for the man to finish the job he had started the night before, with Edmond's presence the motivation for haste. George didn't appear to have any hesitation about drawing a gun on someone—in fact, almost seemed eager to.

Edmond backtracked as far as the Cornwell homestead but again saw no sign of where the horse tracks had gone—or the beef. He caught sight of George near the wagon in what looked like a heated argument with his wife, but no other man was in sight. Only the black mare he'd noted earlier.

Ride in and question them now, or keep his eyes and ears open for a few days to see if any other explanations came to light? If the Cornwells were innocent of wrongdoing, he'd rather not burn bridges he wouldn't be able to repair. George already had enough distrust of him. Edmond would wait.

He picked his way along the river most of the way back toward Cayley in case he missed something along the rugged banks or in the tall grass. The sun was high and the day hot when he finally reached the outskirts of town. He circled to the front of a wagon, hogging the trail.

Frank Walsh turned in his seat and pulled back on the reins. The horses stopped, but not without protests. "I take it Mackenzie got his cattle delivered safe and sound." Frank let out a low chuckle. "Is it wrong to admit that if I knew they were his, I would have been slower to bring the law into play?"

"No, not wrong, but I appreciate you coming for me, all the same. You know how important maintaining order is. More than anyone else in this area."

Frank nodded, weariness adding to the lines at the corners of his mouth. "Sometimes, I wonder if I should have stayed with the Mounties."

"My father told me plenty about how things were when you first arrived out here." If Edmond remembered correctly, Frank came out in the early eighties as a young man and had spent almost two decades in the force. "We owe you a lot for everything you've done to keep the territories peaceful. No one can blame you for wanting a different life."

"Only, that didn't quite work out like I planned either," he murmured.

Edmond supplied a nod. He'd arrived back in the area shortly after Frank lost his ranch to Mackenzie. Strapped for cash, the Walshes had taken a loan from the large ranch owner. When Frank hadn't been able to meet the payments, Mackenzie took the land instead, leaving them nothing but a small herd they'd had to sell to buy a few acres near town.

Frank straightened and flicked the reins. The horses, Bar L stock, gave a start and pushed into the harnesses, wrapping their broad shoulders. "Where are you off to this morning?"

"Need to stop in at the office and write up my weekly report." His least favorite part of his job. "Has the Bar L had any cattle go missing recently?"

"You mean from rustlers? Been years since we've had any trouble in the area." He eyed Edmond. "What haven't you said yet? Are other ranches losing cattle?"

"Don't know, but I'd appreciate you keeping an ear out for anything." Edmond chuckled at how quickly things could change. "And here I thought chicken rustling the biggest of my problems when I woke up this morning." He'd not mentioned the woman staying with them and the fact he wouldn't be able to put her on today's train as he'd planned.

"I heard about Matthew Lawson and Rundle's chickens." Frank cursed. "I swear, that boy is no good. Won't be long before he's doing a lot worse."

"I hope not." But the possibility had stolen more than a few minutes of Edmond's sleep over the past few months.

"Seen too many men go wild like that, and locking them up or fining them don't seem to dent their skulls."

"Then what will?"

Frank shook his head. "I go to church, and I believe as much as the next about Christ's redeeming grace ... but some folks seem to fall a little too far out of that light."

The finality of his tone didn't sit well with Edmond. "I hope that's not the case with Matt." For his mother's sake, as well as his own. The boy had had a rough go of it the last couple years, but before then, he'd been shaping up to be a fine man like his father.

A train whistle sounded, and Edmond's thoughts flew in a different direction. It would be Monday before the next train came through town. If he didn't have to check on Miss Wells' wound, he'd happily—well, he'd be content to—sleep in the jail. At least, that would be the easiest course of action. The last thing he needed was a woman burrowing under his skin.

"Well, I have some errands to run, but say hello to your father for me in your next letter." A sad smile showed in Frank's eyes as much as it did on his face. "Best officer I ever served under."

Edmond thanked him and directed his horse toward the train

station. He liked to be apprised of comings and goings. He'd also heard Lawrence Mackenzie expected a shipment of quarter horse fillies, planned on breeding them to Shadowed Warrior, his prize stallion. The foals would be worth a fair penny with the growing popularity of quarter-mile racing in the province and the breed becoming a ready favorite for ranch work.

As Edmond rode, his thoughts pinged between George Cornwell, Matt Lawson … and Miss Wells. Growth was a good thing for the settlement, but often, life was easier when things didn't change.

By the time the paddocks adjacent to the tracks came into view, the first of the young horses were being herded down a ramp. Heads high in interest, intelligence beamed from their eyes. Though most only yearlings, with a few two-year-olds among them, their muscles showed fine development a man couldn't help but appreciate.

"Fine-looking animals."

Edmond startled at the voice beside him. He usually kept better attuned to what went on around him, but it was hard not to become distracted by what he saw. "Yes, they are."

"Could do worse for yourself."

Edmond laughed and shook his head. "Just appreciating the view."

"No crime in that."

Edmond forced himself to look away from the horses and acknowledge the man. "I don't believe we've met. I'm Constable Bryce."

"Pleased to meet you, Constable. My name's Hank. Hank Mason. Tasked with delivering those fillies to the Mackenzie ranch. At least, most of them. Still have a handful unspoken for. With room in the car, figured we'd try to sell the others while we were here."

Edmond looked back out over the herd, now settling into their paddock. Temptation gnawed. He had some money put away, saved for when he retired from the force. But was now the time? Was this the venture? His five years of service would be up come the end of August. Only a couple months.

It was easy to imagine settling into the homestead and spending his days working with horses. He could breed them, train the foals, and make his profit in sales. But was he ready to lay down his uniform? What would Father think of him for shortening his career? What would he think of himself?

"I best settle up with the station manager before Mackenzie's men come for the horses," Hank said with a knowing smile. "But I'll be out at the ranch for the next week … if you know anyone looking for some good bloodlines. I hear the Mounties are particular about their mounts."

"If anyone comes to mind, I'll let them know where to find you." Edmond touched his hat and directed Ranger toward his office. He had reports waiting on him. Yet it was impossible not to glance back and question the direction he had chosen for his life. Just because Frank hadn't made a go of his ranch didn't mean Edmond wouldn't find success. And maybe something else.

He made it as far as the jail before shoving the idea of change aside. He was needed here and not ready to put away his uniform. There would be enough time for horses in the years ahead.

CHAPTER 8

Careful to keep her weight on the heel of her foot, Lenora hobbled to the door and drew it open. Sunlight streamed from the west in golden ribbons, and she blinked at the brightness. Hands sticky from slicing strawberries for topping the cake Melina had baked for dinner, Lenora headed to the pump. She could have stayed in the house to wash up, but she'd been cooped up with Melina's incessant need for conversation for most of three days. While Lenora enjoyed the friendship the younger woman offered so freely, she was used to more solitude.

A long sigh drew an ache to her throat. Sleeping mornings away after a busy evening performing at the Pot O' Gold. Long afternoons lounging in her room as she flipped through the latest catalogs featuring Eastern or European fashion or preparing for her show. Trying to fill the moments to keep them from feeling so empty. So she didn't need to acknowledge the emptiness growing within her.

The hole that still gaped wide.

The one she wanted to ignore because she didn't know how to fill it.

Lenora turned her attention to everything surrounding her. The small clapboard house draped a coat of brilliant white, dark-blue door and shutters. Cedar shingles followed the roof to a high peak where a stone chimney marked the location of the fireplace below. The smaller chimney above the kitchen was smoke-stained steel.

With one boot on and the other foot dressed in nothing but a thick stocking, Lenora picked her way over the rutted ground, decorated with sprigs of grass and stones. The barn, chicken coop, and smokehouse showed similar construction to the house but without paint. From somewhere beyond the barn, a cow mooed, joining the happy cluck-cluck of chickens scouring the yard for their next savory snack. If she closed her eyes, it would be easy to imagine she'd gone home. So easy to feel safe. To feel peace.

And yet peace remained only an external sensation, far removed from the uncertainty of her future and everything she wished to forget.

"Now what?"

She'd forsaken her job, her dream, the possibility of returning home. She'd run until she had nothing left. Money. Strength. Desire, even. She just wanted to stop. Right here. To not worry about the impossibility of tomorrow.

The long-handled pump waited halfway to the barn, and Lenora plunged her hands into the half-full pail hanging from the spout. Sun-warmed water bathed her hands. When the strawberry juice washed off, she tossed the water out on the ground and reached for the handle. Clear water ran into the pail, but over the squeak of rusted iron, she was unaware of the excited collie until two paws—two very muddy paws—were planted on her waist.

Yelping, Lenora leapt away from the assault, stepping sideways into the cool flow and pail. Water sloshed over the yellow robe as the dog leapt again.

"No! Down!"

At the masculine shout, the animal obediently dropped back on its haunches, tail tucked, but the damage was done.

Lenora swept at the black paw prints marring the pale fabric but only managed to smear the mud. Moisture soaked through her sock, and pain pulsated up her leg. The urge to scream rose in her throat but was killed by the rush of footsteps coming from the barn. She bit her lip and glared at the dog, who already crept forward with the desire to be patted.

"To the house, boy," Edmond commanded, confirming Lenora's fear. He must have come home earlier and been in the barn the entire time.

She attempted a step out of the puddle, but he was at her elbow before she made it much farther. Lips pressed hard, she held back a curse. Especially as his brown eyes looked her up and down. While his brow suggested concern, his lips hinted at amusement. She pulled her arm away and managed another step. "I'm fine."

"Might be more convincing if your teeth weren't clenched," he answered smoothly. The red coat strained against his shoulders as he stooped and swept up her legs. One look at her dripping sock and he shook his head.

"I'm fine." But her protest held no strength as she leaned into him and looped an arm around his neck. For security.

He said nothing but was not completely successful in keeping a straight face.

"You find this amusing, don't you?"

"Just not something I see every day, ma'am."

"What, Constable? A woman being accosted by your dog?" Accosted was a strong word, but it fit the current state of her mood.

"No."

He didn't say anything more, but from the wandering of his gaze, she could very well guess. Her face flamed. What must he think of her? The end of the day, and she still in this ridiculous robe now loaded with mud and dripping water. Never mind her lack of a boot.

Meanwhile, he looked as immaculate and manicured as she'd ever seen a man. This was the final straw. Before she left, Constable Edmond Bryce *would* find her attractive.

"How bad is it, Constable?"

Edmond glanced at Lenora's face and regretted it. A coy smile gave her lips form, and her large eyes teased him. Loose curls fell over one shoulder, only the sides pulled up with a ribbon. He really should go back to thinking of her as Miss Wells but found himself unable to.

Edmond centered his focus, checking the sutures and gash. Doing his best to ignore the shapely ankle and foot resting on his knee, he cleared the tightness from his throat and took the fresh bandage Melina held ready for him. "No redness or festering. Should be mostly healed in another couple of days." Which was good because Lenora's presence in his home the past three days did him no favors. Not with that smile or the way she filled out his sister's gowns. The blue she wore now brought out the brilliance of her eyes.

But it was an earlier vision of her that almost proved his undoing. Of her in that sunshiny robe, nightgown peeking from beneath, and muddy footprints up the side. He'd come to her rescue, and color had bloomed in her cheeks while those blue eyes sparked.

Then he'd held her in his arms, carrying her to the house … where Melina had waited with raised brows and lots of questions.

"Thank you, Constable." Lenora's voice purred.

Edmond held his reply while he wrapped her foot. He could feel his sister's stare burning a hole in the side of his head, but he wouldn't acknowledge her either. She'd questioned him yesterday evening about why he didn't insist—or, at least, invite—that Lenora should call him by his given name. She would neither understand nor accept his reasons, so he'd spared himself the argument by going to bed. That didn't keep Lenora's name from coming to mind frequently enough.

"Bryce."

Edmond's head came up.

"Scottish, isn't it?"

He nodded and returned his attention to her bandage. "My grandfather came to Canada from Scotland with his parents as a lad." If not for Mother's efforts to pass to her children some knowledge of where they came from, Edmond probably wouldn't have known more than his grandfather's name and what was said in annual letters. Father never spoke much of his parents or even life before he'd come west. When he was around, politics and current events on the plains were his topics of choice.

"But your given names are French?" Lenora continued. "Melina.

Edmond." Her voice dipped a little when she spoke his.

"And Auguste. My little brother." Though not so little anymore and almost finished with his training in Regina. Another Mountie in the family.

"Edmond, Melina, and Auguste."

"My mother's people were French." He finished with her foot but left it resting on his knee. "She was the daughter of a fur trader. She and my father met while he was stationed at the fort where her family lived." She'd stolen the heart of more than one Mountie but had given hers to Constable Nathan Bryce. Edmond couldn't help but wonder if she would have done better to keep it. For most of their years of marriage together, she was more of a widow than a wife, raising three children by herself on the frontier.

Lenora Wells shared a similar build to his mother, but that was where the similarities ended. His mother had kept her straight, dark locks twisted in a tight knot at the back of her head, while Lenora let her wheat-colored waves fall loose. Her complexion and eye color were also fairer. Thoughts of his mother fled as he took in the younger woman's full lips that curved with the slightest smile. Did they taste as well as they looked? Would there be any harm in catching a strand of hair and testing texture? He inclined toward her, and the aroma of rosewater and fresh cornbread teased his senses.

"I like your mother's choice of names."

Edmond rocked back. "Yes. I was named for Pépère." The only thing he could think to say. Careful with Lenora's foot, he extracted himself and set it on the chair. Best he kept his distance for both their sakes. The attraction he felt for her was just that. Attraction. He knew nothing about the woman.

"If you excuse me, I think I'll turn in for the night." He stepped past Melina but squeezed her shoulder. "I need to check in on Lawsons on our way to church, but otherwise, I'll be all yours tomorrow." Or should be. One could never be certain what one day to the next would bring. His duty as an officer of the law came first, and his sister understood that.

"Good." Melina followed him to the stairs. "I have plans."

"As long as they allow me a few hours of peace and quiet." The steps creaked under his sore feet. A good night's rest would go a long way to fixing that.

Not bothering with a lamp, Edmond began to work the brass buttons through their holes. He'd barely set the coat aside when much lighter footsteps scurried upward. "What do you need?"

"Are you still decent?"

"Always," he mumbled. At least, since another female had taken up residence in his house. Seemed only appropriate.

"Good." Melina pushed inside, lamp lighting her way, and plunked down on his bed. "There's something I've been wanting to talk to you about, and it can't be put off much longer."

His curiosity peaked. "What's that?"

"I want to invite Lenora to stay longer."

"W-what?" Despite having heard her perfectly, he couldn't help stammering the question.

"Quiet! She'll hear us."

He lowered his voice, but it didn't affect his tone. "Why would she stay here?"

"She's nowhere else to go. I'm not saying she'd stay here forever, though you could make that a possibility if you opened her eyes." Her smirk faded as quickly as it had come. "I know her foot is almost healed, but I don't think she should leave yet. I don't think she's well, Edmond. She's still so tired. She sleeps half the day away and doesn't seem to be improving."

He opened his mouth, but Melina threw up a hand, silencing him.

"It's not that she's lazy."

"I wasn't going to suggest that." Though the consideration had crossed his mind. "Perhaps she's simply not sleeping well. Maybe she finds the bed uncomfortable."

She raised her brows. The large bed was better than anything else they had to offer and nicer than most boardinghouses would supply.

"All right, maybe she is still recovering from her journey here. I don't see how her staying is the answer. Perhaps for a few more days, but not for any real length of time."

Melina surged to her feet. "Why are you so against it? It's not as though you are home very much. In fact, you hardly are. And that's fine. I knew what it would be like. I remember how it was with Father, but …" She shook her head, probably wondering how he could not see what was right in front of him.

But he did. "I'm sorry, Mel. It's nice for you to have someone here while I'm away, I suppose. I thought getting the dog would help."

She gave a rueful smile. "Porter isn't so good at making conversation. He's a lot like you that way."

Edmond started on his shirt buttons, loosening them. The truth came too close and provided all the more reason to remain a bachelor until he resigned from the force. As for Lenora Wells … his resolve already took a hit every time he came near her. He needed distance from her, not a permanent house guest.

He opened his mouth with an argument when Melina's not-so-talkative dog started yapping at the front of the house. A warning.

Leaving his coat over the back of the chair, Edmond took up his holster and slipped past his sister. He jogged down the stairs, double-checking his revolver while he went. He'd heard coyotes earlier, but Porter generally ignored them unless they were poking around the yard. The last thing they needed was one breaking into the henhouse.

A knock thundered against the door just before he reached the front room, where Lenora backed toward the stairs. He instinctively gave her arm a reassuring squeeze on his way past. Late evening visits were not unheard of out here, but not the usual unless someone needed the law.

He paused with his hand on the latch and glanced back at the woman they had voluntarily brought into their home. Could he protect her from what waited beyond the door?

CHAPTER 9

Edmond opened the door to a burly man with whiskers like a bush, despite not appearing many years his senior.

"Good evening, sir ..." The man squinted at him. "Constable Bryce? I didn't know this was your spread."

Edmond stepped out of the way so they could carry on the conversation without inviting the growing swarm of flies, moths, and mosquitos into the house. Trying to remember where he'd seen the man before, he closed the door and clapped a winged bloodsucker between his hands.

"Nice place you have here. I'm on my way to the Bar L, but ol' Burt is done in after the ride up from Fort Macleod, and I'm not inclined to argue."

Barstow. That was the man's name. Edmond could almost see the word sketched into the early pages of his notebook. *Something Barstow.* He'd worry about the *something* later. "You are welcome to spend the night. I think there's some stew and bread left over from supper."

Melina appeared at his side with a ready smile. "I'll put the stew back over the burner for a couple of minutes."

Their guest snatched the weathered slouch hat from his mussed hair. His eyes lit. "Thank you, ma'am."

"Would you prefer coffee or tea?"

The sides of Barstow's beard rose with his grin as he followed her into the kitchen. "Coffee for me. I've never been able to take to a drink I can still see through."

"I guess that includes water," Lenora murmured from her spot against the far wall.

No one but Edmond appeared to have heard her. He didn't like the wariness in her eyes, as though she no longer felt safe. He stepped closer while the others disappeared into the kitchen.

"Excludes most liquors as well," he whispered. "So I can see some benefit."

A two-syllable chuckle rang like the chime of a bell. "Though it does lead one to wonder what the man does drink. Besides coffee."

Edmond leaned into the wall beside her. The low light flickered in her eyes, bringing them to life. "Milk."

She slapped her palm over a burst of laughter. "I'm sorry. I let myself picture that."

He joined with a chuckle. "What is so funny about a man appreciating a tall glass of milk?" His hope of adding fuel to the humor glinting in those blue irises fell flat. She stiffened away.

"I'm sorry, Constable, but I have yet to see a man appreciate a good glass, mug, or any other drinking vessel containing milk. Even my father never drank it. I don't know if his intentions were to save it for us girls or because water suited him fine."

"I can see why a man might abstain for the good of his family."

Her lips thinned. "Are we still talking about milk?"

"What else?" Edmond winked before he had a chance to think better of it.

"What else, indeed," she said flatly.

"You speak as though you know the pain of that path."

She again shifted away from him.

He held his ground. "Mel told me your father was a pastor, so I imagined him above such. A beau perhaps?"

"A beau? A charming word, Constable. But I've never had one." Her gaze dropped to the floor.

Edmond couldn't help but stare, and his disbelief was likely written on his face. She was a beautiful woman and well into her twenties.

"Not a real one, leastwise. I have not had a shortage of admirers,

Constable." She looked past him as though trying to peer through the door to the darkness beyond. "Plenty of men have sought me."

"And you happily turned them all away." Breaking hearts at every turn, no doubt. He pushed aside the unsettled feeling twisting within him. He could hardly match the thought with the woman beside him. Yes, she was beautiful with her inquisitive blue eyes, straight nose, and expressive lips … But he'd never forget the first time he saw her in that awful green gown, hair up in a limp bun. She didn't strike him as a woman who fed off of men's attentions. The somber look on her face painted a much kinder vision.

She straightened away from the wall. "I think I'll retire for the night and let you see to your company."

"I suppose I should rescue Mel." Though he couldn't deny his reluctance to leave, to end their conversation. "Hopefully, she can confirm his name for me. I'm horrible with names, but even people I've met only once expect me to remember them."

She spun to him. "You mean you don't know the man in the kitchen with your sister?"

He motioned for her to lower her voice. "It's not so bad. We're feet away. And Mel is used to taking care of herself—better with a pistol than most of the men on the force. Besides, I do recognize the man. A Mr. Barstow … I think."

Lenora glared at him as though he had committed a crime. "You think? But you will still allow him to spend the night here. After your welcome, I had expected him to be a close friend of the family. Not some …" Her mouth moved as though trying to find the perfect word, one probably better unheard by their guest.

Edmond took her arm and led her toward the fireplace so they at least faced away from the kitchen and its inhabitants. "I think—"

"Ouch!"

He winced along with her. Had he damaged her foot because of his carelessness? "Sorry."

She dropped into the closest chair. "I don't believe that's what you were about to say, Constable."

No, but he couldn't quite remember his thoughts anymore. And her constant use of *constable* as though it was his proper name was becoming an irritant. "Miss Wells ..." The firelight burned like amber in her hair and revealed a vulnerability in her expression that made it difficult to consider anything more than the overpowering desire to protect her. A few other considerations skittered across his consciousness, every one involving her. Her hair. Her lips ...

He lowered into the rocker and scooted closer. In the same action, he pictured his sister and that mischievous gleam in her eyes. She would be all too pleased if she saw them right now, but he fought the impulse to push back to his feet.

"Miss Wells ... Lenora ... you needn't worry about Mr. Barstow." So long as that was the man's name. "This is the way of things out here. We often have travelers stay the night or refresh themselves. Less so now that many travel by rail, but very rarely is any malice intended." He'd not mentioned the incident several years ago when a homesteader was murdered and robbed by a man he had let spend the night. Such cases were rare and pursued with all fervency. The perpetrator had been hanged.

"Perhaps it is easier for you, Constable, as an officer of the law, to feel safe around strangers. But as a woman ..." She stood and hobbled toward the bedroom, keeping her weight on her heel.

"You have nothing to fear so long as you are in my home."

She looked over her shoulder. The firelight and a nearby wall lamp gave light to hope in her eyes—or, at least, the desire to hope. Maybe he needed to listen to his sister and encourage Lenora to stay as long as she wanted. And when it was time for her to leave, to make sure she had someplace safe to go.

The bedroom door clicked behind her, and the rumble of conversation from the kitchen overrode any other sounds. Edmond settled into the rocking chair and looked into the fire. He had just one concern with Miss Lenora Wells remaining. Would he be able to let her go when the time came?

Lenora laid in bed for over an hour, listening to the visiting that had since moved to the sitting room. Laughter, Melina's expressive tones, and the lower rumble of Edmond's voice all tugged at Lenora, making her feel as though she were missing something. A piece of home she'd forgotten. The girls had always been gigglers, much to Papa's complaint. What happy times there had been, though. Laughter, stories, and music.

Lenora wasn't aware she had started humming until the voices in the other room hushed. She rolled over and buried her face in the pillow—so much more comfortable without the derringer underneath. After the first night, she had slipped it into the table's drawer beside her. She'd be safe here—safer than she'd been since leaving home.

The dull but constant nausea that had kept her from eating more than a few bites of stew grew to a roiling within her. She needed to stop thinking about the past and focus on a future. A future not involving a chivalrous Mountie or his kindhearted sister. Though the thought tugged at her center.

A tap on the door rolled her over. "Yes?"

"May I come in?" Melina.

"Of course." This was her room, after all.

The door opened just enough for Melina to slip through. She moved to the trunk against the wall that held extra quilts. "I sent my quilts out to the barn with Mr. Barstow, so I need a few more to make up my pallet by the fire."

"You've been sleeping on the floor?" How had she not considered Melina's sleeping arrangements until now? The girl always retired last and was awake and busy by the time Lenora woke. All she'd seen was the neatly folded quilts on one of the chairs.

Melina shrugged. "It's not as though we don't have a second bedroom upstairs or even a cot, but it is so buried under crates and things my parents and Auguste left behind. The floor has been fine."

"Nonsense." Lenora scooted to the edge of the wide mattress, much bigger than the one she had shared with two of her sisters. "There is plenty of room for the both of us."

"You don't mind?"

"How could I? I feel bad I didn't insist on it sooner."

After slipping into a nightgown and kneeling for a not-so-hasty prayer, Melina crawled under the quilt beside her. "I shall do my best not to kick or elbow you in my sleep," she said with a hint of humor.

"If you did, it wouldn't be the first. Samantha often slept beside me. She is one of the youngest and would often be laying sideways over the rest of us by morning." To think, little Sammy would be on the verge of becoming a young woman by now.

Melina fluffed the pillow under her head. "It must have been wonderful having sisters. Even if they did disturb your sleep."

"It was." A dull ache and wave of sickness returned. Why hadn't she seen more clearly what she left behind? She'd been so determined. All she'd thought about was leaving and proving Papa wrong … and then, awing audiences with her voice.

"Tell me about them."

Lenora closed her eyes, the image of home clearer than expected. She'd done well avoiding thoughts of home until now, but being here in this house, soaking up the warmth that resonated from more than the fireplace …

"You don't have to if it's painful for you."

"It's not that. I—I took them for granted." *I hated how suffocating all the rules were.* Rules for everything. Pastor Perry's daughters would forever be above reproach, always shining examples of obedience and virtue. Lenora had only seen the rules as restrictions, not protection.

"It's easy to take things for granted when you're young. But why not go back?"

Lenora hugged herself, swallowing against the bile creeping up the back of her throat. It was too easy to see herself through her parents' eyes. Wearing flounced gowns of brilliant colors, not much more than glorified corsets, her legs on display for her male audience, she'd sung songs that would make a proper woman blush. She heard again the catcalls of men who let more than just their eyes wander if she made the mistake of getting too close. She'd tried so hard to keep her distance, to never be seen off the stage, unaware that greater danger lurked in the side curtains, applauding her every performance, the smoldering, emerald-green eyes she had once been drawn to watching her every move.

What had been a slight turning of her stomach roared to life like the Missouri River. She clamped her mouth closed and rolled onto her other side. "It's too far."

CHAPTER 10

Edmond woke to the earliest morning light, still a blue haze in the windows, and the muffled sound of … retching? He blinked back sleep and followed the sound to the kitchen, where a form crouched on the floor, leaning over the empty slop pail. At least, it *had* been empty. His stomach lurched at the odor.

Keeping breath to a minimum, Edmond lit the lamp Melina had left on the table.

"I'm sorry I woke you." Lenora's voice cracked. She moved to stand.

He wasn't sure she'd woken him, but it seemed likely. He reached for her elbow, the lack of color in her face warning him of her danger of falling over. "Are you all right?"

Her head wagged with slow motion. "Maybe you should keep your distance. I've probably come down with something."

He'd take his chances. "Let's lay you down, first. Take the bed I made near the fire." He hadn't found sleep in his own bed with her fears pestering. "I needed to be up soon, anyway."

Edmond replaced the slop pail with a clean bowl—the smell alone would have compelled anyone to empty their stomach—then slid his arm around her.

Bowl tucked to her chest, Lenora sagged against him and rested her head against his shoulder. The trek across the floor was quickly over, and he tucked her between thick quilts. Her pale face wore a gleam of perspiration, but touching his palm to the side of her head revealed no fever. He brushed her hair back. His thumb lingered on the curve of her ear.

"Is there anything you need?"

She swallowed, and her eyes momentarily hid behind delicate lids and curved lashes. "Water."

"Even though you can see through it?"

Her lips turned up. "I happen to like liquids I can see through," she whispered.

"So no milk."

Her nose scrunched at the suggestion, and she moaned. "Not tonight."

"This morning," he corrected. "I'll be right back." And yet pulling away proved more difficult than it should. He hurried with the water again, kneeling at her side.

Lenora raised up enough for a sip and then returned the glass. Her gaze never left him.

It was hard for him to look away, as well. "I'm sure this will pass soon. Try to sleep some more." He set the water nearby and pushed to his feet. She'd get no rest with him hovering over her. "I'll get an early start on chores and save Mel some time." That would allow her to primp as much as she desired before church, given she hadn't also fallen ill.

Outside, the morning sat still and cool, seeping through the sleeves of his undershirt. He hadn't thought to put on a shirt or coat. Melina was right. They couldn't send Lenora away until she was healthy, but most likely, a few days would set her to rights. Coming down with a stomach ailment easily explained how weary she'd been.

Edmond made sure the horses had water and then released the chickens from the coop. He tossed them a few handfuls of scratch and grain. The young jersey cow Melina insisted they buy stood at the gate waiting to be milked, bawling for her share of oats. He slipped the halter over her head and led her to the stocks. Soon the tang of steaming milk against the side of a tin pail added rhythm to his thoughts, once again on the woman in his home.

What if he was wrong to not delay her departure longer? Something still unsettled him about her and her habit of sleeping with a revolver. If she had come to Canada to escape someone, might she be in danger?

Then there was Melina. He'd never seen her so happy. Before Lenora came, she'd talked his ear off by the time they finished supper.

If anything, he could let Lenora stay for the sake of his ears.

The cow's leg twitched a warning, and Edmond relaxed his hold on her udder. He'd been doing pretty good, skirting the main reason he wanted her to stay. And leave.

Her effect on him.

What was the crime in admitting that she was a beautiful woman—with her subtle smile cracking a dimple on her cheek or the sparks that often ignited in her eyes when she was upset or returning fire? With the end of his service fast approaching, there was nothing to stop him from taking a bride and pursuing another occupation.

He didn't realize he'd stopped milking until the cow shifted positions, twisting her head to better see what he was doing.

"At least, you didn't have to wait for Mel to milk you," he mumbled. The cow would have probably preferred the wait to the roughness of his hands. Edmond could hardly remember the last time he'd milked a cow. Not since he'd left to join the force five years earlier.

Five years.

He'd not given much consideration to the end of his term of service with the North-West Mounted Police. What else was there to do but extend his time? Just as Father had. He'd not joined up to earn a few dollars and experience the west. It was the uniform he loved, upholding the law, bringing civilization and safety to the wilderness. Duty. Honor.

The ting of hoof against pail preceded a gush of white over his boot.

"No," he moaned, scampering out of the way. He obviously wasn't meant for keeping a farm.

Edmond added a few oats to entice the cow to hold still a little longer and hurried the milking, satisfied with the third of a pail he'd managed to get. The cow was loosed into the pasture and had no reason for complaint either.

The rest of the morning went quickly, giving no more time to his conundrum. He didn't have to make a decision today. Time in church would give some perspective. Perhaps the Good Lord would point him in the right direction.

With Lenora back in bed with peppermint tea and chicken broth, Barstow saddling his horse, and Mel fastening her bonnet ties under her chin, Edmond brought the wagon to the front of the house.

"I feel bad leaving Lenora alone for so long." As usual, Mel was in her seat before he could offer a hand.

"She'll be fine for a couple of hours. A quiet house and sleep are what she needs most right now." Something the morning had not provided. Not with Mel and Mr. Barstow—Elijah, he told them— talking up a storm over breakfast.

"I suppose you're right."

"Course I am." He allowed himself a smile as he shook the reins over the horses' backs.

"Just so we're clear, you're not always right. And only probably. More like a *possibly*." She nudged him with her elbow, but he refused to engage.

A hollered farewell and "thank you" made them both glance at Elijah Barstow. He waved a hand and pointed his horse north.

Mel nearly stood with her wave, and Edmond frowned. "Mr. Barstow seems like a decent enough fellow."

She settled back on the bench. "Yes, he does. Seem like a decent fellow, that is. Do I need to question where the *enough* fits in?"

"I'm not saying anything."

"You think I'm interested in Elijah, don't you?"

"Elijah, is it now? Not a crime if you are."

She laughed out loud. "I can't tell if you are hoping I am so you can get rid of me sooner or hoping I'm not, so you don't have to fend for yourself again. Or maybe ..." She smiled in the most annoying way, as though she knew all his deepest secrets better than he did.

"What's gotten into that brain of yours?" Not that he wanted to know. Edmond shifted, no longer comfortable on the hard bench. He encouraged the horses to go faster. Riding with his sister was often a hazard.

"Nothing." But her smile didn't lose any of its luster. And her voice was much too chipper.

"You're either daydreaming about *Elijah* or scheming something. Well, if you're scheming anything that involves me, don't."

"Of course not. But only because you might not want me around after you take a wife, and contrary to your belief, I have no designs on Elijah Barstow. You are stuck with me a little while longer, my brother. So feel free to explain that to any prospective brides."

How hard could he run his horses on the way to church without committing sin? Thankfully, Melina didn't say anything more until they came into view of the log church the community had built two decades earlier.

"Edmond?" Her voice was small, reminding him of the freckle-faced little girl Mother had just scolded for cutting up one of her dresses to make doll clothes.

Protectiveness rose within him. "What is it?"

"Are you happy with me here? Or would you have preferred I stay with Mother and Father?"

He stopped the wagon in the middle of the trail. "'Course I want you here." He'd likely go a little crazy when some handsome rancher finally snagged her affections, but most important was her happiness. "I'm sorry I grumble and don't show my appreciation. I don't want you to feel stuck with me if you'd prefer to marry."

She chuckled and then sighed. "You are stuck with me for a little while longer, then."

"We'll see." He tipped against her with his shoulder before encouraging the horses forward.

Nothing more was said as they pulled close to the small building and tied the team to the hitching pole. Other families from the area did the same and exchanged welcomes and "good day."

Another wagon stopped near the church but remained on the road. Edmond glanced in his notebook to confirm their names. It appeared George Cornwell had no plans on staying for the meeting. Edmond moved to help Cassandra Cornwell from the high seat beside her husband.

"Thank you, Constable Bryce," Mrs. Cornwell said. "I almost didn't recognize you without your uniform." She lifted her children out of the back of the wagon, now removed of its canvas cover. Heather, she set on the ground while keeping Lindon on her hip.

"I'll be back in two hours," George murmured. As soon as his family was clear of the wagon, he urged his mare into a canter—but not before shooting a glare in Edmond's direction.

"Don't mind my husband, Constable. He likes to keep to himself."

Edmond smiled as though unaffected, but it wasn't George Cornwell's behavior that stirred unease. It was the fear in his wife's eyes and the pleading in her voice.

The young girl tugged on his sleeve, redirecting his focus. "Why aren't you wearing your red coat?"

"Because today, as long as everyone behaves themselves,"—he winked at her—"I don't have to work." He held his hand out to direct the family past him to the church.

Little Heather, wearing a pale purple dress to match her name, followed close to her aunt, but her eyes remained on him. "What if someone does something bad? Lindy eats dirt when we tells him not to."

"In that case, I would need to let your auntie handle him. I'm only here to make sure big laws are obeyed. Like no stealing. Or fighting."

"Lindy sometimes hits me," she stated matter-of-factly.

"Well, that isn't good at all, is it?" Edmond barely contained his chuckle. The girl seemed intent on having her little cousin arrested.

"Let's not bother the constable, Heather." Mrs. Cornwell's smile tightened, and she tugged on the girl's arm to encourage her pace.

Melina met them, and Edmond provided introductions. His sister placed a hand on Mrs. Cornwell's arm and directed her to meet several other women, including the parson's wife who waited on the church steps. Heather remained at his side, a miniature shadow.

"Auntie called you a lawman, but you don't wear a star like they did where we used to live."

"Instead, I wear a bright red coat."

"So people can see you when you're coming?"

"Something like that."

"I'm glad you aren't like those ones with the stars." Heather's forehead scrunched with a downturn of her mouth. "They tried to take my uncle away. They weren't nice to him."

Edmond turned his full attention to the pint-sized child and her innocent tales, but Mrs. Cornwell broke away from a group of women and snatched her hand.

"Don't mind her, Constable." She tugged her niece away. "She makes up stories."

He offered a smile. "Of course." But possibilities pestered while he followed up the several steps. Just inside, the preacher stood talking with Mr … Edmond searched for the name. The chuck wagon driver. If anyone here knew Lenora's past or what she was running from—

A hand clapped him on the back. "Just the man I was hoping to see," Frank said. "I have something you should look into."

"What's that?"

Frank nodded for his wife to continue with their children without him. The three boys hurried on ahead, leaving the youngest, a ten-year-old girl, to walk at her mother's side.

"This can't wait?"

The older man shrugged. "Probably can but thought you might be interested since you were asking about rustlers the other day."

He had Edmond's full attention. "Go on."

"Seems there's been some missing cattle off the Mackenzie spread."

"Stolen or just misplaced?"

"Can't be sure." Frank frowned. "But we're suspecting stolen."

"Who's we?"

He hesitated, and they nodded to a single fellow as he passed. Henry Pettman. Edmond couldn't begrudge the man coming to church but got the impression Melina was the biggest reason for his sudden interest in religion.

"Who's we?" Edmond repeated to Frank.

"Me and Mackenzie's new foreman."

Edmond had heard Mackenzie hired on the former trail boss, but that wasn't what surprised him. He raised a brow at his friend. "Since when are you on speaking terms with anyone from Mackenzie's ranch?"

"Since Greer came to the Bar L asking questions. I told him we hadn't noticed any missing cattle but would be keeping a closer count from now on. Told him he should speak with you, but he didn't seem to take to that idea very well. Got the impression he didn't think much of you."

Edmond withheld the harrumph rising in his throat. "I got the same impression." Greer was just the kind of man to take the law into his own hands. Edmond would need to stay one step ahead of him. "I'll ride out there first thing tomorrow."

Thanking his friend with a clap on the shoulder, he turned back to see he'd already missed his chance to speak with Lenora's friend from the chuck wagon. Most everyone was already seated and ready for the meeting to start. Edmond followed suit. The increasing likelihood of rustlers in the area didn't sit well with him, but at least it gave him something besides Miss Wells to occupy his thoughts.

CHAPTER 11

Achy numbness spread through Lenora's chest, adding to the queasiness in her stomach. She hugged the frilly yellow robe around her. Most of a week had passed, but the nausea hadn't subsided. Though she planted her feet on the smooth wood floor, the desire to stand fled. She remained on the edge of the bed, mind spinning, doom settling over her.

Not this.

The door eased open, and Melina poked her head in. "You're up." She smiled. "I thought I heard you but didn't want to disturb your sleep."

"Yes, I'll be out in a minute." *Or ten.*

"How are you feeling today?"

Lenora smoothed her hands down the front of the robe, trying not to let them linger over her stomach. "Better, thank you." Not exactly a lie. More akin to hyperbole. After four days of hoping the nausea would subside, she had no choice but to acknowledge the one truth that sealed her fate—eating lessened the discomfort. Being the eldest of seven children, she well remembered the first few months of Mama's pregnancies.

Her stomach swooshed and churned along with her thoughts. How would she find employment and start a new life with a growing girth? What would she do with a baby?

"Are you sure you're well enough to be out of bed?" Melina stepped into the room, concern pressing her brows together.

Lenora pasted a smile into place and pushed to her feet. It was time to put away her fears for a few hours and make herself useful. She'd become too dependent on the Bryce siblings and their generosity. How long could it last? "I'm fine."

"Are you sure? Your face is as white as one of our Canadian blizzards."

"Just a little lightheaded." *And panicked*—but Melina didn't need to know that. "Adjusting to being upright is all."

One of Melina's eyebrows cocked higher than the other.

Lenora kept her smile in place and walked past her to the kitchen. At least, her foot was healing and offered no more than a pinch of discomfort. Her nausea, however, raged. She dropped into a chair and plucked a biscuit from the plate. She nibbled slowly, waiting for the nourishment to take effect. There had to be some other explanation for her illness. A fit of nerves, perhaps? Hadn't Mama an aunt who suffered from vapors? Lenora would settle for anything that didn't result in a baby, a tether to all her sins.

This isn't fair, Lord!

She'd given up that life. She sought to start anew.

"I can fix you something to go with the biscuits," Melina offered, circling to the stove.

"Nonsense. These are perfect." Light, flaky, and mild for her unsettled insides. While Lenora ate, she glanced around the kitchen for something she could do. The contents of a large bowl pushed up the thin blue towel laid over the top. "I could form loaves when the dough is finished rising if you like."

"If you feel up to it." Melina lifted the towel for a peek. "A few more minutes should be enough. I can imagine how much bread your mother had to bake for a family of nine. Seven *girls*! That is incredible."

"More giddy and loud than incredible. But wonderful." If only she'd realized that before it was too late. Papa would disown her for sure if he knew she was with child. If he hadn't already. In the end, she hadn't told him her intentions, too afraid of what he might do to stop her or what he might say. Some goodbyes were better unsaid.

"With brothers, all I got were grunts and mutters. And teasing. I think they had a competition between them on who could torment me the most."

Lenora allowed a brief chuckle to escape. "Little sisters are also quite talented at teasing, I assure you."

Melina opened her mouth but was interrupted by the dog's yapping at the front of the house. "Someone sounds excited."

The door opened a moment later, followed by heavy boots across the floor.

"*Someone* is actually home for lunch," Melina said just before Edmond appeared in the entrance, fully outfitted in his police garb. The flat-brimmed Stetson was in his hands, turning circles.

"Thought I'd stop in and see if you have anything I can grab to eat." He tucked the hat under his arm and withdrew a couple of envelopes from a pocket. "And to deliver mail."

Melina leapt across the room to snatch the letters from him. "Wonderful! One's from Mother, and the other..." Her eyebrows peaked. "From North-West Mounted Police Headquarters at Fort Macleod?"

He leaned into the door frame. "Go ahead and open it up. I already read it."

She had the square card out before he finished his sentence. "An invitation? They are holding a ball at the fort to celebrate the formation of the force—its thirty-seventh anniversary. Are you attending?"

"I don't have much choice." Edmond pulled a folded paper from his pocket. "I've been ordered to report to the commissioner in Fort Macleod that same day."

"Oh, Edmond!"

He gave a low grunt, and a frown pulled at his mouth. "Let's try not to read too much into it."

Melina swatted at him with the invitation. "You deserve a promotion."

"But I might have to settle for a new posting."

The siblings stared at each other, and something unsaid passed between them. Lenora itched to slip out of the room. She was a guest and had no place in this conversation, as silent as it was. She diverted her gaze to the remaining biscuit in the center of the plate and reached for it.

A hand at the end of a scarlet sleeve intercepted. Their fingers collided.

"Oh!" She snatched her hand back.

Edmond dropped the biscuit. "Sorry. I didn't know you wanted it."

"No, that's fine." She pushed the plate toward him. "You eat it."

He blocked her and shoved the plate back her way. "I'll find something else."

She countered, bring the plate to a sudden stop. The biscuit skittered past the rim and over the table's edge. She grabbed for the biscuit, but it dropped to her lap.

"Guess that makes it yours." His lip twitched with a smile. Edmond pinched some bread dough from the large bowl and looked back to Melina. "I'll leave it up to you if we stay for the dancing. Pretty sure you'll enjoy it much more than I, with all those eligible bachelors in their scarlet dress."

Melina slapped his hand away from a second helping of dough, the momentary solemnity forgotten. "I think there are enough police in our family, thank you very much. While there is something about a man in uniform, even that loses much of its appeal when I'm the one who has to wash those coats and keep those brass buttons from popping loose."

"For which I am grateful." Edmond winked at his sister, making Lenora ache for the family she hadn't seen in four years. She stared at the biscuit in her hands, the teasing of her little sisters echoing in her memories. Laughter had once come easily, not buried under bushels of concerns and regrets.

"All the more reason to keep you away from a room full of bachelors," Edmond continued. "You might end up washing someone else's coat, and then where would I be?" He plucked the invitation from Melina's hand. "You are officially uninvited."

"That's just fine." She turned to the stove and set a small pot over the burner. A can of beans followed. "If Lenora's still with us at the beginning of August, you can take her."

Any pleasure from listening to the siblings' banter ran face-first into a brick wall. Her cheeks flamed as though she were the one standing over the hot stove. Thankfully, Edmond only spared her a glance before shifting on his feet and mumbling an excuse about August being a long way out.

The sting of his rejection pricked deep, but he was right. Lenora could not prey on their hospitality for another month.

Where else would she go if her fears were realized, and she did carry a child?

Please, no.

"I'm expected at the Mackenzie ranch this afternoon, so I'd best be off." Edmond's gruff tone returned her to the present.

"You haven't eaten yet." Melina gave the beans a quick stir. "Sit down and stop overthinking everything."

Lenora feigned indifference as she finished the last of the biscuit. Her stomach was already settling, so she reached for the bowl of dough to busy her hands. She refused to acknowledge the sting of Edmond's rejection but stole a peek as he settled at the end of the table with an empty plate in hand. His momentary discomfort had passed, and he now seemed completely unaffected. And oh, so bold in his scarlet coat. Stalwart to uphold the right. Noble—the strong lines of his jaw and honest eyes so different from the many men who had visited the Pot O' Gold. She could hardly picture him in that setting unless it were to break up a brawl or drag some fool off to jail for the night. Not to sit at one of the tables nursing a glass of whiskey, his eyes and hands making a woman feel in the same running as the drink—something to offer momentary pleasure, something to be gawked at, used.

Lenora felt a smile on her lips when Edmond poured a mug of the morning's milk and took a long, deliberate drink.

Constable Edmond Bryce—as good a man as they came.

Her heart squeezed, and her smile faded. A man like Edmond would have little use for a woman like her. She could well imagine his reaction if he discovered the possibility of an illegitimate child.

"I'm glad to see you're feeling better," Edmond said, his voice smooth. He set his mug aside.

"Thank you." Lenora twisted off a portion of the dough and began to form a loaf, trying not to consider the truth. She would not let herself drown in self-pity. "Maybe I can be of some help around the farm now. What little I can do to repay your kindness in letting me stay here as long as you have."

"Don't you worry about that." Melina spooned steaming beans onto her brother's plate. "And you are welcome here as long as you like. Isn't that right, Edmond?"

He almost choked on his beans and shifted in his seat but nodded. "Of—of course."

Not exactly an enthusiastic invitation, but she would grab it and hold on for a little while longer. There was no room for pride in survival and no room for the ache to belong here.

For the entire ride out to the Mackenzie ranch, Edmond couldn't shake the feeling that he had been manipulated. By his sister or Miss Wells, he wasn't sure, but he'd bet his money on the first. There was also something about Lenora's smile. As beautiful as a mountain sunrise but as shallow as a creek in August. A front she hid her true feelings behind.

A week of having her under his own roof, and he wasn't any closer to discovering her secrets than solving this case of cattle rustling.

Edmond slowed beside a corral of young horses, the fillies he'd seen at the station in Cayley. They eyed him with curiosity, tails flicking across their backs. Hard not to admire the length of their legs and the sturdiness of their bodies. Maybe it wasn't too late to change his mind.

Someone shouted out his approach, and Edmond pushed thoughts of horses aside, turning to the men who rode out to meet him. Jim Greer and another fellow Edmond recognized but couldn't put a name to.

"So you finally decided to pay us a call." Greer's tone was almost caustic. He cut his horse in front of Edmond's. "We can handle this on our own, Mountie."

"Lawrence Mackenzie seems to think otherwise. Cattle rustling is against the law, and that is my department, so I suggest we work together on this."

Greer grumbled, but nothing intelligible.

"What did you find?"

Instead of speaking, Greer tugged his horse's reins toward the mountains.

Edmond let the two men take the lead. Easier to get a feel for people when you could keep an eye on them. He had nothing against Jim Greer—besides his attitude—but he had arrived just before trouble started, same as George Cornwell.

"One of the boys was out riding boundaries when he came across a passel of coyotes," Greer finally muttered. "They'd found the carcass of one of last year's heifers."

"But you don't believe the coyotes took her down?"

"Not a strong, healthy girl like her. Wolves might have, but I was told they've been scarce."

"They keep themselves higher in the foothills, but a couple have come down this year onto the prairies. You're right about the coyotes, though. A calf or sickly heifer is likely enough, but they don't care much for the challenge of a larger animal."

Greer led them deep into a coulee, the creek in the bottom of the western border of Mackenzie land. "A few other things don't sit right."

The coulee opened to a wide base. Willows and a few spindly pines took up much of the area along with an assortment of jagged boulders, fallen from the slopes of the coulees and washed clean with years of flooding. He heard the flies before he saw what remained of a rust-colored carcass—one of the new Herefords by the look of it. Edmond dismounted. The grass around had been trampled flat by the hungry scavengers, but the cow hadn't been killed here. Drag marks extended toward a stand of low, thick pines. Dark crimson stained some of the once green blades of grass.

Edmond stepped closer, and any hopes of the animal's natural death fell away. A bullet-sized hole had penetrated the skull an inch above the right eye, a killing shot taken at close range.

He crouched, taking in the rips and fang marks but also the straight edge of even cuts along the thigh and shoulders. Someone had been in a hurry with their knife, and it would have been easy to blame the marks on a coyote, but the heifer had indeed been butchered. The rustler probably stashed the carcass in the thicket, hoping it would go undetected. As the last one might have.

Coyotes had a way of sticking their noses where they didn't belong, but this time Edmond thanked them.

He followed the trail into the shadows of young evergreens. The closer to the river, the softer the ground. A cluster of heel prints from a boot marked the original location of the carcass.

Edmond knelt to mark the size of the boot while Greer approached from behind. "These aren't yours, are they?"

"No. I took a good look around but wasn't fool enough to spoil your evidence." Despite the hint of scorn, Greer remained far enough back that Edmond could examine the area. The first sign that he might be able to work with Mackenzie's new foreman.

"Appreciate it. How far did you follow the tracks?"

"Just to the river." Greer motioned for him to lead the way.

The boot tracks led across the river, no attempt made to hide them. Probably in too much of a hurry to be bothered, and he would have been loaded down with cuts of beef and forced to make several trips. The tracks joined with those of shod hooves. A worn branch lay across the trail. Gnawed through. The rustler's horse had likely tired of waiting and taken to cribbing. Seemed to be a trait of this particular horse.

Edmond glanced behind him. The second man had followed them across with the horses, and he and Greer mounted. Edmond took Ranger's reins but stayed on the ground. It was too easy to lose a trail on the rutted prairie. And once lost, not so easy to find again.

They walked for miles, Edmond not taking his eyes off the ground but very aware of the restless men behind him.

"You can head back to the ranch if you wish, and I'll report what I find," he suggested.

Greer's grunt made it clear what he thought of his idea. His voice carried the same tone. "We'll see this through, Constable, if you don't mind."

Edmond chanced a look at the foreman with brows lowered in a glower. A smoking ember sitting on a keg of gunpowder. He'd have to be on guard to make sure Greer didn't try to enforce the law on his own. Enough stories from south of the border painted a rather unruly settling of the American West. The purpose of the North-West Mounted Police was to make sure the same didn't happen here.

With the two cowhands on his heels and the muscles in his neck burning down into his shoulders, Edmond tracked southeast toward Cayley before veering directly south onto Lawson land.

Edmond pulled up short, his suspicions hitting his gut like a rifle butt. *Please, Matt. Not you.*

"What's wrong?" Greer demanded.

"That's as far as we're going today, I'm afraid."

"You lost the trail?" he shouted.

Edmond shrugged. "I'll do my best to see if I can figure out what happened back there, but you two best head to the ranch. Let me know if you see any other signs of rustlers."

"You want us to sit back until they make off with more cattle?" Greer swore. "I'm not winning any gratitude from Mr. Mackenzie. He's not lost cattle to rustlers in years. A delay could cost me my job."

"I understand, and you have my word, I will do my best to locate the culprit and bring him to justice before that happens." Though he'd not be sorry to see the man leave.

Greer glared for a full minute before straightening in the saddle. "Fine, *Mountie*. Let's see what your word is worth." He nodded to his companion and reined hard to the north.

Edmond watched until they rode over the next hill before turning back to the tracks barely etched into the prairie soil. He shot a prayer heavenward that the trail took another turn.

CHAPTER 12

The stiff breeze that had blown most of the day finally gave way to a calm. So very different from the storm that continued to rage inside. Lenora leaned her arms across the top plank of the fence, watching the horses nibble sprigs of green. Edmond's bay gelding joined the small mare minutes ago, and his coat still bore moisture despite a thorough brushing.

The rumble of voices rose and fell like the wind over the prairie, increasing the agitation churning her insides. Melina had joined Edmond in the barn when he returned, and Lenora could easily guess their discussion.

"This is ridiculous." Wasn't it her right to know where she stood with them? Lenora made it as far as the large, wide-open doors.

"You believe it was the Lawson boy?" Melina's voice.

Lenora stopped just out of sight and leaned into the door. Maybe she shouldn't listen in, after all.

"I need more evidence," Edmond said, "but I can't put it past him. Not with all the trouble he's already been in. Unfortunately, motive is strong as well. They lost a lot of cattle two winters ago and more since. I should have done something before it came to this."

"So you are convinced."

Lenora felt his sigh as much as she heard it. "No. There was no sign of the beef on the property. It was pork in their smokehouse. Mrs. Lawson said she and Matthew butchered one of their hogs a couple of days ago. Plus, their horse isn't shod, hasn't been since Mr. Lawson's death."

"But if not Matt, then who?"

The pause extended, and Lenora almost moved away.

"I have some ideas," Edmond finally said, "but nothing I can share yet. Not on a hunch."

"Of course." Melina hushed her tone, making it hard for Lenora to make out her words. "Though I assume you've also considered Matt or an accomplice could have already sold the meat. You said there were two pairs of tracks the first time. He could be working with someone."

"Possible." But doubt was also evident in his voice.

"What will you do if he is one of the rustlers?"

"What I'm commissioned to do. Take custody of the boy and see him stand trial."

The sorrow in his voice was so tangible Lenora couldn't help but steal a peek at the lawman. He kept his face shaven, allowing nothing to obstruct the strong slope of his jaw. His eyes were hooded but not able to hide the heart the man had—as large as the wide blue sky overhead.

What was it about seeing him so saddened that cracked open her heart a little for him and this boy he so wanted to believe was innocent? Was it possible he'd see her in the same light? Innocent until proven otherwise? Worthy of trying to save?

Lenora sank back against the door until she heard footsteps headed in her direction. Her heart took flight, as did her feet, carrying her to where she had leaned against the fence. Still too close for comfort, she bent low and slipped through the planks into the pasture. One horse, and then the other, looked at her. Ears perked, they started her way. She took a step back.

"They don't scare you, do they?"

No more than you. She held her tongue from expressing that sentiment. "Of course not. I didn't wish to distract them from their dinner."

"Thoughtful of you."

She moved to the fence but stayed on the safer side, several feet from where he stood.

"I make you nervous, don't I?"

She put her smile in place and faced him. "Of course not."

He chuckled. "Just checking, because I'm aware I have that effect on certain people."

Certain people? Like silly girls who couldn't help but be swept away at the look of him in uniform, hat perched just a little to one side?

"But I'm quite confident it was not the law you wished to escape in coming here."

She startled and checked her thoughts.

Earnestness softened his features. "I will stand by what I said earlier. You are welcome here as long as you wish, but ..." He leaned closer and lowered his voice. "But I can't protect you if I don't know what you are hiding from."

She straightened. "I am not hiding." The partial lie singed her tongue.

"Then, running?"

"No." She caught the question in Edmond's eyes and shook her head. But even as she did, Channing's words whispered in her ear. *You belong to me.*

"Then what is it?" Edmond stared at her as though peering at the pages of a book. How easily did he read her? Could she trust him with her pathetic tale? Oh, to confide in someone. To not feel so alone. His face wore an open invitation, and he slipped through the fence to join her. What would it be like to step into his embrace and soak up his strength?

"It's my future I ..." *I fear.* "I'm uncertain of."

"Why is that?"

She gripped the sides of her skirt, keeping her hands from their destination over her stomach, still flat. How long would that last? The more she considered the possibility, the less she doubted her condition. "I'm not sure what to do next?"

"Understandable, but you would find ample opportunity open to you in a city like Calgary. I'll see that you are set up in a nice boardinghouse and with a suitable occupation. There is plenty available with the growing populous. Washing, mending, teaching, tutoring—you seem a well-spoken woman. Is there reason to hide away here?"

She opened her mouth but couldn't find her voice. So that was his offer of comfort—to encourage her on her way? Why not simply ask her to leave without pretending to care what became of her? For his sister's sake, probably.

She blinked back the sting of disappointment and … something more. A hurt that penetrated her ever-crumbling reserves. "Of course not, Constable. Now that I am well enough, there is no reason to wear out your hospitality." She flashed her prettiest smile and turned back to the horses, now the friendlier option. "Calgary sounds like a fine prospect. I am sure everything will work out for the best." If she had the money for a ticket, she'd board the next train. Her pride was too bruised to speak with the good constable about her dilemma.

"I'm sure it will."

"Thank you, Constable. I feel much better now." Her biggest lie yet. The hurt continued to slice through her, making her eyes water. So much for remaining indifferent to him.

Edmond folded his arms and leaned into the fence, mentally beating himself with the butt of his rifle. Lenora strode away from him across the pasture, no longer as shy of the horses. The image of her perfect smile nudged his conscience. He had yet to see it reach her eyes. And he hadn't helped matters at all. Just as she'd started to talk and open to him a little, he'd opened his big mouth. Edmond had never seen walls thrown up so quickly.

He silently groaned at the sound of Melina's approach.

"Where's Lenora going?"

"A walk."

"What did you say to her?"

"Why do you immediately assume I'm to blame?"

She cocked a brow, condemning.

Or was that his own conscience?

"Maybe you aren't to blame, but I'm guessing you didn't help. She's angry. And probably a little hurt."

Edmond looked from Lenora's departing form to his sister and back again. "And you can tell that, how?"

Melina patted his arm. "I'm a woman. We have our own language that doesn't require words. Look at the way she's walking, the tightness in her shoulders, her folded arms."

"And that's all my fault?" He wasn't sure whether he was asking or stating.

"No one else is around to point a finger at." Melina squeezed his elbow. "Why don't you go apologize?" She patted his back then moved away as though she had no doubt in his compliance. Maybe she was just saving herself from an argument. Edmond was not short of one.

He swallowed it, though, and started in the direction Lenora had gone, matching her pace to maintain the distance between them. He had some thinking to do, and she probably did as well.

She crossed two fences and walked down to the shallow creek supplying water to most of their land. Near the shore, a thick willow branch that had fallen in a late snowstorm that spring provided a perfect bench. He'd planned to buck it up for firewood in the fall, but now he wasn't so sure. It overlooked the creek and the mountains on the horizon. For the first time that week, it was easy not to worry about cattle thefts or who might be involved. Especially when Lenora glanced back at him, her expression disarmed.

"Constable?" Her voice held as much uncertainty as he felt. He should have made his presence known sooner or should have left her alone and not intruded on the intimacy of this location.

"I'm sorry."

Her eyebrows rose. "For what?"

A long list of possibilities bombarded his consciousness. Sorry he had made her feel unwelcome. Sorry to have insinuated she hasten her departure. Sorry for the thudding in his chest that made all other apologies slip between his fingers like the silt along the nearby bank. He stepped closer and saw the red in her eyes and the residue of moisture on her lashes. *I'm sorry I made you cry.* He had to stop himself short from wiping her tears away as he might have done for Melina in a situation such as this. Well, when she was younger. He couldn't remember the last time he'd seen his sister cry.

Lenora turned back to the river, probably giving up on his reply.

"I don't mean to intrude." He moved to sit beside her.

Her shoulder lifted. "How can you intrude? This is your land, so …"

She didn't finish the thought, but he could hear it linger between them. *I'm the intruder.*

And yet she brought new purpose, new life, to this farm.

"A fine piece of land," he murmured. "Finer than I deserve."

"What do you mean?"

He nodded to the view. "We have a hundred and sixty acres. The government awarded my father most of them at the end of his second term with the force. But other than the house and a few fences, we've done nothing. Some of the blackest soil and lushest pastures you'll find, and here it lays. Wasting. Waiting."

"For what?" Her voice was so small, he almost didn't hear it despite her nearness.

"For a farmer. A rancher. Someone who knows more than how to mount a horse and pursue the letter of the law." Edmond took off his hat and turned it over in his hands. Why couldn't he be that man? He'd be more inclined to ranching or to horse breeding, but nothing was stopping him from walking away from the force when his term expired in the fall. He would be free to take a wife and raise a family. Easier than ever to imagine sitting in this very spot with a good woman … but without the distance between them.

What would it feel like to wrap his arm around a woman who belonged with him, one he loved? And why could he not imagine holding any other woman—wanting any other woman?

When Lenora looked at him, he gave a half smile. "Mel will probably end up marrying someone a little more suited to the land than I. More than one cowpoke has had his eye on her."

"I imagine so. She's a beautiful woman. Through and through." Lenora's gaze dropped to her hands, cupped on her lap.

Edmond nodded while his heart sank. He was foolish to let himself fantasize about the woman beside him. Any man would be drawn to that smile and eyes so blue. What man wouldn't want to sink his fingers into the gold falling from her hairpins? To pull her close enough to taste those lips …

But all that was only the surface of a woman he knew little about. He couldn't force her away either.

"What I said back there, about other options." He pushed the hat back onto his head. "You don't have to leave until you're ready. You are welcome to stay as long as you desire." He'd not consider his own desires in this moment.

She raised her chin. "I'm starting to feel I have overstayed my welcome. And I can't fault you." Her gaze stayed on him, seemingly taking him in. She moistened her lips. "Perhaps it is best I leave. As soon as possible."

"No." His earnestness surprised him, and he stood for the sake of a reasonable distance. "I understand very well how frightening an unknown future can be." Especially with his own hinging on one choice. "Take your time." He shoved his hat back on his head. "I have work waiting, but you might as well enjoy the view. The sunshine will do you good."

She mumbled something about no longer being a burden, but he ignored her and strode away. He needed to track down Melina and set down some rules. If she wanted Lenora to stay longer, there could be no more matchmaking schemes. He was already far too drawn to her.

CHAPTER 13

Three days later, Edmond pushed his suspenders up on his shoulders as he walked into the kitchen, bereft of the usual early morning aromas. No fried eggs, bacon, or steak. The subtler scent of fresh biscuits gave some pleasure, but all he saw on the stove beside the steaming kettle was a pot of boiling water. A fury of tapping rose from the bottom of the pot. He laid his coat over the back of a chair and stepped closer to peer around his sister.

"Why are you boiling our eggs?"

Melina shrugged. "Why not?"

"Because we never eat them boiled." And the thought of spongy insides did nothing for his appetite.

"What's the harm in trying something new?" She breezed past him with a hot plate of biscuits.

He snagged one before she made it to the table and juggled it to keep his fingers from searing. "Because I know how I like my eggs. And you know how I like my eggs." What was the point of trying something he knew he didn't like?

"Good morning." A surge of understanding accompanied Lenora's quiet greeting. This change was likely on her behalf. But why? She never ate eggs in the morning—just a piece of toast or biscuit before disappearing out to the latrine or back to the bedroom. Come to think of it, most mornings, he didn't see her before he left.

"Morning." He took a bite of his hostage biscuit and held out a chair for her. Yesterday's fresh air must have been good for her because she had more color in her face than usual. Her blonde waves hung unruly from a night's sleep, held at bay by a simple string. A few escapees graced her cheeks and neck. He distracted himself by grabbing three plates and finding a chair. Ogling at their house guest like an adolescent was unacceptable. He bowed his head and asked a blessing on the food. With another glance at Lenora, he stole two more biscuits and slathered them with butter. My, but she was a beautiful woman.

"What awaits you today?" Melina's question jolted him from his contemplation. She joined them at the table with a bowlful of eggs buried in cold water.

"First thing is to ride out to the Mackenzie ranch and see if they've had any more trouble." While he was there, perhaps he'd track down Lenora's friend. The old cook might be more forthcoming than their guest about her past if he knew anything. "And then on to the Bar L. If there are any more missing cattle, that may take the rest of the day."

Melina set an egg, still encased in its shell, on his plate.

He eyed it. "I also plan to drop by Lawson's."

"Hoping that if Matt sees enough of you, he'll be too afraid to get into more trouble?"

"Something like that."

She returned to the stove for the kettle. "Would anyone care to try some peppermint tea? I picked fresh leaves this morning."

That brought his head up. "What? No. Just coffee if we have it. We do have some, don't we?" She'd not mentioned the need to buy more.

"Of course." She poured him a mug, an amused twist to her mouth. She was up to something.

"Peppermint sounds nice." Lenora nibbled crumbs from a biscuit. "Thank you."

Nothing more was said as Edmond finished off his biscuits and cracked open the egg loitering on his plate.

Lenora followed suit, albeit cautiously. A strand of gold fell over her cheek. She peeled back the top half of the shell and spooned out a small portion. Her eyes closed with the bite but not with pleasure so much as acceptance.

"How is it?" Almost finished with her first egg, Melina looked expectantly between the both of them.

Edmond tested a bite to appease his sister. "Edible."

"Very good, thank you." Lenora's was by far the kinder reply, but he couldn't get past the texture. He liked eggs flat and stuffed between two halves of a biscuit or slices of bread—not rubber leaking liquid gold off the end of his spoon.

He forced down the egg in as few bites as possible and drowned it with coffee, then grabbed three more biscuits for the walk to the barn. Food in one hand, he took his coat with the other and hurried out with thanks thrown over his shoulder. He appreciated his sister cooking for him but sure hoped she didn't get the idea that changing their menu was a good idea.

Ranger made quick time over the prairie, and Edmond started to relax. The morning was mild with a breeze rustling the grasses, the sun rising steadily in the east, and the mountains still shadowed in the west. He filled his lungs with the cool air and looked heavenward with a prayer of gratitude. He loved this land and his role in taming it. He was exactly where he wanted to be—exactly where God wanted him.

Why, then, was it becoming increasingly difficult to banish a certain woman from his thoughts? Or not wish she was here to witness this beauty with him?

Edmond encouraged Ranger faster. The distraction of having Miss Wells around was temporary and had no place in his choice whether or not to continue with the force. The decision was between him and God, and right now, he felt led to extend his service for another five years. Besides, he was only twenty-six. Thirty-one was still young enough to take a wife and raise a family. He had his whole life ahead of him.

He grinned at his own foolishness ... but couldn't keep his gaze from wandering to the pen where he'd last seen Mackenzie's new fillies along with the few left for sale. A handful of cows and young steers occupied the area now. Edmond's chest tightened with a disappointment he'd not expected. Maybe he should have bought a filly when he'd had the chance. Wouldn't have changed anything, but she might have been a nice addition to the farm. No rule against a Mountie breeding a few horses in his spare time.

The Mackenzie spread buzzed with early morning activity. A couple of men hitched horses to the latest model of a Massey-Harris binder, headed out to cut hay to supplement the cattle's forage this winter. Other hands saddled horses. A few men looked over a pen of what appeared to be cow and calf pairs. Jim Greer wasn't anywhere in sight, so Edmond directed Ranger toward the main house. Constructed almost three decades earlier, the two-story Victorian home stood proudly with red brick walls and black shutters open at the sides of the large windows gracing the front.

The door burst open before he was able to dismount.

"Constable Bryce!" The daughter of the house hurried to meet him, eyes bright and expectant.

"Good morning to you, Cora."

"Are you here to talk to Father about the missing cattle?"

"I am." He swung down and looped Ranger's reins over the hitching post. "Any new developments?"

"Not that I know of." She glanced at the ground, toeing the powdered dirt with her polished boot. "How's your family? Melina? Is she well?"

"She's good." Usually a fireball, why did she tend toward shyness when asking about his family?

"And your parents?"

"Good." He started up the stairs, ready to address his business here.

"And Auguste …" Cora's voice changed pitch. "He's enjoying his training?"

Edmond shrugged. "Haven't heard much one way or another."

"Oh. Melina thought he was. Said he was doing really well, especially in his classes. I honestly could see him better suited as a lawyer than a Mountie. But as long as he's happy. And he is so good with horses."

Edmond eyed her much as he had his boiled egg—neither made any sense. If she knew the latest news and so much else, why ask him? "Yep," he answered. "Is your father around?"

"Sure. Just finishing off his breakfast. I'll show you in."

Edmond opened the door for her and followed inside. As always, he had to pause and take in the stained pine panels reaching to the ceiling and thick wool area rugs giving the home an elegance rarely seen this far west. Nothing was too good for Lawrence Mackenzie in his desire to make a comfortable home for his wife, three daughters, and young son.

Cora hurried ahead of him into the dining room. "Constable Bryce is here to see you, Father."

The large man grunted and rose from the oak table, dominating most of the area. "Ah, good." He straightened his coat over his girth while coming around the table, then extended a hand. "Thank you for coming out. Have you any news on that cattle rustler?"

There was nothing flabby about Mr. Mackenzie, including his grip. "Not yet. Just thought I'd come out and check in on things. Any more missing cattle?"

"None we've noticed so far. I have my boys keeping a pretty close watch, though." He motioned back to the table. "Can I offer you breakfast or coffee?"

Tempting as it was to take the man up on his offer and help himself to some eggs cooked right, Edmond shook his head. "I'm fine, thank you."

Mackenzie directed him back toward the front of the house. "Have any of the other ranches lost cattle?"

The morning sun met them with a brilliance Edmond didn't remember being there minutes ago, and he tipped his hat forward. "One from the Bar L that I know of. On my way over there next."

"But none of the smaller outfits?"

"Not that have been reported."

Mr. Mackenzie nodded, but his expression remained hooded.

"Do you have any thoughts on who might be behind the rustling?"

He shook his head. "Greer's been doing some digging and says he has suspicions. I'll send someone out to find him. Told him to help you with your investigation. The sooner we catch the culprits, the better, don't you agree, Bryce?"

"Of course." He didn't like the tone Mackenzie used, as though he was suggesting Edmond purposefully delayed an arrest.

"Good."

At least, he knew the man's expectations, but Edmond didn't answer to the cattle baron. He looked toward the bunkhouse and neighboring kitchen. "I don't suppose the cook who rode with Greer is still here."

"McRae?" Lawrence Mackenzie squinted at him, the tips of his mustache pulling down his mouth. "He is. Not sure what he would know about the cattle thefts, though. You don't think—"

"No. I had another matter I hoped to speak with him about while I wait for Greer." Not that it was his business to pry into Miss Wells' past, but she was staying in his home and becoming a fast friend of his sister.

"McRae's probably cleaning up breakfast. Should be easy enough to find."

"I'll walk you down." The chipper female voice rotated Edmond to where Cora stood behind him, a smile on her face.

He thanked her father and took his leave, the girl's lilac skirts swooshing alongside him. The oldest of her siblings, she was quickly becoming a young woman and a handsome one at that. Not a beauty like Lenora Wells, Cora had a subtler attractiveness with her large, green-brown eyes and oval face.

"What are you wishing to speak with Mr. McRae about?"

"A personal matter." He removed his hat to look less official, but he couldn't remove the pole keeping his spine straight as he considered the questions he wanted to ask the man. "Is it all right if I visit with him alone?"

"Of course." She continued at his side. "You don't suspect him of anything illegal, do you?"

"No. We have a mutual friend."

Cora's face brightened. "You mean the woman who came with them on the cattle drive."

He nodded, hoping that information would suffice.

She seemed to get the hint, but her smile grew. "I'll let you go on, then. Say hello to Melina for me."

Another nod. Edmond waited for her to start back toward the house before taking out his notebook to record McRae's name and what he knew of him. Not a lot. The main thing was not forgetting his name again. Tucking the book away, Edmond shoved into the cookhouse. The heavenly fragrance of eggs and steak almost knocked him over, and he paused for a moment to fill his lungs with the aroma.

"Sit yourself down, and I'll fix you a plate."

Edmond turned to the man who had spoken and tucked his hat under his arm. "No, that's fine. I'm just here to speak with—"

"You can do your speaking between bites, can't you?" Two steps took McRae, tall and lanky, to the stove and a smoking pan sizzling with meat. "I know a hungry man when I see one."

Edmond took a seat. "All right." It would be a long day, after all, and some things were too hard to walk away from. Like a thick steak. "But only if you'll sit with me for a few minutes. I have a couple of questions."

The older man tipped his chin and slapped his hands across his long apron. "So do I."

Minutes later, McRae lowered his thin frame onto the bench across from Edmond with two plates loaded with eggs and crowned with a slab of perfectly browned meat. He slid one across the table.

"You must mean to keep me here for a while." Edmond took a bite and almost moaned aloud. So much better than boiled eggs.

"For as long as it takes." McRae lifted his fork but didn't it put to use. "Been anxious about Miss Wells and if she's gotten settled."

At least, the subject of conversation was mutually agreeable. Edmond swallowed another bite of eggs, the seasoning sprinkled over them teasing his tongue with a hint of lingering heat. "Somewhat. For the time being."

"What does that mean?"

"Miss Wells is staying with me—" At the look in the older man's eyes, Edmond hurried to finish. "With my sister. I'm rarely home. Too much to do to sit around while womenfolk …" He caught himself and tried again. "What I mean to say is, my sister is only a little younger than Miss Wells and enjoys her company while I'm away on duty."

McRae's glare broke with a chuckle.

Edmond cut a piece of meat and popped it in his mouth. He'd earned it.

"Good," the older man said. "Makes me feel better knowing she has someone looking out for her."

Edmond didn't answer, allowing his reward to waken his taste buds. His sister tended to overcook steaks. McRae's inclination was apparently the opposite, but it sure made for tender meat.

"What did you want to ask me?"

He took a second to chew. "About Miss Wells, actually. I was wondering if you knew much about her. Where she came from and so forth."

The man straightened and folded his arms across his chest. "Is this an official inquiry?"

"Official? Um, no. Not official. She's done nothing wrong."

McRae's eyes narrowed. "So a personal inquiry."

The meat Edmond had just swallowed lodged halfway down. "As I said, she's staying with us. I don't know how to help her if I don't know anything about her."

"So she's not talking to you either." McRae relaxed his pose. "All I know is she grew up somewhere in Oregon. Father is a preacher. Near as I gathered, she ran into some sort of trouble out in Wyoming and traveled all the way to Montana to get away from it. Except it followed. That's where I came upon her. Only a few coins and an old ring to her name and desperate to get away."

Edmond considered that while eating more of his steak before it cooled. "You don't think it's the law she was running from?"

"Do you?"

He shook his head. "Doubt she'd still be here if she were."

"What are your plans for her?" McRae reached into his pocket, withdrawing a small pouch. "I don't have much, but I'd like to help if I can."

Edmond held up his hand. "If it's for her upkeep, I'm not concerned about that. If it's for starting over somewhere else, it's probably best coming from you." The last thing he needed was for Melina to think he was trying to send Lenora on her way.

"All right, then." But McRae still dug into his pouch. "I would like you to see this is returned to her." He withdrew a ring and set it on the table between them. A small ruby glistened in a lacy gold setting.

"This is hers?"

"Gave it to Jim Greer in trade for passage. Seemed important to her, though, so I bought it from him after Mackenzie paid us."

Edmond picked up the ring between the tips of his fingers. The band appeared to be gold with the ruby gripped by tiny prongs. A tiny pearl graced each side.

"I'll trust you to see she gets it back." McRae pushed to his feet and headed to the rear of the cookhouse where his stove waited, large pots steaming.

Edmond slipped the ring into his breast pocket and finished off his breakfast. He pushed to his feet. "Thank you for this. Best meal I've had in a while—only, don't tell my sister."

"Kitchen's always open to you, Constable."

Setting his hat back on his head, Edmond turned to leave.

"One last thing."

He looked back.

"I might be wrong, but if you do mean to help her, you should know. I don't think she's using her real name. Her given name may be right, but she acted a mite strange the first few times I called her Miss Wells. Seemed to get used to it over time, but not in the beginning."

Edmond thanked the man again and took his leave. Jim Greer met him at the door and questioned what he'd discovered about the cattle thefts, none too happy with Edmond's lack of results, but neither was he forthcoming with anything he'd found. Even then, it was hard to think or care about missing cattle and possible culprits with Lenora Wells—or whoever she really was—on his mind.

After a full day of riding, tracking, and talking to the local ranchers, Edmond was no closer to finding the rustler than before. He let his horse walk the last few miles home, though he wanted nothing more than to pry the boots off his feet and put them up. And supper. He'd not had time to stop in town earlier in the day, and the steak McRae had fed him was no more than a pleasant memory.

Porter yipped and darted to greet him and Ranger. The gelding snorted but otherwise ignored the dog, staying his course to the barn, no doubt just as anxious as Edmond for food and rest. He curried Ranger and treated him to some oats before turning him out in the pasture with Melina's mare for the night. Too bad Molasses, as they called her, was so small and had years behind her. A fine riding pony, but not worth breeding. Not like those fillies he'd passed on.

Edmond hooked the gate and started toward the house, giving the dog a vigorous scratch behind the ears before he pushed inside. The wonderful aroma of roasting chicken hit the hole in his stomach like a punch. "Smells good in here."

Melina flashed him a smile while setting a lid over a boiling pot. Potatoes, by the look of it. "How was your day?"

He moved to sit down, but she waved him back up.

"I was about to tap on the bedroom door and let Lenora know supper is almost ready. If you don't mind." Again, that smile of hers, except the pleading one that got him to cater to her far too often.

He turned to go.

"But first …"

He glanced back. "What?"

Melina's smile was gone, uncertainty in its place. "About Lenora." She stepped past him to close the kitchen door, breaking a dusty cobweb that had linked it to the wall.

"This must be serious."

"I'm worried about her," she said in a whisper. "I want to take her to Calgary."

"Oh?" He attempted to cover the pang of disappointment with indifference. As much as he'd suggested Lenora move on, he wasn't ready for her to leave.

"She's not well. She's constantly fatigued and already sleeps far too much. While I have my suspicions—"

"If she's not well …"

"I want to take her to the doctor there."

"Oh." He wasn't sure what else to say. If she was ill, a visit to a doctor was in order. "I'll come with you."

Melina's eyes lit. "You can get away? We won't be able to come back until the next day. I also hoped to shop for some fabric and sewing supplies. Lenora needs more than the one dress, and mine are short on her."

At the thought of following women around while they shopped, accompanying them to the city lost some of its appeal, but he shrugged. Things were relatively calm at the moment, contrary to Greer's assessment. The town could survive without him for twenty-four hours. He wasn't comfortable letting two women travel alone. Not two women he cared about.

CHAPTER 14

The wagon jostled over the trail leading to Cayley, boards creaking and hooves pounding the path under them. No one said much. Lenora seemed especially solemn, as though on her way to jail instead of a doctor. Edmond almost chuckled. After all, she had been the one to try and convince him to let her stay in jail that first night. At the time, it had simply seemed wrong for an innocent woman to sleep in a cell. Now, the thought of her uncomfortable in any way hit him on a more personal level. Melina reclined in the back of the wagon, letting Lenora take the space beside him on the bench. It would be too easy to slip his arm around her, pull her close, and keep her safe.

The sharp whistle of the train announced its arrival at the station. Cayley was the high point between Fort Macleod and Calgary, so the stockyards were often one of the busiest in Alberta. Today the Bar L had cattle to load, so there was no need to hurry. Edmond paused long enough at his office to grab some reports out of his desk. He'd meant to mail them this week, but delivering them by hand would save postage.

"Whoa." He pulled the wagon up to the station. "You can purchase tickets while I take the wagon to the livery."

Melina jumped to the ground before he rounded the wagon, but Lenora waited on the edge of her seat like the proper lady she was. He derived far too much pleasure from wrapping his hands around her waist and lifting her down. Despite illness, her middle had thickened a little since her arrival, which was good. She'd been far too slight when she'd arrived.

"Thank you." Her brief smile did not hold its usual confidence.

He released her and straightened his coat—another employment for his hands. "I'll be back in a few minutes."

He climbed back onto the bench and headed toward the livery. Hal Rogers curried a horse just inside the stables and raised a hand in a wave. Edmond returned the gesture. "Have room for these two overnight?"

"Sure do." He set the brush down and walked over. "You heading out of town?"

"We are. I'll be back on tomorrow's train."

His head jerked up. "Your sister is going, too? Not leaving us for good, is she?"

"Just for a day of shopping. You know women."

"Your sister isn't like most other women." Hal grinned a little too wide.

"I reckon she's not." But she was still his little sister, and the interest in Hal's eyes was too obvious to ignore. Not that Edmond hadn't suspected Hal's attraction before. Melina turned a fair number of heads in the area. "I need to be off. I'll pay you extra for unhitching them."

"Don't worry about it. Least I can do."

Edmond nodded and started away. As much as he'd like to think the man was just grateful for all Edmond contributed to the community, he had a feeling that was the last thing on Hal's mind. Not that he'd be a bad suitor for Melina. A hard worker with a thriving business. He was building a house in town and would always be close at hand if Melina needed him.

Glass shattered against the side of the building, and Edmond spun back toward the livery. Laughter followed, then a heavy grunt. He rounded the corner to where Matt Lawson shoved another boy against the wall. Travis Walsh, Frank's oldest at fourteen.

"What are you two doing back here?"

"Ain't doing nothing, Constable." Matt pushed away from the younger boy and started walking, distancing himself.

"Hold up, Matt." On the ground, dark brown glass shards lay under a splattering of liquid staining the wall. The area reeked of whiskey. "You want to talk, Travis?"

He held up his hands, but his eyes sparked with a defiance Edmond had never sensed in him before. "Matt was the one drinking. I told him he shouldn't."

Edmond walked past Travis, taking a sniff as he did. Clean.

Matt had stopped in his tracks but faced away.

"You want to explain yourself?" Edmond gripped his shoulder and inhaled the same rancid odor that hung to the side of the building. "Where did you get the whiskey?"

"Found it."

"You know it's against the law for a boy your age to be drinking."

He jerked away. "I ain't a boy no more."

"Then why are you acting like one?" Edmond pulled him around. "You can't walk away from this."

"What's going on back here?" Hal rounded the corner at a jog. He took in the situation with a glance. "You need any help, Constable?"

Edmond looked to the boy and then to the broken whiskey bottle. His teeth hurt from the pressure of them grinding together. "Yeah. Hitch those horses back up and drive over to the train station. Let Mel know I won't be able to go with them after all."

Focused on nothing but what was required of him, Edmond told Travis to go on home and then led Matt toward the jail. The train whistle blew a warning for its departure. The sound penetrated deeper than it had in a while. He'd never liked the sound after all the times it had signaled his father's absence, but he'd made peace with that over the years. Until now. He was letting his sister down. Never mind missing a day spent with Lenora Wells. He hadn't realized how much he'd looked forward to it until he was stuck with a headstrong kid who didn't understand how much trouble he was making for himself. Or how much he was hurting his widowed mother.

Edmond sat on the edge of his desk and squared off with the boy. "You want to tell me where you got the whiskey?" He motioned with his head to the cell at his side. "Or do you need some time to think on it?"

Matt's chin jutted, but at least his eyes showed fear. "I found it. I wasn't doing anything wrong."

"Illegal possession of alcohol. That usually amounts to upwards of a five-dollar fine."

His jaw loosened a notch. "We ain't got that kind of money."

"You think I'd let your mother pay for your crime this time even if she could?" He shook his head while a prayer broke heavenward that the boy would start to get a sense of the path he was on. "Five dollars or time in jail. If you want to contest it, we can ride to Calgary to let a judge decide."

A bead of sweat trickled across Matt's temple, and he glanced at the floor. "How long?"

"How long will it take to ride to Calgary?"

The haunting whistle sounded again, this time farther from the station.

"Seeing as we just missed the train, it's not going to be a quick trip."

"I meant ..." Matt gritted his teeth.

"One week." Edmond gave him a few minutes to let the silence work on him before opening the barred door and motioning him inside. The boy was slow to come but finally rose and walked past. "I'll ride out and talk to your mother."

"Why involve her? I'm in here, ain't I?"

The bitterness in Matt's voice ate at Edmond's hope. "You think it's right to let her worry about you?"

Matt sank onto the cot but didn't reply.

"I won't be long." Edmond locked the cell and headed for the wagon waiting outside of the livery. There had to be a way to reach the boy, but Edmond was quickly running out of ideas. And patience.

Small iron wheels rattled over the straight rails, taking the train farther and farther from Cayley … and Edmond Bryce. As soon as the engine had heaved forward, she'd felt the tug of his absence pull on her, the news that he couldn't join them still echoing in her ears. At first, she tried to convince herself she felt relief that he wouldn't be looking over her shoulder, interrogating her about the doctor's verdict. But now, miles between them, she missed him. And she dreaded that she might never see him again. She'd made up her mind that if the doctor confirmed her fears, she would tell Melina and Edmond the truth. Better while in Calgary, where she had a chance of finding new accommodations and employment.

"Don't worry." Melina squeezed her arm. "Everything will be fine."

Lenora tried to hold to the words, but how was it Melina seemed to read her mind? Could she possibly suspect?

No. A woman like Melina, as generous as she was, would offer no comfort if she knew the truth. Polite courtesy, no doubt, mindful of her Christian duty, but she wouldn't want a stained woman in her home. And certainly not anywhere near her brother.

Lenora forced her lungs to expand against the growing ache in her chest.

"Wait and see."

She compelled a smile for her friend's sake, already hurting for the loss that would soon be hers. "I'm just tired." She settled into the firm seat and closed her eyes, wishing time to pass more quickly … or freeze completely.

A while later, Melina shared the lunch she'd packed, more than enough for the two of them with Edmond's portion unspoken for. Melina told stories of the area and its gradual settlement. Hills, green with summer, spread out toward the rugged peaks of the mountains, which still bore traces of snow. Deep ravines and gentle rivers. Not so different than parts of Montana or even Wyoming, and yet unique.

The whistle sounded, and Melina leaned over to better see out the window. "Almost there."

She sat back, and Lenora peered out. Sure enough, buildings and homes spread over the valley in neat blocks backed against green buffs and cupped in the elbow of a river. Calgary was much larger and more developed than what Lenora had pictured this far to the northwest. Helena, Montana, couldn't be more than a quarter the size, if that. The possibility of employment opportunities in a city this big sprang within her with budded hope.

"That's the Bow River," Melina supplied.

Lenora looked back to the sharp bend of the river. "I can see how it got its name."

They both chuckled and braced for the train's lurching stop. It took little time to gather their bags and reach the platform. Melina led the way away from the station to a streetcar, which they rode into the heart of the city. Tall sandstone buildings lent an elegance to the frontier. They left their belongings at a hotel and ate lunch, then started on foot toward the clinic.

The two-story, red brick building looked more like a business than a doctor's office—at least, the ones she was used to seeing. Only the pale-yellow curtains blowing in open windows offered any welcome. She paused and stared up at the solid wood door. A few steps separated her from the truth she wanted to escape.

"Are you all right?" Melina waited at the top of the stairs.

Lenora didn't trust her voice, so she nodded and hurried to join her. Too late to turn back.

Despite the chandelier hanging in the middle of the reception area and the open windows, it took a moment to adjust to the dimness of the room and the strong odor of floor polish and chlorine.

A petite woman with the first traces of silver in her dark hair stood from a small desk and moved to greet them. "Good afternoon, ladies. How can I help you?"

Melina saved Lenora from answering. "Miss Wells is hoping Dr. Jensen might have time to see her today."

"You're from out of town?"

"Yes. From Cayley."

The woman looked Lenora up and down. "And the reason for

your visit?"

"I, um …" Lenora compelled a smile to her face. "I wish to discuss that with the doctor."

The woman's dark eyes narrowed, but she nodded. "Have a seat, and I'll show you back in a few minutes."

"Thank you," both Lenora and Melina murmured.

A row of chairs sat against the opposite wall, and Lenora tried her best to sit quietly. She and Melina had already spent most of the day on hard seats and the chair's rigid back ignited spasms down her spine.

About ten minutes later, a woman came out of the back room with a baby in her arms, not more than a few months old. So tiny. So helpless.

Oh, God, I'm not ready!

Any horrible disease—consumption—would be preferable to pregnancy. How could she keep a child? Care for it? She didn't even have the means to take care of herself, existing on the charity of others.

"Doctor Jensen will see you now, Miss Wells."

Lenora propped herself onto unsteady legs.

"I can come in with you if you like." Melina touched her sleeve.

Lenora squeezed her friend's hand but shook her head. This was something she had to do on her own.

CHAPTER 15

Hard to close the door without extra force, but Edmond managed to control the frustration gushing through him. Dinner dishes in hand, he hurried across the street to the boardinghouse to return them. As good a cook as Mrs. Newton was, the burn of indigestion suggested Edmond needed to step away and let his temper cool. He should saddle Ranger and go for a long ride. Maybe if he made the rounds he'd forgone this morning, he'd be better able to deal with his young prisoner.

Charlie opened the door of the boardinghouse with a smile, and Edmond passed him the load with a quick "thanks" before hurrying back out.

"Wait up, Constable. You ought to see this."

Edmond turned slowly, not sure he wanted to deal with anything else today. "See what?"

Charlie disappeared inside for a moment before reappearing with a paper that looked an awful lot like a hand bulletin for a saloon. A woman adorned the center, dressed in not much more than a frilly corset, the full length of her shapely legs displayed. The Lovely Miss Perry, according to the advertisement. Edmond focused on the man holding what should be kindling. A married man should know better than to—

"It's her, isn't it? The girl you brought by here, the one who's been staying out there with you and Mel."

Edmond snatched the bulletin, this time searching the shades of gray portraying the angles of the woman's face and light ringlets laid over bare shoulders. Soft eyes. Straight nose. While there was no way to be absolutely certain if the portrait was Lenora's, he'd looked over enough wanted posters to know what to look for when identifying a suspect. This was the woman he'd been housing for the past couple of weeks.

"Where did you get this?" The poster read, *The Pot O' Gold Saloon, Cheyenne, Wyoming*.

"A man stayed here last night before taking the train to Calgary. Says he's been looking for her."

Edmond again examined the picture and allowed himself to acknowledge anger, though he wasn't sure who to aim it at. Anger and protectiveness. This man had likely been on the same train as Lenora and Melina. Were either of them safe? "Did he say why he's trying to find her?"

"Not a word. Didn't take much to get the poster from him, though. Had at least a dozen of them."

"And you? You didn't say anything about her?"

Charlie shook his head. "Figured I'd best mention it to you first."

"Thanks," Edmond murmured, turning away. Two steps and he rotated back. "What did he look like?"

Charlie's heavy brows pushed together. "Tall man—not much more than you. But had a gut on him." He patted his own less-than-small middle. "Light hair with some white, though all I saw was his mustache. Big, ugly thing."

Edmond nodded and started toward the livery. He needed that ride more than ever now, but it'd be hard not to drive his horse north. He took another look at the bulletin, and his stomach dropped. It had to be Lenora—or Miss Perry, as the fancy script read. Made sense that she'd change her name if she were running from someone. Did this man intend her harm? Why take refuge with a lawman if running from the law?

Edmond groaned and pivoted toward his office. He didn't trust a stranger who had hunted Lenora all the way from Wyoming anywhere near his sister. Or Lenora until he knew the full story. If he rode hard, he could make the forty-some miles to Calgary before morning. He'd catch up and return with them on the train tomorrow. He'd planned to go with them in the first place, so he'd not need to return to the farm tonight anyway. The only thing holding him in town was the seventeen-year-old sitting in his jail.

What was he supposed to do with that boy?

Edmond took another hard look at the face in the poster. And marched into his office.

Matt jerked upright from where he reclined on the cot.

Grabbing the keys from his pocket, Edmond shoved them into the lock.

"What are you doing?"

"Letting you go." He swung open the door but stood in the way. "On three conditions."

The boy's expression asked the question loud enough.

"One, you go clean up that glass you broke. If I come back and see so much as one shard, you're going back in here for twice as long as I was planning to keep you."

A stunted nod and Edmond plowed forward.

"Second, you go home, and you start helping out your ma on that farm. If you leave your property before you hear from me again, you're going right back in here. Do you understand?"

It took a moment, but compliance finally came. "Yes, sir."

"And lastly, when I do come for you, it will be with jobs around the community. You're going to do them without one word of complaint or …" Edmond nodded to the cell. "You get the idea."

"Yes, sir," came the subdued answer, despite the tightness around the boy's mouth suggesting the desire to rebel.

Edmond held his gaze for another full minute before standing aside. "Then get on with you."

Matt hurried to comply. As soon as he was clear of the jail, Edmond leaned into the bars. He could only hope this was the right course of action. For now, he had little time to contemplate. He needed to lock his office and get his horse.

It took another fifteen minutes before he had Ranger saddled. He usually liked to pack a bedroll and supplies in case the trip took him longer than planned, but he couldn't spare the time. Each minute he lingered set him on edge. Who knew what the man's intentions were when he found Lenora or what he was willing to do to get what he wanted.

Finally mounted, Edmond nudged Ranger with his heels and whipped ends of the reins against the saddle. "Yha!"

Ranger bounded forward, out of town and past the full stockyards. Just outside a loaded pen of young bulls, Jim Greer stood toe to toe with George Cornwell. A string of curses spewed like scalding coffee from the latter's mouth as he shoved away from Greer. Biting back the desire to release a curse of his own, Edmond slowed Ranger and reined him to the two men and the gathering crowd—more men from the Mackenzie ranch.

"What do you want, Constable?" Cornwell snapped.

"That depends." Edmond nodded toward the herd, trying not to let his frustration show. "What seems to be the problem?"

"Nothing at all, Constable Bryce," Greer crooned. "Mr. Mackenzie sent us to pick up these bulls he had shipped in. That's what we're doing."

"While trying to rob a man blind." Cornwell crossed his arms over his thick chest and glared at the other man.

Edmond held up a hand, trying to steal back both of their attention. "What's your interest here, George?"

Both men spoke at once, trying to override the other man and making either impossible to understand over the buzz already in his brain.

"That's enough! Shut your mouth, Greer, or you'll have to explain to Mackenzie why you didn't make it back to the ranch today."

"What's that supposed to mean?"

"Give it some thought. I think you can figure it out. While you are doing that, I want to hear Cornwell's side."

George's mouth showed the hint of a smile. At least, someone was amused. "One of those bulls is mine, Constable. He was shipped the same time as Mackenzie's cattle, and the railway shoved them all together, but I have my bill of sale."

Edmond waited, expecting something more, but nothing was forthcoming. "May I see that?"

With a grunt, George pulled a stained sheet of paper from his shirt pocket and thrust it out.

Edmond scanned the handwritten auction bill and nodded. "Says here you have a three-year-old Hereford bull. But there are no shipment dates."

The man's glower narrowed at him. "Because I went there myself and brought him back. I should have taken him home immediately, but I had to fix a pen for him. I hadn't planned on buying a bull so soon."

Edmond glanced down at the sale price and understood why George had been unable to walk away. "Which one's yours?"

"That large bull in the corner."

Large was right—a good hand over the backs of the others in the pen and heavy. No wonder Greer had balked at separating him from the others.

"Sounds legit enough to me, Greer." Edmond passed him the bill. "What's your complaint?" He peered down at the foreman, daring him to have one that would add to the delay. The ride to Calgary was not getting any shorter, and the need to leave scratched at Edmond like a thorn bush.

"Mr. Mackenzie told me to come to the station and pick up thirty new bulls. That's all I counted in that pen."

Edmond's last nerve stretched to the breaking point and began to fray. He didn't have time for counting penned cattle—an ever-flowing tide. "How do you know the mistake wasn't at the other end? I have something more important to attend to. Let Cornwell take his bull, and you haul the rest back to Mackenzie. Suggest he do a good count, and if he has a problem, he can see me later."

Smugly, George tucked his bill into his pocket while Jim Greer murmured something under his breath and then shouted the order to his men.

Edmond managed to sit tight a minute longer to make sure everyone complied before he spurred his horse again toward the north. Too many delays already. He'd never forgive himself if anything happened to Melina … or Lenora. But he couldn't have ridden away from his job either.

"I understand, Doctor." All too well. No longer needing to submit to the quiet torture of the firm examining table, Lenora pushed into a sitting position on its edge and closed her eyes against the burn of approaching tears. Now wasn't the time or place.

The doctor crossed the room as though eager to put distance between them. "Given your uterus' position, you are probably about not much farther than two months along." The terseness in his tone became more edged. "Do you know the date of conception?"

How could she forget? There was no possibility of that now. "The tenth of May."

She watched him silently calculating. "So that puts you at about nine, almost ten, weeks. Another month and your nausea and tiredness should ease."

One more month. She waved a hand over her nose, the air too thin and laden with horrid scents. Sterile, tinny smells that made her stomach want to heave.

"And then you will begin to show."

She swallowed hard as the bile crept higher.

"Am I right to understand that you are unmarried?"

"Yes." The word clung to the back of her throat, drenched in shame.

"Is the father willing to do right by you?"

Her head snapped up. Channing Doyle? Want anything to do with the child? To commit? To marry? He might take her back, but he would never marry her. He'd made that clear enough in the past. No, Channing was free from responsibility, while she … "The father can rot in—"

"Now, Miss Wells, that is not a sentiment that will do you any favors now."

"I don't want any favors from him." Not from Channing. Everything came at a price where he was concerned. She looked away, unable to shutter the hot moisture before it rolled to her cheeks.

"I see. If that is the case, I suggest you go see Father Chism. He is a priest at the large sandstone cathedral on First Street and might be able to help you. Not here in Calgary, but I believe he has connections to a home in Edmonton open to women in your ..."— he made a strange noise in the back of his throat—"your condition. They are often able to place the child with families shortly after birth."

Lenora nodded and straightened her dress.

The child.

The birth.

Both seemed so separate from her, distant. Not her baby. Not what was happening within her.

"Thank you, Doctor."

"Good day." Curt and precise. She was dismissed.

Lenora moved to the door, where she took a moment to dry her face. Chin high, she walked out. She only paused briefly to be informed that Melina had already seen to her payment.

"Are you all right?" Melina met her in the middle of the entry.

"Of course, I am. I shouldn't have come here, though." Lenora hooked her handbag on her arm and started for the door. "A waste of your money." She took the stairs two at a time, but Melina remained on her heels.

"But he was able to confirm everything for you? And the baby. All is well with the baby?"

She made almost the full length of the block before Melina's words caught up with her. She spun back. "You knew? How long have you known?"

"A few days." Melina touched her shoulder gently, testing

Lenora's reaction. "I did half suspect from the beginning, though."

Lenora pressed a hand against her chest, over the ache rising through her. "You thought so little of me?"

"Of course not. I have no idea what you have been through." She tightened her hold. "But this is part of the reason you've been hiding, isn't it?"

Lenora hugged herself. So much for being a wonderful actress. She glanced around to make sure no one was in earshot. The rest of the population seemed content to mind their own business. How long would that last? Another month or two before fingers started pointing and tongues wagging? "Does ... your brother know?"

"I doubt it."

That explained why she hadn't been asked to leave. She certainly couldn't go back and face him now.

The thought of never seeing him again tore at the corner of her heart.

It's better this way. To not see the disdain in Edmond's brown eyes or feel his silent rejection.

"Why don't we find someplace quiet, and you can tell me whatever you are ready to." The gentleness in Melina's words made Lenora believe it was an offer for her own sake and not merely of curiosity.

She followed Melina toward the river, where willows arched like huge parasols to provide relief from the July sun. They strolled west, away from a sawmill and other buildings of industry, to where a lone bench had been constructed to overlook the full rush of the river. Melina sat and waited.

Lenora would have preferred to keep walking, but she lowered beside her friend and focused on the river. What she wouldn't give to let it sweep away all her troubles, burying them within its murky depths.

A wild goose ventured near, nibbling at the ground as though expecting an offering. Melina reached into her bag and tossed a fragment of biscuit. Large, silver-and-black wings struck the air but not in flight. The blackhead bobbed down and grabbed the morsel.

"I'm here to listen. No judgment, I promise."

Lenora filled her deprived lungs. No more running. No way to escape her past. She started her tale with leaving home. Then singing at the saloon and trying to get ahead. The times she thought to leave. The threats and lack of funds that held her in place. The leering men. The night Channing had insisted on *speaking* with her in his office after she'd finished her performance.

Her last performance.

A comforting arm encircled her shoulders. "What he did wasn't your fault."

The sentiment fell flat against reality. "Wasn't it? My father taught me a woman protected herself with her modesty. That if she flaunted herself, she was responsible for the ideas she gave men." That was the least of her sins.

"My mother taught my brothers that a man had better be the keeper of his own thoughts and actions."

If only it were so simple. "It doesn't matter now."

"What did you do? After, I mean."

"Ran." From herself as much as from Channing. For all the good that did. "I pillaged a poor box outside of a church for a modest gown and—"

Melina fingered the hideous green fabric of the skirt, and Lenora nodded.

"Seemed suitable." Something Papa would approve of.

The goose moved away, seeking food elsewhere.

Lenora laid a hand low over her stomach and closed her eyes against a surge of tears. She had no time for emotions now with a baby to plan for. The doctor was right. The child would be better off with a mother who had a husband and means of providing for him or her. A mother whose past wouldn't taint its life. She had nothing to offer.

Lenora stood and faced her friend—that is how she would always consider Melina. Even now, no guile or revulsion marked her face. Lenora extended her hand. "I want to thank you for all you have done for me. For allowing me to stay in your home. For your kindness. I'm sorry I wasn't more use to you during my stay. I would have liked to repay you for … everything."

Melina stared at her proffered hand. "What are you talking about? You're coming home with me. I can help you. And we have an excellent midwife in the area." She joined Lenora on her feet. "Where else would you go?"

Lenora grasped for a satisfactory answer, one to appease Melina's generous heart. "The doctor informed me of a home run by a church. They might have a place for me." She squared her shoulders, hoping to disguise how badly she didn't want to say goodbye.

"Is that what you want?"

"What I want?" Her resolve crumbled like Melina's fresh-from-the-oven biscuits. "What I want has little bearing on what must happen. I can't turn back time and make different decisions. I can't *want* away this baby."

"I'm sorry."

Lenora threw up her hands. "That's half the problem. You have nothing to be sorry for. You've done more for me than I deserve, and I can't ask any more from you. Or your brother." A laugh broke from her throat. "What do you think he will have to say about all this?" She could easily imagine and didn't wish to experience the reality.

"I honestly don't know. And it doesn't matter. You're *my* guest." Melina gripped her arms. "You're my friend. I'm being purely selfish, Lenora. I don't want to go back to that empty house. Not without you. I'm not good at being alone. I thought I would be, but I don't like it."

"Then why stay?" Melina had parents who would gladly accept her back into their home. She wasn't trapped.

"This is where I'm meant to be." A sad smile crept up at the side of her mouth. "Have you never felt led by God?"

Lenora looked at the river—anywhere but Melina's innocent face. If He had tried to lead her, she'd never listened.

"You do believe in God?"

"I suppose so." Lenora honestly didn't want to think about Him right now. And most likely, He didn't want anything to do with her. If He was as all-wise and all-knowing as Papa taught, God had probably washed His hands of her long ago.

The rush of the river and two geese arguing filled what otherwise would have been silence, haunting the crevices of Lenora's heart. She sunk back to the bench. Pa had been correct about everything. She reaped the consequences of disobedience and walking away from God. She felt the displacement—the shame, the stains on her hands and soul—but knew in her head there was a way to return. How to find such an obscure path in the darkness surrounding her? Utter blackness pressed her into the solid bench. Easy to imagine remaining here until she wasted away to nothing.

Warmth covered her hand and squeezed. "God is waiting."

Lenora glanced up. "For what?"

"For you to remember how much He loves you."

A tear rolled free, and Lenora swatted it away. She shook her head. A lovely platitude, but an impossible reality.

CHAPTER 16

Morning's glow filtered through the draped curtains of the hotel room, as welcome as the rainbow after Noah's flood. A merciful sign the night had passed. Lenora rolled onto her side and focused on the slivers of light, dim with the earliness of day. Her eyes burned from lack of sleep, and she feared her tossing and turning may have kept Melina from resting well in the second bed only feet away.

Stay or go?

The question had stalked Lenora most of the night as she'd considered the child growing within her. She should ignore her friend's request that she return to Cayley and figure out how to build a life here in Calgary. Now, before her pregnancy became obvious and no one wanted to hire her. Closer to her time, she could contact the priest and go away to have the baby, leaving him or her in their care, trusting they would find a good family.

That would be the unselfish thing to do. She'd spent far too long thinking only of herself. Melina and Edmond owed her nothing, and she had taken advantage of their kindness.

Yet the thought of leaving them, of saying goodbye and walking away...

She pushed off the bed and quietly dressed. Hunger pinched her stomach, followed by the swoosh of her insides. She unfolded a napkin she'd kept from last night's supper with two slices of bread tucked inside. Piece after piece, she broke off to pop into her mouth while continuing to fasten her skirt. A little snugger than yesterday. She sighed. Melina was right—she'd need a new dress soon, one made to expand with her growing middle.

"Awake so early?"

"I can't sleep." Despite the exhaustion wrapping her tight. "I thought some fresh air might do me good." Maybe then, she'd return and try to sleep for a couple more hours.

Melina pushed her blankets back. "I'll come with you."

"No. You should sleep. I won't be long."

Though Melina relaxed, her gaze followed Lenora. "Are you sure?"

Lenora hugged the shawl around her and nodded. "You rest." She slipped out the door and down the flight of stairs to the open lobby. No one was about, so she stepped out the front door and breathed deeply of the cool morning breeze. At the edge of the stone walk, she leaned into the wide pillar. Loneliness grew inside of her, an ache expanding in her chest. Why was doing the right thing so much harder than following her heart? Why couldn't she be more like Melina, whose heart led her in the direction she should go? Like a compass.

Change my heart.

The plea slipped from her, and she glanced toward the royal-blue awning above. Lenora had never doubted a God existed but spent her adult life ignoring Him. She'd always considered it a mutual arrangement. What use would a God of absolutes, of judgment, of punishment, have of her until she met her end? She had decided as a child, listening to her father's sermons, that she could never please God, so her only chance of happiness was in this life.

Another mistake.

A few people were out at this early hour, readying wagons or preparing their shops for opening, but she drew little attention. In her awful green gown, hair braided down her back and tucked under a shawl, she was no different from any other hardworking woman busy in the early hours of the day.

Head throbbing from lack of sleep and thoughts unsettled but restless, she started walking. She didn't much care what direction she took, but the mountains across the western horizon drew her. They stood majestic as the sun touched their peaks and deepened their rugged contours.

A horse tied across the street whinnied, and she glanced that way. A man loaded the back of a wagon with large sacks of who knew what. He nodded at her, and she returned the gesture, keeping her pace steady. Uneasiness followed her. She glanced over her shoulder, but the man had resumed his work. And no one else on the street paid her any heed.

She continued walking, head down, refusing to acknowledge anyone else but unable to ignore the prickle of hair rising on her arms—the sensation of being watched.

Edmond tied his horse to the pole outside the hotel, his motions more instinct than effort. He straightened his hat, dusted the trail from his red coat, and started up the stairs. A man in a dark suit stood near the front desk, instructing one of the kitchen staff about the breakfast provided in their dining room. Upon Edmond's entrance, the man's words halted, and he stared. The benefit of wearing a uniform.

With a motion of dismissal, he sent the cook away and approached Edmond with an uncertain smile. "Good morning, Constable."

"Good morning." Though Edmond had yet to test that sentiment. "My sister and another young lady were supposed to have stayed here last night. Melina Bryce."

He followed the man to his desk, where he glanced down a ledger. "Yes. Miss Bryce and guest. They arrived yesterday evening and are scheduled to depart this morning."

Edmond closed his eyes for a brief respite, tipping his head back with a silent prayer of thanks. They had made it safely this far. "What is their room number?"

"Number fourteen."

"And you can confirm they retired here last night?"

The attendant tapped his pencil on the corner of the ledger, then nodded. "Yes. I remember the two young women pausing for their key shortly after their dinner. I have not seen them since."

"Thank you." Edmond headed for the door. Might as well let them sleep. He found a bench out front and sank onto it. Now that he knew they were safe, nothing could keep his eyes from closing for a few minutes. He drifted in and out of consciousness as the street gradually woke to activity.

A hand gripped his shoulder, jerking him awake.

"What are you doing here?"

Edmond tipped his hat back and looked up at his sister. The ache in his eyes spread through the rest of his body, begging for more sleep and preferably a place to lay down.

"Edmond?"

Unfortunately, he'd have to answer his sister's questions first, or she'd never leave him be. "Came to make sure you were all right."

She raised a brow. "Why so concerned? I wasn't alone."

Which was the problem. "Where is she?" It was difficult to use her name—maybe because he wasn't sure which to use.

"Lenora? She went out for some fresh air about an hour ago. I was becoming concerned, so I came down."

He shoved to his feet, blood again pulsating through him. "You don't know where she is?"

Melina's eyes widened. "What's wrong, Edmond?"

He took a breath but couldn't ease the tightness from his lungs or the dread welling in his gut. He thrust the bulletin into his sister's hands. "She might be in danger. I don't know. She's not who we thought she was."

"We didn't know what to think, remember?" Melina barely glanced at the paper before handing it back to him. "Who's after her?"

Edmond gripped the bulletin, trying not to dwell on the image of Lenora's shapely form. How did the photograph, or any of this, not bother Melina? Surely, the truth of Lenora's risqué past justified more than a passing glance. "I don't know who's after her. Charlie Newman got this from one of his boarders, and that is Lenora, isn't it?" He couldn't keep his frustration from his voice, couldn't swallow the bitter taste of what felt like betrayal.

"Yes, it's her. She told me what happened." Melina walked to the edge of the street, searching left and right.

Edmond thrust the bulletin back into his pocket. "When?"

"Yesterday. Here." Her hands twisted at the fabric of her skirts. "Maybe it'd be best if we split up. Or maybe you should go to headquarters, tell them what's happened and that you need help tracking her."

"We don't know that something has happened!" He wiped a hand down his face and regulated his tone. Exhaustion was no excuse for losing control. "You said she went on a walk. She could be back at any time."

"But what if she isn't?"

He didn't want to consider the possibility he'd arrived too late. Didn't want to consider losing her. Even though he should want nothing to do with her ... beyond what was his duty.

What was his duty toward Lenora Perry? "Fine. Let's start looking. I'll begin at the train station. Then the liveries."

With a hasty nod, Melina hurried off in the opposite direction.

"Meet back here in an hour," he hollered after her and caught her nod.

Edmond started out on foot. Though Calgary boasted a population of over forty thousand, the train station was only blocks to the east, and many of the liveries were in the near vicinity. He jogged around the next corner and directly into a young woman. She yelped and jerked back, but he caught hold of her arms.

"Lenora?"

Gasping for want of air, she stared up at him. Relief washed over her features, and she fell into his arms. He couldn't help but hold on tight while he caught his own breath. Nor could he ignore how good she felt in his arms, or the surge of protectiveness flowing through him, giving strength to his embrace. If not for the photograph of her burning a hole in his pocket, he might not be able to let go. But she was not his to hold. Neither was she the kind of woman he was willing to sacrifice his career or heart to.

He released her and took a full step back. Distance would do him good. "What happened?"

Her face became an unreadable mask, and her arms fell stiffly to her sides. "Nothing. Just my imagination." She squinted up at him as though seeing him for the first time. "What are you doing here?"

"I …" He shook his head, not sure how to explain. "I was able to get away, after all."

Her brow furrowed briefly. "I'm going back to the room." She sidestepped him, her steps clicking down the boardwalk and into the hotel.

Edmond straightened his coat and followed her as far as the hotel. He mounted Ranger and rode in the direction Melina had gone. Minutes later, he joined her on the ground and explained that he had found Lenora—Miss Perry.

Melina slipped her arm through his as they returned to the hotel. "You had me imagining the worst with that handbill and talk of someone after her."

He'd not mention his own feelings on the matter.

"Let's not say anything to her about the man yet."

"Not tell her?" Edmond wiped his hand over his eyes, still burning and full of grit. A steady ache started at the base of his skull and radiated to his temples, attacking his ability to think coherently. "How would it benefit anyone to keep her in the dark? A man is hunting her. I have questions I need answered. We have decisions to make. We can't—"

"I know!" Melina released a gust of breath. "But not yet. Not today."

"Mel …" He understood she wanted to protect her friend, but this wasn't protection.

"She hardly slept a wink last night. She has so much else to decide right now, so much on her mind. Let her work through one problem at a time."

"What do you mean?" Somehow, he had forgotten the reason for this trip. "What did the doctor say?"

"He only confirmed what she and I already suspected."

"Which is?" He lifted his hat and pressed fingers against his temples in a massaging motion, fighting the desire to shake his sister for making him work for every morsel of information.

Melina looked at him squarely, her mouth straightening into a line.

"Mel!"

"She's pregnant, Edmond. She's pregnant."

He stared, the words not quite penetrating the painful fog. They spun through his head, reverberating off his skull. Pregnant? Unmarried and pregnant? Or maybe she was married after all, and that was her husband looking for her. Or, at least, the father.

Melina was still talking, something about keeping his mouth shut, that it hadn't been her place to say anything, but she thought he needed to know. Of course, he needed to know. The woman had been living in his home.

"Edmond."

"I … I need to see to Ranger before I take him to the station." Though right now, a long ride home sounded about right. He started away with the horse. Either way, Ranger needed a rest and prime hay. He'd pay for a serving of sweet oats as well.

"Edmond?"

"I'll be back." After he figured out what to do with what he'd been told. He wasn't sure why he was even surprised. One look at the *Lovely* Lenora Perry's photograph and any fool could tell exactly what kind of woman she was. No wonder his feelings were in such a tussle. She was a professional at seducing men, at playing with their affections.

CHAPTER 17

A bell jingled overhead, and Lenora stifled a yawn under her hand as they exited yet another shop. The third one they had visited. Oh, to curl up in bed for a few hours while she tried to sleep off both her exhaustion and humiliation. Thoughts of throwing herself into Edmond's arms brought heat to her cheeks every time she looked at him. An action not easy to avoid since he'd insisted on accompanying them—though not more than a step into any of the stores. He loomed near the door like a guard, where, from the looks of him, he needed a nap even more than she. Several times, she caught him covering his own yawn behind a closed fist or wiping a hand over a reddened eye. He must have ridden all night. But why go through all that just to return to Cayley with them in a few hours?

"Why don't we stop for lunch before heading to the station?" Edmond stuffed Melina's packages under his arm and followed behind.

His sister looked back at him with a shake of her head. "We have plenty of time. I have one more shop I want to visit. Cunningham's always has the best selection of fabrics."

"Then why didn't we go there first?" Impatience edged his voice.

"Why don't you go back to the hotel and rest, Edmond? I still have the key to our room." Melina paused and faced him. "We'll be fine."

An extended gust of air emptied his lungs. "No, lead the way. You need someone to act as a pack mule."

"Are you sure?"

The glower he shot his sister dared her to question him again.

Melina glanced at Lenora and led the way across the street. They'd walked a block when a large red brick building came into view, the sign over the double doors stopping Lenora in her tracks.

Edmond bumped into her but managed to grab her arms before she stumbled forward. He released her just as quickly.

She tried to ignore his withdrawal and focused on Harrington Theater. Not a saloon or tavern, but an actual theater where her voice could be appreciated without the need to lower herself to the gutters of men's minds.

"Are you all right?"

"Quite. I was just admiring the—"

"The theater," Edmond finished for her, words tight. He stepped around her with a mumble under his breath.

She moved to follow, but not without stealing a few more appreciative gazes over her shoulder at the crimson of the brick, the gold tassels hanging from the awning, and large posters declaring the feature performance of Shakespeare's *Macbeth*. What would it be like to perform in such a place? Not at all as impressive as the photographs she had seen of grand theaters and opera houses in the East, but elegant and inspiring in its own right.

Hand pressed over her stomach, Lenora tried to push such thoughts aside. She was in no condition to pursue her career. At least, not until the baby had been delivered into the arms of parents who were better suited for the position. Then what would stop her?

A scarlet wall abruptly blocked her way, and she jerked to a stop—just short of slamming into Edmond's back. Melina stood at the door to a shop, waiting for them to join her.

Edmond motioned Lenora past and took his usual place just inside the door, his interest more on the street than the fabrics lining the walls and spread across tables.

"Oh, look at this pink!"

Lenora stepped to the first table where Melina stood, a dusty-colored rose fabric between her fingers. Lenora touched the light muslin. Perfect for a summer gown, but impractical in every way for life on a farm … or any working profession.

But if she were to return to singing … someday. If she found a home for her baby. Until then, any other plans fell flat. "It would look beautiful on you," Lenora said before moving on. She'd already fallen prey to frivolous dreams. It was past time she based her decisions on reality.

"I was thinking it'd be perfect for you. More suited for your fairer complexion."

She didn't need something lovely, something with frills, something to ply upon her vanity. Mother had been right to steer her far away from such extravagances. Useful. Durable. Like the rooster red at the end of the table. As Lenora drew near, she changed her mind. A heavier gingham, it would hold up well with work but too closely resembled burgundy, a color she had worn often on the stage. Except those garments had been satin, and most could not be referred to as gowns.

A cinnamon bolt of the same fabric sat beside the red. A horrible shade of brown but completely suitable. Very reminiscent of the colors of her youth. Earth colors. Practical. Modest.

Melina brushed against her sleeve, leaning near.

"I like this one," Lenora stated.

"Brown?"

"It's sensible."

"Yes, but maybe too sensible." Melina squeezed her arm. "I think a blue would be nice. You looked so well in that skirt you borrowed from me. We could choose a darker shade if you prefer."

Lenora glanced across the room at the vast array of blues. Much prettier than the bolt of cloth in her hands. Was it a sin to wish to dress attractively? To be beautiful?

Favour is deceitful, and beauty is vain …

The Bible verse her father had compelled her to commit to memory answered her unspoken question. She forced a smile and held to the cinnamon. "This one is good." At least it wouldn't be as horrible as the green currently hanging off her.

She glanced at Edmond manning the door and had a twinge of regret. How she wished she could dress to please him. He met her gaze, but all his hooded expression revealed was a degree of distaste. Was it aimed at her choice of fabrics or at *her*?

Another look to the blues and her resolve weakened. "Maybe …"

Melina snatched the brown from her arms and dragged her across the room. "A deep blue would wear well."

Lenora didn't dare glance at Edmond but could feel his gaze follow her. She nodded. "All right."

Grinning, Melina collected the fabric and moved to the counter where a matron measured off nine yards, cut it, and wrapped it in brown paper for safe transport.

Lenora headed in the opposite direction, pretending to examine a collection of buttons in small jars along a shelf. She had done nothing to warrant the kindness or generosity she'd received from Melina or her brother. Lenora had eaten their food and imposed upon their hospitality. What a useless wretch she was. She should decline any more favors from them and find her own way … but here she stood, trying to ignore the guilt pricking what remained of her conscience.

Ranger snorted as the train heaved out of the Calgary station. Edmond rubbed the animal's neck. "Easy, boy." A few hours, and they would be home. But then, what? Keep his mouth shut and pretend everything was the same as it had been a day ago before he'd learned Lenora's true identity and her secrets?

He wasn't so talented an actor. Not like her.

Edmond swallowed the rising bitterness every time he considered Lenora Perry and the façade she had put on. A pregnant saloon girl who had weaseled into their lives and played with their heartstrings. She'd used them.

Ranger nudged him, mouthing his sleeve, and Edmond stepped out of reach. "Not now, boy." He was trying to think and not doing a very good job at it. He'd not been able to think straight for the past twenty-four hours, and following Melina and Lenora around while trying to see past her act hadn't helped a bit. As soon as he'd situated them both safely in a passenger car, he'd left to settle Ranger and couldn't make himself return. The thought of sitting across from Lenora and those large blue eyes …

Edmond knocked his fist against the wall of the stock car and cut his thought short. He'd not let his mind consider the depth of her sad eyes or the gentle slope of her jaw, drawing his attention to full lips. Never mind the golden waves she often allowed to flow loosely over her shoulders. He was a man who prided himself on control and a sound mind, and he'd not allow himself to be manipulated.

When the train pulled into Cayley, the sun was nestled in the peaks of the Rockies, and Edmond's resolve was in place. It was time to discover the full truth about Lenora Perry's past and the man who hunted her. Then Edmond would make a decision on what to do. Hiding her on the farm indefinitely, or even until her baby arrived, was out of the question.

He waited until the door to the stock car opened and led Ranger down the ramp. Melina and Lenora waited on the platform just outside of the passenger cars. He motioned in the direction of the livery. He'd be back in a few minutes with the wagon.

"How was the trip?" Hal called from the door of the stables.

"Fine." Edmond's polite reply came out blunt. Honesty would open a can of nightcrawlers he had no wish to dig through.

"Want me to hitch the wagon for you?"

Edmond handed over Ranger's lead. "Please." He wandered to the door of the livery and stood in the shadow of the wide door. Melina and Lenora crossed the dusty street, each toting a stack of packages in their arms. Both appeared young and innocent, reality well hidden. Releasing his breath in a huff, he strode to meet them, reaching first to relieve Lenora's arms. If she were with child, over-exerting would be unwise. She already looked far too peaked.

Pregnant.

The mere thought of her carrying another man's child sank deep in the pit of his gut and soured.

Her arms fell limply at her sides as soon as he lifted the burden. "Thank you," she murmured.

He grunted a reply and turned to the wagon. By the time he'd loaded all their packages into the back, Hal was finishing with the harnesses.

"I'll settle up with you tomorrow."

"No problem." Hal handed him the reins, hardly looking at him. Not with Melina smiling from the back of the wagon where she had already made herself comfortable.

Lenora stood with her hand on the tailgate as though considering climbing in as well. As tempted as he was to let her manage on her own, Edmond swallowed his anger and offered her an arm. "Come sit up on the seat. It handles the ruts better." A preferable option in her condition.

She glanced at Melina as though torn but finally nodded. "Very well."

He boosted her up on the bench, his hands again at her waist, but this time very aware of the weight she had put on in the past few weeks. A result of the child growing within her, no doubt, not just a healthier diet since her arrival.

He circled the wagon and climbed aboard. While they jostled over the narrow road leading to the farm, he could not help but be aware of the woman beside him. Her slumped shoulders, white pallor, bowed head, and the way her hands clasped on her lap did not escape his notice. What was going through that brain of hers? Or was she merely weary from the journey?

Edmond stiffened his spine. Whatever trouble she was in was, no doubt, the result of the lifestyle and occupation she had chosen. The consequences were her own.

"I told Edmond." Melina's stark words just before they'd pulled into the Cayley station hammered through Lenora's thoughts.

What must he think of me? Melina's confession explained the scowl on Edmond's face. A wonder he'd not balked at allowing her to come home with them. Shame lit a fire within her chest, and Lenora wished she'd known before she agreed to return. She would never have conceded if she'd sensed such strong disapproval. If she wasn't so exhausted, she might have insisted on remaining on the train, returning south. Shouldn't Channing know he was to be a father? Was she heaping wrong upon wrong by staying away?

He'll never marry you. So what was the point of returning? Nothing would change. If he knew, he would only treat her pregnancy as another reason to keep her under his thumb.

Lenora allowed Edmond to assist her from the wagon and lingered long enough to grab a couple of packages to carry with her to the house. She took them directly to the bedroom, laying them on the lone chair before dropping onto the bed she shared with Melina.

"What do I do now, Lord?"

A useless prayer, but she had nowhere else to turn.

Melina tapped on the door before stepping in with more packages. She set them with the others. "No, don't get up. Lay down until supper's ready."

Lenora nodded her thanks and dropped her head back as soon as the door closed. She shut her eyes, but the rigid expression on Edmond's face remained. Utter disapproval. She couldn't stay here knowing what he thought of her.

The melody of her mother's favorite hymn played in her memory, the words coming on their own.

Rock of Ages, cleft for me ...

"Let me hide myself in Thee."

Oh, to be hidden away from the shame and the reality of her situation.

"Let the water and the blood, From Thy riven side which flowed, Be of sin the double cure, Cleanse me from its guilt and power."

Was such a cleansing truly possible? Papa's sermons tended

to run more on the duty of the individual to forsake sin and do good continually. But he had spoken of repentance too. Would it be enough to wash her clean?

She sang the verse again, clinging to the hope it planted in her heart.

The door opened a crack, and Melina's face appeared. "I had no idea you could sing like that." Awe tinged her voice.

Heat rushed through Lenora. She'd tried to sing softly. "I hadn't meant to disturb anyone."

"Far from a disturbance." Melina smiled though her eyes glistened. "I wish everyone could hear you sing. Would you consider it?"

Lenora pushed up. "Consider what?"

"Singing for the community. At church. Your voice is angelic, and that song … I can't think of anything more uplifting than listening to you."

While the suggestion was flattering, Lenora hadn't sung for an audience in over two months. And she'd not sung in a church, never mind entered one, for much, much longer. Years. Who was she to bring others closer to a God she had estranged herself from?

"You don't have to. I won't pressure you." Melina slipped out of the room as quietly as she'd come.

Lenora sank her head back into the feather pillow. Sing again? Part of her ached to stand before a congregation of any kind and move them with her voice, but she was more suited for a theater than a church. God looked down on such vanity. To sing praises to Him for the sake of her own pride would be one more sin to add to the growing pile.

I couldn't sing for them. I'd be an impostor.

Edmond's boots sounded out a path from the front door to the kitchen. His voice mumbled through the walls.

Oh, how she would love to sing for him, to see that same appreciation and awe Melina had shown.

With a groan, Lenora rolled over and buried her face in her

pillow. A pretty voice would have little effect on Edmond's opinion of her now that he knew of the baby, of the sin she'd committed. No one would want her in their church once they knew her past. God included.

Why deceive herself?

CHAPTER 18

Edmond's mood was still as sour as the crabapples growing at Widow Bagley's the next morning as he headed toward Cornwell land. A new corral, wood still moist and green, held George's bull, which snorted as he approached. Enough to bring George's head up from where he crouched with a hammer and nails near the start of a one-room house, fastening a board onto the framed wall. Behind the house, they had set up a tent that sang with children's giggles and squeals. The little boy burst through the door wearing nothing but his birthday suit.

"Lindon!" His mother darted out behind him and snatched him up. Her gaze cut toward Edmond and her face reddened. "Morning, Constable Bryce. Excuse me, I've yet to wrestle these youngsters into their day clothes."

He chuckled and nodded. "Looks like you have your work cut out for you."

"That's the truth." She ducked back into the tent.

George stepped over the low wall, hammer still in hand. "What are you doing here?"

Edmond dismounted. "Just checking in to make sure you got your bull home with no further problems from Greer."

"As you can see."

"Good." Edmond approached the house. "Do you need a hand?"

"Not from you," George grumbled. "We're fine."

Edmond tightened a smile and walked to the corral, where he hooked Ranger's lead over the top rail. "Glad to hear it." He started toward the black horse grazing closer to the river, front legs hobbled.

"Been admiring your mare. How old is she?"

George followed. "She's not for sale."

"No matter. Can't help but appreciate a fine animal like her, all the same." He let the mare sniff his hand before scratching her neck, across her shoulders, and down her long leg. He unfastened the hobble and lifted her hoof. Not shod, but freshly trimmed. No way to tell if she'd been involved in the cattle rustling. He released her leg and slipped the hobble back around her pastern.

George waited with arms across chest, and a glower leveled at him. "What are you really doing here, Constable? What are you looking for?"

"Nothing, anymore." Edmond nodded and headed to his horse.

"Is there something you want to accuse me of?"

He glanced back. "No, George. I have nothing against you." He swung onto Ranger and tipped his hat to Mrs. Cornwell, holding a fully clothed boy at the door of the tent. "Good day to you."

The interchange with George pestered his thoughts as he made two more stops, and then Edmond rode toward the Lawson farm. As much as he hoped for George's innocence for the sake of his young family, there was something about him that unsettled Edmond.

At the Lawsons', a handful of children milled around the yard, playing or busy with chores. Mrs. Lawson had six children, and all were accounted for but the eldest. Matt. The others provided a warm welcome, two young girls running up to grin at Edmond.

"Hello, Constable Bryce," the ten-year-old said, brushing her braids back over her shoulder. "Are you here to see Mama?"

Edmond swung down from the saddle. "And Matthew. Is he around?"

The girl's eyes widened. "Are you here to arrest him again? I heard—"

"Hush, Lucy!" an older sister chided. "Mama said not to talk of it."

A flicker of movement in the shadows of the barn door drew Edmond's gaze. Matt stood with his hands in his pockets, shoulders slumped. Edmond shook his head. "I'm just here to speak with him. He's going to give me a hand with my rounds today."

Mouths widened to match the roundness of the children's eyes. "You mean like a deputy?" the youngest boy asked. Not more than seven, admiration glowed on his face.

"You could say that." If Mounties had deputies. He'd not lower their eldest brother in their eyes and inform them of the truth. Respect was important to a man. Especially one who was still finding his way out of boyhood with no father to look to for approval.

Maybe they had more in common than Edmond had considered. Maybe Matt needed someone to show him how to be a man more than he needed the fear of the law.

Edmond maneuvered past the children toward the barn. The others flocked around like hungry chicks. "I have a few things I need your help with today, Matt. I'll speak with your mother if you want to finish any chores and saddle up."

The boy's jaw flexed, but under the scrutiny of his siblings, he kept his mouth closed and gave a curt nod.

Satisfied, Edmond moved toward the cabin, though he didn't have to go far. Mrs. Lawson met him halfway. Her hands worked her apron, and worry filled her gaze as she cast a glance to her eldest. "Is there some trouble, Constable?"

"Nothing to concern yourself over. Matthew agreed to give me a hand for a couple weeks. I'll allow him some time in the mornings to help out here, but I would appreciate it if you could spare him for a few hours each day."

Mrs. Lawson stood silent for a moment. Her nod came slow but held deeper understanding. "Of course, Constable." Her eyes glistened. "Thank you."

The weight of the widow's hope fell heavily onto Edmond's shoulders. She was trusting him with her son ... and he wasn't sure how much good he could do.

The children swarmed him asking questions until Matt started across the yard with his pa's horse in tow. Despite the tension the young man emitted, the large Morgan plodded along, black tail flicking against its deep red coat. Gaze like flint, Matt mounted and waited for Edmond's directions.

Keeping his expression relaxed, Edmond swung into his saddle and nodded to the youth who should be his prisoner if he were going by the book. In this case, the spirit of the law would have to do. "Let's head out." He quirked a smile. "Deputy."

The furrow deepened between the young man's eyes, but his siblings cheered. Hopefully, Matt would take that to heart.

Edmond led the way to Widow Bagley's home. During his last visit, he'd noticed her dwindling firewood supply, and it was past time to fulfill his promise to bring in some more logs for her.

Mrs. Bagley met him at the door with a ready hug.

"I brought some extra help today." He nodded to Matt, who hadn't budged from his horse.

"That the Lawson boy?"

"Yes, ma'am."

Something akin to concern flickered in her gaze, but she smiled. "Well, bring him back when you two are done, and I'll have some cookies waiting."

"Will do." He'd never admit her baking was one of the main reasons for his frequent visits.

After grabbing two axes from the shed and a sharpening stone for the older one, Edmond instructed Matt to tie his horse near the trough and then led him into the nearby coulee where stands of old willows waited with dead branches aplenty. He set to work, giving directions as needed. Gradually, Matt's jaw relaxed, and they fell into a steady rhythm together. Conversation was sparse, and that was all right. Edmond had enough to occupy his mind while sweat ran freely down his neck. He set his coat and hat aside and rolled up his sleeves.

After the branches were felled, Edmond had Ranger drag them closer to the house. A double-handled saw made quick time, laying out foot-long lengths. Other than the scowl that had returned to the young man's brow, Edmond was grateful for the help.

"Not so bad, is it?"

Matt mopped his brow with his sleeve. "Would have been better off relaxing in jail."

"Might have been more comfortable, but a jail doesn't make a man. An honest day's work. Service. That's the kind of man your pa was."

Matt pushed away from the saw's handle. "Don't talk about my pa."

Edmond kept the blade moving until a length of log fell loose. "Your pa was a good man. He'd be pleased with the work you've done today."

Arms folded tight against his chest, Matt took another step back. "What do you know? You ain't him."

The venom in his voice gave Edmond pause. "I'm sorry." He crouched and began loading his arms with logs. Some would have to be split, but that would hold until another day. He'd stack what they had while the boy cooled off and then see if Mrs. Bagley's cookies would sweeten either of their moods.

Another half hour found them mounted and on the trail again but with Matt as sour as ever. Edmond was tempted to take Matt home and head out to the Bar L on his own, but wisdom suggested it would be unwise to part with the strain between them. A few miles might shake loose whatever chip Matt wore on his shoulder … though Edmond didn't hold out much hope.

"I think it best that I leave." Lenora pulled a sprig of yarrow from the row of carrots and glanced at Melina, who had armed herself with a spade against an infiltration of thistles in the raspberry patch. "If I wait much longer, what chance have I of employment?"

"Why leave at all? At least until the baby comes. There is little employment available for women out here, anyway. And how long will you work? What if it becomes too much as the pregnancy continues?"

I don't know! Uncertainties threatened her resolve, but if she admitted as much, Melina would never let her leave. Lenora snatched another weed from the ground and tapped loose the soil from the roots. If she felt she had a choice, she would stay here and help where she could. Melina, bless her heart, enjoyed her company, and even the truth of Lenora's circumstances had not changed the easiness between them. It was almost possible to forget the dark shadow that hung over the house every evening when Edmond returned. He hardly acknowledged her presence unless his sister gave him no choice. Easier to go to bed early than pretend the sting of his disapproval didn't affect her.

"I simply see no reason for you to go away when you're welcome here."

"Am I welcome?" Lenora bit the inside of her cheek. The words had slipped out and escaped on the breeze before she could stay them.

Melina sunk the spade deep and left it standing. She wiped her dirty hands on her apron as she stepped near and crouched to assist with the smaller weeds. "Give Edmond time. He's used to everything being black and white, right and wrong. But life isn't like that. It's an array of grays. Like a photograph. Otherwise, we'd hardly have need of a savior, would we?"

"I suppose not." Lenora sighed. Melina made the past seem so easily reconciled. But those shades of gray clung to her hands and soul like ink to the pages of a book. Ingrained in her very nature. That was probably what Edmond saw. He was not so naive as his sister.

"I'm not helping, am I?" Melina gave a sad smile before she gathered up a pile of weeds and hauled them to the edge of the garden to be added to a larger heap. Yarrow, lamb's quarter, thistles, and grass. Keeping a garden clean during summer seemed a never-ending battle. Pull a weed only for another to spring up in its place after the next rain.

"I don't blame your brother for his uneasiness around me. He's a good man." Much better than she deserved ... everything she wished she were worthy of. If she could ever get her inner garden clean enough.

"And I believe you are a good woman."

Lenora laughed out loud, though it came out a little strangled. "You don't know who I was. Who I became."

"Maybe, but you left that. You fled just like Joseph from Potiphar's wife. You are trying to start anew."

Perhaps, but Joseph had fled before relinquishing his virginity. He'd stayed pure.

Porter yapped and was joined by a horse's whinny. A surge of anticipation died a quick death at the hands of reality. Edmond was home, and her welcome had long since worn thin.

"I guess that's our cue to wash up and finish dinner." Melina headed around the corner of the house, leaving Lenora unwilling to abandon her hiding place. She picked weeds until the end of the row and then started on the next, in no hurry to be back under the scrutiny of Constable Edmond Bryce. She'd rather remain out here and do something useful.

"Rock of Ages, cleft for me, let me hide myself in Thee." The line never lingered far from her thoughts since first coming to mind. Lenora clung to the words, the meaning. To hide away until she woke from this nightmare. Sitting back, hands resting on her lap, she continued to hum the melody softly as to not be overheard this time.

A shadow wavered on the ground beside her. Tall. Flat-brimmed hat.

She twisted to the intruder and immediately wished she hadn't. He looked far too fine standing there in his red coat, gun holstered at his side, hardly a scuff on his tall boots despite being worn all day.

"I'm sorry I disturbed you. Melina asked me to bring in some of the fresh greens for a salad. I didn't realize you were here."

She shrugged and focused on the weeds. The last thing she wanted to do was start over-thinning the carrots, and she wasn't far from that.

"You two have been busy." His voice grew closer before shifting toward the patch of lettuce and spinach.

"What you see is a result of Melina's hard work. Naturally, I am quite useless to her." She kept her voice even and chipper. Why not confirm his own beliefs?

"I doubt that." Yet his tone suggested uncertainty.

She turned a smile at him. "Now you question my word?" She stood to face him and began to dust off her ugly green skirt. She and Melina had started sewing another dress in blue, but this one seemed the most appropriate for kneeling in the dirt. The most appropriate for standing in Edmond's presence. If she could remain on her feet. Darkness clouded her vision and a wave of dizziness threatened to knock her over.

A strong hand gripped her elbow. "Are you all right?"

She waited until her head cleared before answering. "I merely stood too quickly. I'm fine." Lenora attempted to pull her arm away, but he held fast.

"Not sure I should let go until you are out of the sun and seated."

Of course, chivalrous to the end, no matter what his personal feelings. "Don't bother yourself, Constable. You've already done enough." The words came out edged, and she hated her lack of control. Hated what this man did to all her reason. She pulled away and turned from him. She'd prefer to keep company with the weeds a while longer than return indoors with him. "I'm not finished here."

"There is nothing that can't wait until tomorrow. You've already overworked yourself." He almost sounded concerned, but Lenora knew better.

"I simply stood too quickly. Now leave me alone."

He was silent, and Lenora closed her eyes and prayed he'd go. Losing her temper at him did not help her plight or salvage her respectability.

But he remained in place. "Why are you angry with me?"

Tears pricked her eyes, and she did her best to blink them away while keeping her back turned. "I'm not angry." Leastwise, not with him. She was angry at herself for letting this man hurt her, for caring so deeply about his opinion while knowing how low she ranked.

CHAPTER 19

Edmond should walk away as Lenora had requested, but his feet refused to budge. He sighed. Knowing her real name hadn't changed how he thought of her, and despite everything else he knew about her, he didn't like seeing her hurt. "Look at me and tell me you aren't upset."

Her shoulders squared, but she didn't turn. Gradually, her breathing steadied. When she finally looked at him, a small smile curved her lips, but otherwise, her expression gave no clues. Only the gloss of moisture in her eyes indicated deeper emotion. "I have no cause to be upset, Constable. You have been very kind to me." Her voice was as smooth and sweet as fresh honey butter. Too sugary for his tastes. "Please, go back in the house and enjoy your dinner. I want to finish here. I assure you my head is clear now. Very clear, in fact."

Edmond nodded because he had no reply. How could he argue with her? How could he tell her it was perfectly normal to have dizzy spells when pregnant or insist she allow him to walk her to the house? Maybe if she were his wife and carried his child, not a saloon girl who had sold herself …

Now he was the one who needed to turn away. How could his feelings about someone be so displaced from what he knew about them? The facts remained solid and undeniable. He'd seen her scantily clad photograph. Her pregnancy had been confirmed. All that remained was to keep his distance until she left. He took her suggestion and started back to the house. Maybe he'd send out some telegrams asking about assistance available to unwed mothers. There were plenty of churches that believed in benevolence and redemption.

Perhaps they could help her move forward with her life.

For he could not—without risking himself.

Melina was busy placing dishes on the table when he entered the kitchen. He dropped into a chair. Could he have done or said anything different to soothe Lenora's feelings? Had he come across as being too callous?

"Where's Lenora?"

"Finishing in the garden." Edmond stared at his empty hands. He'd completely forgotten the greens Melina had requested, but his appetite wasn't much. Not anymore. "She said she'll be in later and not to wait for her."

Melina blew out her breath and dropped the platter on the table before heading to the door. "Can you not even be civil to her anymore?"

Edmond's chair squawked as he shoved it back. "I was civil. But how can you suggest the truth of her identity and … everything else … has no effect on our relationship with her?"

"Which *relationship* are you referring to?" She cocked a brow at him.

"You know what I mean." He crossed his arms. "She needs to find a suitable place to live." His arm pressed against the small lump in his breast pocket where her ruby ring resided. He'd carried it with him for far too long, looking for the right time to return it to her. The appropriate moment never seemed to present itself.

"What's wrong with here? Mrs. Walker is an excellent midwife."

"In Calgary, there are both midwives and doctors." And the sale of the ring would allow her a comfortable start.

Melina stepped to the table and slipped into the chair across from him. "There is something else I've been meaning to discuss with you. I want to talk to Mrs. Walker on Sunday, ask her about the possibility of her taking me on as an … as an apprentice."

"Apprentice?" The word broke with a little more force than necessary.

Melina stood and took a stance similar to the one Lenora had minutes earlier. "I won't sit here wasting my life, contributing nothing more than a fine quilt on occasion."

"You contribute plenty." And not just to his comfort, but as an active member of their church and community.

"I need more, Edmond. I want to help women bring their little babes into this world. I want to feel a part of something bigger, greater ... more divine."

The light in her eyes was hard to ignore. "This isn't because of Lenora?" *And her baby?* He'd not voice the last. The intensity of his feelings on the matter was irrational, but he couldn't help himself. Couldn't help the itch under his skin, too deep to scratch, the spike of his temperature or knot in his chest at the thought of Lenora's offspring.

"I'd thought of it before," Melina continued, "but honestly, yes, Lenora and her situation have affected my desire. The thought of a woman going through pregnancy and labor without anyone at her side who cares for her and her baby ... She deserves better than that."

It wasn't their place to determine what Lenora Perry deserved. Edmond opened his mouth with one last argument, but Melina spoke first.

"It's not just Lenora and her situation, Edmond. I can't be a Mountie like you and Auguste. I need something."

Edmond leaned back in his chair and massaged the tightness in his right shoulder. The day had stretched over a dozen hours of riding, confrontations, manual labor, tracking, and trying to plant a little common sense into a kid who'd have none of it. Truth be told, Melina might have made a better Mountie than him. If she'd been born a boy.

"We don't have to decide anything today."

"Seems like everything's already been decided." He scratched his fingers through his hair. "Don't mind me. It's been a long day."

She lowered back into the chair across from him. "Did things not go well with Matt?"

"As well as I expected. But we found another carcass. This time on Bar L land."

"No."

He nodded. "Frank came upon it while hunting strays. Tracked the rustler through Mackenzie land before we lost the trail." He wouldn't tell her the direction they were headed, but he planned on sending out a couple of telegrams in the morning inquiring into the past of Mr. George Cornwell.

Thankfully, Melina didn't pepper him with more questions like she used to do. They ate dinner in relative silence. Almost halfway through, the front door opened. Lenora appeared a moment later.

Melina jumped from her seat. "Come and eat."

Lenora moved to the far side of the table from him, but Edmond beat her there and held out the chair. No reason to act ungentlemanly. She murmured her gratitude and then fell into the quiet that felt almost natural now.

Melina was the first to break it. "I meant to ask earlier, Lenora, but with the Sabbath tomorrow, would you consider joining us for church?"

Edmond almost rolled his eyes. Didn't they know enough about her and her previous life to already know the answer? She'd always found excuses in the past.

"I would like that, thank you."

He jerked to look at her.

She already watched him, a shallow smile upon her lips.

Channing relaxed into his chair and downed his bourbon as the chant rose to the ceiling, pressing against the rafters. The voluptuous blonde strode into the center of the stage, lighting it with the flash of a smile and sparks in her eyes. Her satiny gown hung low to her ankles, but a quick jerk brought it to her knees, revealing shapely legs. Men cheered.

A clap on the back returned Channing's attention to the man seated beside him. "Miss Nell has them eating out of her palm.

Maybe her voice isn't as cultured as Lenora's, but she's reeling the men in just as well."

Yes, she was. The Pot O' Gold had been filled to the brim the past two nights.

"Guess you can pull Anderson off the hunt now."

Channing's smile faded.

"Surely, finding her isn't worth it."

"That's for me to decide." He stood and returned to his office. Miss Nell's serenade followed. Her voice was good, and she had charm Lenora had never flaunted in front of the customers. He'd had to discover it on his own.

He closed his eyes for a moment. The crowd loved his new singer, and they were right too. She belonged on a saloon stage. She would neither challenge him … nor drive him mad.

Not like Lenora.

He struck his fist against the desk, and numbing pain spread across the side of his fist. They were right. He was wasting thought and money on a pointless search. Lenora was no longer within his reach or his power. And nothing ate at him more. All along, she had inferred he would never be enough, just as the Pot O' Gold wasn't enough. Everything he had worked for and built from nothing … not good enough for the likes of her.

Would Da agree?

Channing dropped onto the corner of his desk and ground his teeth. Another cheer erupted from the main room. Glasses clinked in celebration. Why wasn't he celebrating? What sort of fool was he?

"Boss?"

Harvey poked his head through the doorway, and Channing waved him the rest of the way. "What is it?"

"A boy just dropped off this telegram."

Channing held out his hand. A short line of type sprawled across the paper, and he smiled for the first time in weeks.

Found her.

CHAPTER 20

L enora should have politely declined or come up with another excuse to stay at the farm. Any excuse. But no, when Melina asked if she'd accompany them to church, Edmond's expression had been clear on what he thought of the idea. He'd been confident of her reply. Lenora had not been able to walk away from the challenge.

The wind pressed from behind the wagon as though God Himself wanted to make sure she didn't back out. She might have believed that if the wind ever blew from another direction, but most days, it swept over the mountains with equal force.

Edmond remained silent at her side on the bench as the wagon jostled over the ruts to the rustic church, complete with roughhewn steeple. The scattering of wagons and mounts suggested that most of the congregation had already entered the building. Though not everyone. A larger wagon approached from the west. A woman held a young boy on her lap, and the driver held a scowl. Sleeves rolled to his elbows and dirt staining his pants, the man paused the wagon just long enough for his wife to get down and lift two children after her. Not surprising. With a slap of leather over the horses' backs, the wagon returned the way it had come.

Edmond tied their horses to a pole and hurried to offer a hand to his sister and then to Lenora. No sooner than her feet touched the ground than he excused himself and moved to help with the children. The little girl quickly attached herself to his side, hand in his—quite the image. One could almost picture the stalwart Mountie with children of his own. It probably wouldn't take much for a child to melt the man's heart. Children were still innocent.

Lenora laid a hand over the slight swell of her stomach, still unnoticed by the rest of the world. For now. If only she could provide a father like Edmond for her child. Maybe a family would be willing to take the baby after its birth, but to entrust her baby to strangers? How would she know for certain what kind of parents he or she would have?

A pang of loneliness wrapped Lenora's heart as she followed Melina up the church steps. She carefully tucked her hands at her sides, forbidding them from revealing her secret. Church-going folks would have no use for her if they knew the truth. Most would react the same as Edmond. Her parents would probably take it worse.

"Are you married to Constable Bryce?"

Lenora twisted to the girl who had forfeited Edmond's hand to come alongside her.

"I …" She made the mistake of glancing at the man in question. His face wore both shock and a hint of red. "No, I'm not." Lenora stilled her own heart's thumping and crouched to meet the child eye-to-eye. With her sun-bleached hair hanging in two braids, she was like a memory of happier times, of family.

"But you aren't his sister."

Lenora chuckled. "No. Miss Melina is his sister. I'm just a friend."

"I want a pretty friend like you."

"As do I. Will you be my friend?"

The girl's eyes widened. "You can be my friend too."

"I would like that." The child's silky braid slipped between Lenora's two fingers. "You remind me of my little sisters."

"I want a little sister. All I have right now is Lindy, and he isn't near as nice. I have to watch him all the time, and Auntie makes me play with him. But he just wants to play with rocks and eat sticks."

Lenora smiled while her heart wept. "I used to have to watch my younger sisters too. One day, you'll see how much you really do love Lindy and will miss playing with him."

The girl started to say something more, but her aunt's hand guided her aside. "Come, Heather, we need to sit down." The gentleness in the woman's gaze fell on Lenora. "Thank you," she whispered as they stepped to the nearest pew.

Lenora stood, warmth rising through her at the realization of attention she had garnered from those seated nearby. Only Edmond looked steadfastly to the front of the church from the pew he had chosen. Melina slipped in beside him, and Lenora hurried to do the same as the parson stood behind the pulpit in his dark suit. Chatter hushed, and the middle-aged man looked over the congregation. His dark eyes bored into her. As though he saw through her mask and knew her deepest sins. Papa often had that ability—to discern the heart of people. What if this man of God already knew she didn't belong here?

Was it too late to bolt?

Melina's arm slipped around her shoulders and squeezed while the parson offered an invocation. Then the congregation stood and sang. Lenora followed suit but kept her mouth closed. She didn't know that particular hymn. Even still, the words tugged at her heartstrings with thoughts of her childhood, memories of singing praises to God with her sisters and mother surrounding her. Home.

Lost in nostalgia and trying not to let shame drive her from her seat, Lenora hardly heard the sermon. Something about the story of Paul's mission to the gentiles. Finally, the congregation sang the concluding hymn. One she knew well.

"I need Thee every hour, most gracious Lord; no tender voice like Thine can peace afford."

Mama had loved this song. How often she had sung it while kneading bread or busy in the garden. How easy it had been to learn by heart. Even now, Lenora was helpless but to raise her voice and sing along.

"I need Thee, Oh, I need Thee; every hour I need Thee …"

The words reached deeper now, deeper than ever before. No longer just a song but a plea to God above.

"O bless me now, my Savior, I come to Thee."

A tear warmed Lenora's cheek, and she ducked her head to bat it away. The rest of the congregation had hushed, their eyes on her.

"I'm sorry." Lenora slipped from the pew. Head down, she hurried out the door and down the steps. She didn't bother following the road. Though distant, the mountains called to her, and she fled toward the west, facing the steady force of the wind.

I need Thee, O I need Thee.

The prayer continued in her heart, beyond her control to hush. She had forsaken God. Had forsaken everything her parents had taught her ... but she still longed for it. She longed for home, but she didn't know how to return. Or if she'd be welcome.

"What have I done?"

Her hem snagged on a rose thorn, and she tugged it free and then paused, this time her attention caught by the perfect five petals of pale pink encircling a circle of gold. Careful of the thorns, she stooped and plucked it from its stem. Such an unassuming flower, but as pretty as its fragrance was sweet. Oh to be like this rose. Simple, clean, and strong enough to endure even the strongest winds.

The subtle racket of a wagon on the road to her right stiffened her shoulders. She stood and hastened her steps, trying to ignore the heavy thud of hooves as they grew louder. Finally, she released the rose to the wind and glanced over her shoulder.

Edmond sat high on the seat, guiding the animals over the open field. He was almost upon her. Retreat was impossible.

"Let me help you aboard. I'll take you home."

That would be dandy if she had a home. But her parents would never accept her back. God had no use for her. And Edmond ... he didn't want her either. "Where's Melina?"

"She decided not to put Henry Pettman off any longer and is allowing him to take her on a drive. They will be along later." He jumped from the seat and moved around the horses. "Are you all right?"

As if he cared. "What does it matter?" She started walking again.

He led the horses along, keeping pace. "You told us your father was a pastor. Was that the truth?"

"I've never lied to you." Not really. Not in anything important.

"Not even about your name?"

The toe of her boot caught on a ground squirrel's mound, and she stumbled to a halt. "What do you know?" Melina had said she'd only told him about the pregnancy. Not about her past. Melina didn't even know so much.

"Your name is really Perry. But you say Wells wasn't a lie?"

"I wasn't the one who told you my name. Mr. Greer did the honors." Lenora sighed. She had allowed the untruth to be perpetuated. She wiped at the gathering moisture on the back of her neck. The sun overhead grew much too warm. "Wells is my mother's maiden name. I had to use it because—" How much dare she tell him?

"Because you were running from someone? Large man with a blond mustache?"

Her mouth opened on its own. "How ... how do you know all this?"

"It's my job to know."

She hugged herself. "And what do you know, *Constable?*"

"You worked in a saloon in Cheyenne, Wyoming. A performer. A singer. The Lovely Miss Perr—"

"Don't." Even the title made her feel dirty. The memories of men chanting it as she took the stage.

"It's true, though, isn't it?"

She met his hard gaze briefly. "Yes. It was true." But she didn't want it to be.

Edmond stood back, unable to ignore the guilt prickling his conscience at his interrogation. She'd committed no crime. Her past was her own business, despite how personal it felt. She'd done nothing against him. So why did his chest throb as though she'd inflicted a wound?

"You must think me a horrible person. No wonder ..." She shook her head and tipped her face away.

"It's not my place to judge you."

"Isn't it? Good Christians, like my father, speak of God being the judge and yet seem the quickest to throw the proverbial stone. Unseen though it may be."

An unseen boulder struck him in the chest. "Sometimes, good Christians forget to trust fully in the hand of God. Sometimes we forget how imperfect we ourselves are."

She spun to him, the wind catching her hair and whipping it across her face. "Imperfect? The infallible Constable Bryce. Surely, you speak of others."

He chuckled, but her dagger met its mark. Ranger pawed the ground behind him, tempting him with an escape—to put this conversation behind them.

"I might say it in jest," Lenora continued, "but I almost believe it myself. You are one of the best men I know, Edmond. One of the very best."

Yet, as she said the words, he felt himself driven lower.

"I don't know what conclusions you've drawn about me or who I was, but I don't imagine they are far from the truth. I gave up my family and even God to pursue fame. I allowed myself to sink to depths I had sworn never to sink to. And now, possibly too late, I realize what I want more than the greatest praises of man."

When she didn't say anything more, Edmond couldn't stay himself. "What do you want?"

Her eyes glistened, and her hand hovered over the almost unnoticeable swell of her stomach, over her unborn child. "Peace." She looked up at him with pleading in her gaze. "I want peace." A tear rolled free, and the wind pushed it sideways across her flushed cheek.

Edmond released his hold on Ranger's harness and caught the hot moisture with his thumb. He opened his arms, and she fell against his chest with a sob. Her shoulders shook, and he wrapped her tight. She fit so well against him, her warmth soaking through his shirt where his coat fell open. Who was he to judge? His duty was to forgive.

Forgive?

In truth, she had done nothing against him. Her past was between her and God.

Lenora's sobs eased, and he glanced down to see her eyes closed. A look of torture crumpled her face. "I can't."

Can't what? He held the question and pressed his mouth to the top of her head. Nothing felt so natural. So right.

His heart lurched into a full trot. He had no right to feel this way about this woman. Never mind the past. What about the future? In a few months, a child would arrive. Family. Responsibility. A complete change in directions from the course he was on.

He needed to make the decision he'd avoided so well.

Lenora pushed away. "I'm sorry. I shouldn't have …" She swiped her hand over a wet spot on the front of his shirt. "I'm making a fool of myself." The last was mumbled as she turned away and stepped out of reach. "Such a fool."

"It's my fault." He turned to the horses and pretended to straighten the harnesses over their necks and across their backs. "Let's go home."

She didn't move for a few minutes, and he remained in place. He had let his mind travel farther than he had any right to, and it was still hard to catch his breath. When she finally did come to him, he splayed his hands around her waist and lifted her onto the seat.

Keep moving.

Because if he paused at all, he might say or do something he couldn't retract.

He climbed aboard and took up the reins. "Giddyap."

The horses complied, and the wagon rocked forward over the rutted prairie back to the road. At one point, he reached out to steady Lenora on the seat but withdrew as soon as they had cleared the roughest terrain.

Miles passed under the large wheels, taking them closer to home.

"Thank you, Constable." Lenora stared at the mountains looming in the west. "I probably would have gotten horribly lost." Her palm circled low on her abdomen.

"Are you sure you are feeling all right?"

Her shoulder lifted ever so slightly. "Just a little achy."

Concern tied his stomach. "You should lay down for a while once we get back to the house."

He almost didn't see her nod.

"I haven't decided if this is punishment or the Lord trying to bring something good from something horrible." She glanced at her stomach, her hand continuing its circling. "And yet, what a wretch I am. Even while I speak of God and wanting his forgiveness, I miss being beautiful. I miss singing."

He wasn't quite sure what she was talking about now. She was beautiful—one of the most beautiful women he knew. And she had sung like an angel a short time ago. "Singing in church doesn't count?"

Her head bowed, and strands of gold fell forward over her shoulders. "I suppose it does. Except, for the first time in my life, I was embarrassed that people heard me."

"Because your song was for God." An understanding washed over him as he said the words that were reflected in her eyes.

"I guess it was. It became more than just a song."

A praise-filled prayer. For God's ears alone.

Edmond cleared the thickness from his throat. "You do have a beautiful voice."

Red rose to her cheeks, and her smile blossomed. "Very kind of you, Constable."

"Edmond." He tapped the reins over the horses' backs, encouraging their gait. "I'm not in uniform." He was simply a man beside a woman he could no longer ignore, with his heart disobeying all orders.

"Edmond," Lenora repeated softly.

She abruptly straightened in the seat and gripped his sleeve. A gasp broke from her throat. He followed her wide-eyed gaze to where a dun horse stood tied to the corral near the barn. A man stepped into sight, hat tipped low on his forehead. Not low enough to hide the large, sandy mustache cascading from his upper lip, never mind the gut that sagged over his belt.

CHAPTER 21

Lenora released her hold on Edmond's coat long enough for him to assist her to the ground. He watched her far too closely, so she forced a smile before facing Fred Anderson.

"Good day, folks," Fred said easily, hardly giving her more than a glance. "This here your farm?"

"It is." Edmond hooked her hand over his arm, securing her to his side, and led her forward. There was something protective in the action, almost possessive. A silent message that with him, she was safe. "You're new to the area?"

"Passing through." Fred addressed Edmond, acting as though he didn't know her. Lenora was fine if that was the way he wanted to play. It gave her more time to consider her options. "My horse is done in, so I was looking for a place to rest till morning."

"You are welcome here if you don't mind bunking in the barn." Edmond nodded to the empty corral. "You can haul your horse some water and fill the manger. We'll see about rustling you up some dinner, as well."

"Thank you, sir. That's kind of you."

"Think nothing of it." Edmond took the final step and extended his hand. "I'm Constable Bryce with the North-West Mounted Police. And you are?"

For a brief moment, Fred's façade of confidence faltered. "A Mountie, huh?"

The corners of Edmond's lips crept up. "That's right."

"Heard a lot of impressive things about your outfit back when I worked for the Pinkerton Agency."

"We've done business with them from time to time." He smiled and patted Lenora's hand. "Excuse us while we step into the house. I'll be back out to care for my horses in a few minutes."

Lenora began breathing again as they walked arm in arm through the front door, though she could feel Fred's gaze burning holes in her spine. Should she tell Edmond why he was there and encourage him to run the man off? Or keep her distance and wait to see what happened? Now that Fred knew Edmond was a Mountie, he might do nothing more than collect information to send back to Channing.

Edmond released her and closed the door. "Do *you* want to tell me who that is and why he's here exactly?"

She released the last of the air from her lungs and hugged her arms. She had no right, nor reason, to hide the full truth from Edmond. "Fred Anderson. He works for my last employer."

"He's here to take you back?"

She faced him, raising her chin while trying to hide the tremble in her knees. "I'm not going." Though, what if she should? Channing was the baby's father. Maybe he would take care of them.

And consign herself and child to that life forever?

She shook her head.

"He's who you've been running from."

"I knew he'd followed me as far as Helena. That's why I stole a ride on McCrae's chuck wagon. I thought this was far enough away."

Edmond nodded, but she could see the thoughts churning behind his eyes. "And why is Anderson—or your employer—so determined to find you?"

"My employer, Channing Doyle ..." She couldn't look at Edmond while speaking of Channing. Just the thought of him made her feel stained. She paced the length of the room. "The longer I worked for him, singing in his *establishment*, the more possessive he became. He hated that I wanted more or that I planned on leaving. He ..." What else could she say about him or his growing fixation with her? At first, she had thought his obsession proof of her power over him.

How wrong she had been.

"He's the father?"

Lenora almost didn't hear Edmond's question, but she provided the required nod.

"He forced himself on you."

This time he hadn't asked a question, and she wasn't sure if she could answer even if he had. Her vision swam, blurring his stricken face. What would he think of her if he knew the truth, knew that in a moment of romance and passion, she had given herself to a man who had no intention of offering her anything more than pretty gowns and a place on the stage?

"You were just a singer. You weren't a ..."

The relief in Edmond's tone drove his meaning deep into her center. She wiped her eyes clear. "You thought I sold myself to the highest bidders?"

A single thought broke through the anger. *Didn't you?*

Edmond's face took on a reddish hue. "I didn't want to, but what was I supposed to think with a photograph of you on the front of a saloon bulletin? And then I'm told that you're pregnant." More color crept over his ears, bringing him close to the shade of coat he usually wore.

Her own face heated. No wonder he'd known her name. No wonder the disdain. "When? When did you ... and how did you see the bulletin?"

Edmond shifted from one foot to the other. "Mr. Anderson's been through the area already asking about you."

"You never warned me?"

"Mel suggested we wait." He nodded toward her midsection. "You had enough on your mind at the time." Raking his fingers through his hair, he cleared his throat. "Speaking of which, you were planning to lay down."

Lenora's fight slipped away.

"Don't worry about Mr. Anderson. I'll take care of him." Edmond pushed his hat back on his head, looking surprisingly official despite his lack of uniform. Even in a plain pair of slacks and brown tweed jacket, he wore his duty for all to see.

"How?"

"I'll have a chat with him."

Lenora wished she shared his confidence. "Edmond ..." Though she had already used his given name, there was something more intimate about this moment. Maybe the small confines of the empty house. Standing so close with so much uncertainty and a sense of danger lurking nearby. "Please don't say anything yet. I need to think, to figure out what to do next."

His eyes sparked. "I should think that obvious."

"Running him off won't change anything. Fred Anderson is just the tracker. If he's here ..."

"Then he's probably already reported your location." Edmond's lips pressed thin. "So we threaten his boss, tell him just what will happen if he comes anywhere near you again."

Could it be so simple? A cloud passed over her vision, and she closed her eyes to wait for her head to clear. Why this? Why now?

Fingers wrapped her shoulders, steadying her on her feet. "Don't worry about anything right now. Lay down for a while, and we'll discuss it when you are feeling better."

Lenora gave a short nod. The ache in her lower abdomen had subsided but not disappeared, and the day had left her emotions frayed. She turned to the bedroom, ready for a quiet retreat.

"And Lenora?"

She paused, loving his use of a name bound to days of innocence and family. If only she could return to the naivety of her childhood.

"I'm sorry for my crude assumptions. If it helps, what I thought I knew never matched the woman I see you are."

His sentiment almost had the strength to warm her ... except he still had no idea what sort of woman she truly was.

Edmond blinked the red from his vision but couldn't lock the anger away. It raged through him at every thought of Channing Doyle and what he'd done to Lenora.

Channing Doyle. He'd not be forgetting that name. If that man ever stepped over the border into his territory, it'd take every ounce of willpower not to take the law into his own hands.

He leaned his palms against the doorframe and breathed deeply, an attempt to compose himself before going out to unharness the horses. If Lenora hadn't asked him to wait, he'd have some choice words for the man who loitered in his yard. As it was, he'd do his best to pretend nothing was out of the ordinary. To keep his mouth shut and his fists from demonstrating what he thought of the man and his employer.

Anderson leaned against the barn, gaze on the house, horse tied in the same spot. When he saw Edmond, he tipped his head forward with a nod.

Edmond had made it halfway across the yard when the wind carried the clatter of Henry's buggy. The matching sorrels moseyed along, their driver in no obvious hurry. Probably the opposite. Melina didn't often accept rides from the eligible bachelors in the area.

Melina alighted from the seat almost before the buggy rolled to a stop, not giving the man enough time to do more than twitch with his desire to assist her. "Thank you, Henry. We look forward to seeing you next Sunday."

With no further invitation, and Melina already moving away, he had little choice but to offer Edmond a half-hearted wave and turn his rig around.

"You found Lenora?" She barely reached him before the question was out of her mouth.

"I did."

"Good." She raised her brows, pressing for more information.

"And your ride? It went well?" he countered, not ready to vocalize what he learned without pummeling someone into the ground.

"Fine, I suppose. Were you able to talk?"

"With whom? Henry? How could I have talked to him if he was

with you all this while?"

She glared. "Haha. You know who I mean. You and Lenora. Is everything … you know … good between you?"

"It's just fine. And between you and Henry? Didn't you want to invite him for dinner, or to come calling again sometime? With Father up north, I do hope you informed him that I expect to be spoken with when he's ready to declare his intentions toward you."

Red flamed in her face. "I don't think you need to worry about that anytime soon." She elbowed past him toward the house, mumbling, "At least, I hope not." She made it another two paces before pivoting back. "Who is that man by the barn?"

"Oh, you noticed him, did you? I thought you might have been too distracted."

"If anyone drives me to distraction, it's you." She quirked a smile as though implying she'd won a round.

"He said he's just passing through and wanted to rest a spell. I told him he's welcome to the barn and that we'll bring dinner out to him when it's ready."

"Bring it out to him?" She gave him an inquisitive look. "Most people we invite to our table."

"You're right. Most people we do." Edmond pressed a flat smile and headed to where Ranger and Molasses waited. The first with ears flicking, eyes alert, the second with head down, stretching for a morsel of grass. Not a well-suited pair.

Anderson had since moved to unsaddle and tend to his animal, keeping a healthy distance between them. All the better. Edmond wasn't sure how to react to the man yet—punch him in the face and run him off his land with a promise of worse if he ever came near Lenora again or cite him the legal consequences of stalking a lady. The first idea pulled harder, and after all, he wasn't in uniform.

Twenty minutes later, he finished with the horses and returned to the house. The lace curtain in the front window wavered, and Melina met him at the door. "You want to fill me in on the story behind Mr. Blond Mustache?" she said as soon as he breached the threshold.

"Bounty hunter. In essence."

"He's the one looking for Lenora?" Her jaw tightened, and her hand settled on her hip. He'd probably be concerned if she were the one armed.

Edmond nodded.

Melina started to say something more, but the bedroom door creaked open. He held up a hand to quiet her as Lenora stepped out, sleep in her eyes, and one cheek flushed from its rest on the pillow.

"Did you sleep?"

"No." The other cheek flamed to match the first. "I need to step outside for a minute."

Took a second to gather her meaning. "Of course." Straightening his jacket over his revolver, Edmond hurried to lead the way, not about to let her go alone.

Halfway to the outhouse, Lenora stepped from his side.

"Maybe you should keep an eye on *him* instead of me." She glanced between him and the small building.

"Ah, yes." Edmond hid his smile and took up a position near the well. He'd fetch Melina some water while here. All appeared quiet at the barn, and he had a clear view of Anderson's horse.

With a full pail waiting, Edmond found a stick to throw to Porter. The dog only brought it back half the time, but it gave him something to do. Just like any relaxing Sabbath if not for the stranger in the barn and the woman he had committed to protecting.

He cast a glance toward the outhouse.

"I hear you've been having trouble around the area with rustlers."

Edmond jerked to Anderson, who stooped to pick up the forsaken stick. He flung it through the air, and Porter raced across the yard.

"That's right." Edmond eased the words out, not letting the man or the fact he could have jumped him while his guard was down unnerve him. "But we're getting close."

"Good." He wiped a hand down his mustache. "Mind if I give

you some advice?"

Edmond folded his arms. "Go ahead."

"Back ten or so years ago, I rode for the Pinkertons, made most of my money from wanted posters. I got really good with faces."

"And tracking."

His mouth tipped up. "Yep. Got good at following a trail. After a while, not even a few years or a full beard could disguise a man from me."

Edmond suddenly realized this conversation wasn't about Lenora. "What are you trying to say?"

"I remember a poster for a young man by the name of George Bates. Wanted for cattle rustling. One of the other Pinkertons brought him in, but I don't know what became of him. Reckon he didn't hang, though, because I saw the same man or a near relative in that town of yours today."

A sinking sensation skittered through Edmond. "The man, he'd be in his thirties now? Medium brown hair. Eyes to match."

"That's right."

"You're talking about George Cornwell. Man with a wife and two children."

Anderson laughed. "You already suspect him but are holding off on account of the family. Family don't change men, Constable. People don't change. Not in my experience."

"I disagree."

"Take a singer I once knew. Beautiful woman and a voice to match, but she didn't have a heart in that pretty chest of hers. You flatter her, and she'll bat her eyes at you, but she'll do the same to the next man too. She might put on a good act, but that's what she is, a performer. And when the curtain closes, and she's gotten everything she can from you, she'll be on her way to the next stage."

"Good evening, gentlemen." Lenora's voice came from behind him, and he turned to see the perfectly affable look on her face as she approached.

"Evening, ma'am. Just talking to the Mountie here about rustlers and the like."

She stepped to Edmond and slipped her arm through his. "He'll catch them. Only a matter of time. What is it they say, a Mountie always gets his man?" She leaned into his shoulder, resting her head there. "And his woman."

Anderson didn't bat an eye. "I've heard as much."

"Good. Then you can go home and tell Mr. Doyle I am never coming back. I am happy here … with my husband."

This time Anderson's expression cracked. "Constable Bryce never mentioned that."

Edmond slipped his arm around Lenora's shoulders. Now that the lie had been released, to disclaim it could put Lenora in danger. "Our conversation never got that far."

Anderson looked between them, his eyes thin slits. "That didn't take you long, Lenora. Does this man know what he's gotten himself into? Do *you*?"

"We've been very happy together so far, and I trust that will continue." She spoke with confidence, but Edmond could feel her tremble in his arms. "So please leave. Tonight."

"Very well. I will forward your news to Mr. Doyle. I'm sure he'll be very pleased for you." But the way he said it, pleasure was the last thing on Fred Anderson's mind.

CHAPTER 22

"Married!"

At Melina's exclamation, Lenora groaned and leaned her face into her hands, elbows braced on the table. Telling Fred she was married to a Mountie had seemed like a good idea at the moment. Before she considered facing Edmond afterward.

"While perhaps not true, that would be easy enough to fix." Melina grinned at the two of them.

Edmond's eyes brooded while his face remained passive. Never a good combination with him.

"I couldn't think of anything else to say," Lenora said, the closest she could come to an apology.

Edmond leaned against the wall, arms across his chest. "You asked me to speak with you before confronting him. You couldn't have done the same?"

"He was my problem. Not yours."

"How could he not be my problem? The man was on my land, threatening my *wife*." The smallest hint of amusement twitched his lip.

Lenora pushed up from the table, her palms clammy against the flat surface. "I need to step outside for a moment." Because sitting here any longer with her *husband* and his sister staring at her was too much.

Edmond reached for his hat.

Lenora waved him back. "Fred's already left." And she didn't plan on going farther than the front stoop.

"We assume he left. It'll be getting dark soon."

Heat swept through her. "I just need … air."

Instead of standing back so she could move by, he took her arm and led her out the door. A gust of wind almost pushed her back, blowing even stronger than it had that morning. There was the air she'd been looking for. And yet, it was hard to catch her breath with Edmond leading her along, his presence beside her overwhelming.

"Where are we going?"

"On a walk."

"I think I've walked far enough today." Especially with the wind constantly pushing against her, trying to compel her back.

His boots halted, and he looked at her. "Are you still feeling unwell?"

"No, it's not that. I'm fine." Aside from the usual queasiness. Perhaps a slight tenderness in her lower abdomen, but nothing to cause concern.

His gaze pinned her in place. "You wanted to get away from me, didn't you? Not just the kitchen. Not Melina."

She wanted to deny it, but that would be as much a lie as saying they were married. "I know what Melina, and even the kitchen, think of me. I know what they expect. But you …" She kept walking into the wind to avoid the reply she both longed for and dreaded.

He made none.

Past the yard, the view opened to the mountains in the west and the sun lowering toward them, a brilliant ball of gold. Higher still, arched a long cloud ridge, alight with hues of gold and a dozen shades of pink, touching every dip and sway of the clouds. She slowed and then stopped, the scene too beautiful not to pause and take in.

The sun sank lower, and the clouds above them darkened, heightening the contrast of a perfect blue sky under the arch and extending behind the mountains.

The colors gradually faded. The world grew dark.

The wind sighed a breath almost as soft as a baby's. A calm settled over the earth. Oh for this moment to never fade. To take that calm and wrap it within her. To keep Edmond at her side.

Edmond's voice rumbled. "Wasn't that worth the short walk? Even with the present company?"

"Yes. Thank you. I wish it would last."

"You don't think you would get tired watching sunsets?"

Not with you at my side.

She closed her eyes and breathed deeply of prairie grass and hope. Warmth encircled her shoulders, and she looked up at the face she had long since memorized. She didn't need the light of day to sense the twin lines on his brow, suggesting deep thought and maybe the reason for his hesitation.

"Edmond ..." How could he stand there with such longing in his eyes? And if he did feel so much for her, why not say something ... or kiss her.

Once the thought took hold, it wouldn't let go. His mouth was inches away. A slight push onto her tiptoes, and she could claim them. She spared a glance toward his eyes and found them lowered. Did that mean he wanted her as well? At the saloon, she'd gotten good at reading, and avoiding, men. Everything about Edmond's posture and gaze spoke of desire. But still, he didn't move. Knowing him, he was probably analyzing everything about the situation, about her past, about the possibility of a future, whether or not he wanted to be saddled with someone else's child. The last thing she wanted was for him to talk himself out of kissing her. Lenora gripped his shoulders and touched her mouth to his.

Just a touch ... and yet there she remained, his arms encircling her to secure her in place. No movement, no passion deepening the kiss. The softest touch. How, then, did it reach to her toes and fingertips? How, then, did it anchor her soul?

His lips brushed hers and then moved to her forehead. He tucked her under his chin. His heart pounded under her ear. Though still in his arms, doubts set in. Did he hold her to keep her from kissing him again? To keep her from making a greater fool of herself? Had she misread the want in his gaze?

"We should go back." His husky voice rumbled in her ears as

he released her and stepped away. Edmond barely glanced at her, straightening his coat and turning toward the house.

Lenora followed slower, sure of one thing. She couldn't go back. Not to the way she had felt about him before today. Not to how things had been before she'd realized she'd fallen in love.

Edmond donned his scarlet coat and pulled his hat onto his head. The weight of his holster seemed heavier than usual. But then, so did his boots. Did he dare leave Lenora alone with only Melina and Porter to keep her safe should Anderson return?

"She'll be fine." He said it out loud with hopes of easing the uncertainty that had grown steadily since their kiss last night—along with the desire to never let her out of his sight again. To never let her go. Even hours later, he still felt the pressure of her lips against his and his need for more. But indulging in his passions would be both imprudent and improper. Besides, what did he know about kissing a woman? Before last night, he hadn't given much more than a passing thought to the matter. Mother and Father had not been ones to show affection other than the occasional embrace or brush of their lips after being apart for months.

Not that he hadn't seen most everything at the academy when the men went into Regina to get away from the rigors of training. Everything from the chaste peck to the fully passionate embrace that should be kept for after matrimony.

Lenora was obviously more comfortable with kissing than he, but he didn't want to consider what practice she might have had. Not with Anderson's words still buzzing in his head.

He pushed his last button into place and again shifted his hat. The letter in his front pocket crinkled. He'd read it again this morning, trying to straighten out his thoughts. In one more week, he would ride to Fort Macleod to meet with Commissioner Aylesworth Perry, the highest-ranking officer in the North-West Mounted Police. Edmond had decisions to make and fast. If he received a commission, would he take it, along with any transfer? Or would he resign and try his hand at a different life? One that might include a wife. And child.

The ruby ring burned in the bottom of his pocket, still waiting to be returned to its proper owner.

"Please guide me, Lord," Edmond breathed—because he sure wasn't in any condition to make a rational choice. Not when his only desire was to hurry down the stairs and kiss Lenora like he had wanted to last night.

He took the stairs slowly, steeling himself to see her in the light of day.

Melina smiled up at him from the table where she scooped eggs onto two plates. "Lenora wasn't feeling well this morning, so I took her in some toast and peppermint tea to help her stomach settle."

"I thought she was doing better." He poured coffee into his mug and drank it black. Bitterness suited him this morning.

"She is. Most days. I spoke with Mrs. Walker about it, and she said nausea can last a full pregnancy or come and go throughout. The worst is usually the first three months, though, so she should start feeling better."

"Good." He drank more coffee and stole a biscuit.

"Don't you want some eggs?"

"I need to get going." And he honestly had no appetite. One last swig and he set the mug aside. "Remember what I said about keeping to the house as much as possible until I get back today. And keep the rifle loaded. I'll try to be home by early afternoon."

She nodded, following him to the front door. "There is a slight chance I'll be called away to help with Mrs. Jenson's baby. It's due any day, but if you think it best I stay here with Lenora, I'll let them know."

"I think that would be best. At least, until I'm sure Anderson has left town." His first order of business this morning. He'd not be able to think of much else until he had proof the man was gone and Lenora was safe. His next task would be to try and make progress on the rustler case. Without blinders on, this time.

CHAPTER 23

With his business completed in town and no word of Fred Anderson, Edmond detoured past the sites where the remains of the missing cattle had been found. There must be something he had overlooked that would reveal the identities of the rustlers. But what? He mulled over and over again what he knew. The chipped hoof of one of the first horses. The cribbing habit of the second. A black coat. Every time, the trail had led a different direction before being lost. Whoever was stealing the cattle was trying hard to lead him astray. Almost as though they knew what he would be looking for and made sure he'd find just enough to keep him hunting.

Suspicion pointed toward George Cornwell—or George Bates if Anderson told the truth. If he had an accomplice.

Unless the first cow Edmond had found was unrelated to the others.

No, they all had to be connected.

He slowed Ranger as he neared the coulee that marked the beginning of Mackenzie land near where Greer had shown him the second carcass. The creek ran low in the gully's bottom, depleted from a lack of summer rain. The futility of his search struck Edmond with renewed force. What was he doing here? There would be nothing to find this long after the rustler had been through here. He should check on Melina and Lenora to make certain all was well, and they'd not seen more of Anderson.

"Come on, boy."

He tugged Ranger's head to the side, but the horse turned a full circle, returning to its original position. Ranger gave a high whinny, stretching his neck to see deeper into the coulee.

"What's down there, boy?" Edmond stood in the stirrups and craned his neck.

Another horse answered the call, its nicker low.

Instinct dropped Edmond from the saddle. He led Ranger down the steep slope toward a stand of trees. The wind whipped through the coulee, bringing with it the crush of undergrowth and muffled voices—someone in a hurry.

Edmond reached the creek about the same time the rider—or riders—mounted their horses. A flash of black moved through the trees. Edmond swung back into the saddle and raced across the water. A spray of cool drops peppered his clothes. As they reached the other side, Ranger tossed his head and dodged to the right. Smoke billowed from the grove. Crackling flames followed, hardly touching the trees with the force of the wind behind them.

Edmond drove Ranger around the fire, searching the foliage for another glimpse of the culprits. Man and horse had vanished, and he could not give pursuit. The flames continued to grow, chased by the strong gusts pushing from the west. The creek was his best bet. Stop the fire now or lose it on the open prairie.

Stripping off his coat, Edmond doused it in the shallow water and confronted the flames on the northeast. He ignored the heat searing his face and the burn of his muscles, slapping the flames down until the charred edge of grass smoldered and the fire lapped at the last of the tall reeds along the creek. He bent over to catch his breath. He'd done it. Only a matter of time before ...

A hard gust swept over the mountains, shaking the high branches of the willows behind him and flattening the grasses low. Ash stung his eyes and made them water. He blinked hard and swiped at the tears while staggering back from the press of heat.

The flames rose in a fury, pushing past his firebreak, licking the ground and leaving it blackened. He ran to the creek and slapped his coat through the murky water. Then froze, his throat clogging with more than smoke. Small orange tongues scored the dried grass on the far side of the stream, leaving smoldering black in their hasty trail.

Edmond sprinted through the knee-deep water, not caring that it sprayed his clothes and soaked into his boots. He tried to get ahead of the ever-growing flames, but they raced beyond his reach, growing with intensity as they breached the top of the coulee. Their roar of victory joined the taunts of the wind. Coughing out a mouthful of smoke, he dropped his blackened coat to the ground. He was powerless against the force driving the fire. All he could do was try to outrun it with a warning to anyone in its path. And pray that the wind eased enough to give them a fighting chance.

He ran back through the stream to where he'd tied Ranger and then galloped toward the east. There were a handful of farms between here and Cayley but little else in the fire's path to slow it down.

God, please help us stop this fire before someone gets hurt.

Edmond drew his rifle from its sheath alongside his leg and fired into the air. He was still a couple miles from the closest homestead, but the sound would travel faster and hopefully raise some eyes to the horizon and the growing cloud of smoke.

After another mile, two riders came at him from the north. Edmond reined to meet them. "Frank." Just the man he wanted. Someone who could keep a straight head in all of this.

"What happened? We heard your shots. What's the smoke from?"

"Wildfire," he panted. "I couldn't slow it." He dragged another breath into his deprived lungs. "Get Mrs. Bagley away from her farm. I'll warn the Shaws and see what we can do to head this fire off."

With a quick nod, Frank kicked up his horse, his oldest son on his tail. Without a miracle, there wasn't much they could do for the Bagley homestead, but if they could get some plows breaking earth, they might be able to slow the fire. Did he dare chance a backburn? Might only make things worse—if that were possible.

How could things possibly get worse between her and Edmond—or more awkward? Lenora couldn't stop thinking about their kiss. Not that it should even be considered a kiss. He'd not returned it.

Blinking away another swell of tears, Lenora scrubbed harder against the washboard. Pregnancy had made a mess of her emotions. She stopped before she wore a hole in the already thin bed linen. Wouldn't that be the fine thank you for all Melina had done for her? And Edmond?

Lenora wrung out the sheet as best she could and hung it on the line before picking a pair of pants from the basket of soiled clothing. Dark with a gold strip down the side. The strength went from her arms, but she forced them into the water and rubbed soap into the knees of the trousers. He'd knelt in the dirt, probably while helping someone. Or saving the day. What a strange sense of fulfillment came from the simple act of washing his uniforms, as though she had something to contribute to the community and to all the good Edmond Bryce did.

She hung the pants on the line while trying to forget how fine he looked in them, his coat gone, his suspenders hanging at his sides. Of course, he looked equally dashing in full uniform, his flat-brimmed Stetson pulled low on his brow.

Oh, what a complete mess she was! Romanticizing laundry. Another menial task she had tried to escape, only to find purpose in it now. Satisfaction in a job well done and in meeting the needs of people she cared for. No wonder Mama never complained. Lenora hadn't understood at the time, couldn't fathom how anyone could be happy cooking for and cleaning up after a husband and children, day in and day out ... but at the moment, that sounded like the perfect life. A husband. A baby.

Lenora laid a wet hand over her stomach. Everything might have been different if Edmond had kissed her in return and if he desired her to stay. Then she'd be allowed a moment to the dream of family and home here on the Canadian prairie with a man she respected and—

"Don't say it." She grabbed a pair of his socks and thrust them into the washbasin. She couldn't afford such fantasies. She had no choice but to leave in the near future and give the baby to a family who could provide the home she could not. With the baby given to new parents, Lenora might continue her singing career in the theater. There was no reason to give up her dream completely.

Lenora paused and shook a few more flakes of soap from the Sunlight box into the water. A deep breath tinged with the sweet scent of suds and smoke from the kitchen stove did little to ease the throbbing in her chest. The best she could do was ignore the longing buried there and hurry with the task at hand.

She was almost to the bottom of the laundry basket when Melina stepped from the house with a pail of dirty mop water. She dumped it behind the house on the garden before returning. The wind snatched dark strands of hair from Melina's bun and slapped them against her face. "Let me dump that water. You shouldn't be lifting."

Lenora took the last towel from the water and wrung it. "Thank you." She stretched her back. "Are you cooking dinner already? Such a hot day."

Melina's eyes narrowed with bewilderment, and she glanced toward the house. "I don't have a fire started."

"You …" Lenora followed her gaze to the chimneys. Not a hint of smoke rose, but the odor of burning had grown, and the western sky wore a thick gray haze.

"No." Melina dropped the pail and raced around the house to the road.

Lenora followed, lifting her skirts from her ankles to keep them from tangling. She had thought the dark tinge to the west a low-lying cloud as she'd often seen when the wind blew like this. Edmond had called it a chinook arch. But this was different.

"A wildfire." Melina spun and darted for the barn, leaving Lenora to stare at the rise of smoke and the glow of orange hugging the horizon below the mountains.

Melina returned minutes later with the wagon hitched to her small mare and hurried to gather all the pails and an armful of burlap sacks. Lenora climbed aboard and held the horse in place while Melina loaded the back of the wagon, then scampered onto the seat beside her.

Melina grabbed the reins. "Giddyap!"

The wagon lurched, and one of the pails jostled over the side, but Melina didn't stop. She drove the horse west for the first mile and then turned toward the north.

"But the fire—" Lenora started.

"With this wind, they can't fight the fire head on. Most likely, they'll try to head it off."

Lenora held the rest of her questions and concerns until they came over a rise overlooking a wide valley. In its heart, a handful of wagons with almost two dozen men and women at work cutting the prairie with plows while smaller fires dotted the length of the fresh-turned soil. She searched the group for Edmond but only recognized Jim Greer and a couple of his men. She didn't see Edmond's flat-brimmed hat until they pulled to a stop alongside another wagon. He hefted pails of water from the back of the other wagon, coat gone, shirt stained gray and black.

"I've brought buckets," Melina said, remaining on the seat. "We'll fetch more water."

Edmond looked up, but his gaze never made it as far as his sister. Frozen on Lenora, his eyes darkened with what looked like anger.

Before either could speak, the wagon pulled forward, Melina guiding it deeper into the valley. They had plowed their line from the edge of the river and out toward the south, paralleling where the fire should come, probably hoping to pinch it between the barren banks of the river and the wasteland they were creating.

Melina thrust the reins into Lenora's hands before the wagon came to a complete stop. "Hold her here." She bounded over the side and grabbed pails from the back to begin hauling water from the river.

How useless. Lenora chafed at remaining on the high seat. Was this all she was good for, holding a horse that probably wouldn't move, anyway? The mare had no interest besides the grass under her hooves. If only Lenora could prove to Edmond that she was more than just a pretty face with a nice voice. More than a saloon singer.

By the time they returned with the water, smoke hung on every breath, stealing desired oxygen. Her head began to ache from the deprivation, but there was no time for thoughts of herself. They were working to save homes and livelihoods. With every minute, the wildfire closed the distance to them.

"Help us stop this fire, Lord." Melina spoke aloud, and the words stayed with Lenora as they set to beat out the smaller fires with wet sacks and blankets.

Lord, stop this fire. Please, calm this wind.

Hadn't Christ already performed that miracle? On the Sea of Galilee with His disciples, He had calmed a storm with words so simple. *Peace, be still.*

If only she had enough faith.

"What are you doing?"

Lenora spun toward Edmond in the same moment that he ripped away her sack. She opened her mouth with a retort but coughed on the taste of ash.

"Get back on that wagon."

She attempted to snatch her sack from him. "I'm trying to help."

"We don't need your help. I have enough to worry about." He grabbed her shoulders and shoved her away from the rising flame. "Wagon. Now!"

She stumbled out of the way while he took her place over the fire, pounding it out with a rage she'd not seen in him before. Well, if that was the way he felt about her presence, she would leave him to his fire—all of it.

Over the bellowing wind, he shouted at Melina, demanding to know what she'd been thinking, barking at her to leave.

Melina threw her sack toward a pail of water and stalked away. She caught Lenora's arm and hauled her the rest of the way to the wagon. "We'll ride into Cayley and make sure everyone knows what's happening. If this doesn't stop the fire, they're in a direct line."

The whole town? It was easy to forget her own hurt and anger when so many people were at risk of losing everything. She spared one glance at Edmond and the fire barreling down the valley toward him. Impossible to guess who would move aside first. Stubborn man.

Oh, Lord, please keep him safe. Stop this fire. Calm this wind.

Instead, it seemed to howl with greater force, both across the prairie and through her.

Maybe God could no longer be bothered to speak words of peace or perform miracles. Maybe it wasn't only her He ignored.

CHAPTER 24

Even after the wagon rolled away, taking Lenora from sight, Edmond couldn't put her from his mind—or his frustration at Melina in bringing her out here. This was no place for a woman with child. Not with the smoke so oppressive and danger pressing nearer with each minute.

He shouted at the others. "Get those fires out!"

The heat from the wildfire wafted over them, carried with clouds of smoke and ash. Time was short. He'd already ordered Jim Greer to move the plow and horses out of range of the fire. He was on his way back to the Shaw homestead to begin breaking ground there in case the flames got past them.

A yelp spun him to Mrs. Shaw, who battled the remaining flickers of her backfire. A tongue of flame clung to the hem of her burgundy skirts. She scampered backward with no escape.

Edmond sprinted across the smoldering ground, Lenora in his head. What if she had stayed? What if it were her with her skirts on fire? He grabbed the hem and smashed the fabric together, smothering the flame until only the singed edge remained.

"I'll finish here." He ripped the fire-eaten blanket from her trembling hands. "You head home with your husband and move your livestock and what you can from your house."

Black soot lined her blanched face as though war paint. Her mouth opened, but instead of speaking, she nodded and hurried over the furrows of plowed prairie to her husband, who loaded empty pails into a wagon. She paused in front of him, and he bent over to kiss her head. For the briefest moment, she leaned into him before straightening her shoulders and climbing onto the seat of the wagon. They had already sent their children to stay with a family in Cayley, but they stood to lose everything they'd worked to build over the past decade.

Edmond fought down the last of the controlled burn and waved for the wagons and horses to be moved to a safer distance. The men from the Bar L and Mackenzie ranches would be able to fall back to the Shaws' homestead, but most would want to return to their own homes and make preparations, whether it be fighting the fire or moving anything of value to a safer location. A necessity if the fire wasn't stopped.

"Please, Father." Edmond let his plea escape in the wind. *We've done all we can. We need a miracle.*

They needed this wind to break long enough to gain control of the blaze.

The heat increased as the fire tore across the plains toward them. Edmond mounted and rode Ranger to the top of the bluff where the smoke wasn't as oppressive. There was nothing more they could do here but pray.

"How's it looking?" Frank said from behind him.

Edmond shook his head. "Too soon to tell."

They waited together.

"I forgot to mention, Mrs. Bagley asked me to express her gratitude. For sending help. For doing what you could."

His stomach dropped. Frank's voice carried the same remorse as when he'd reported an hour earlier. They had done nothing to save her farm—there'd been no time. Most of the livestock had been rounded up and moved, all but an ornery, old cow that had refused to budge and a few elusive chickens. All the outbuildings, the frame home, garden—everything had burned.

"The grass will grow again. Barns can be rebuilt. As long as we can keep people safe."

Edmond nodded, but he didn't remove his gaze from the billowing smoke and lapping orange below. The roar grew with the yowl of the wind. His jaw hurt, but he couldn't unlock it. People were what mattered. Lives. Not land. Not buildings. Not even a man's livelihood was more important than the people in his life. That was where Father had been wrong. He'd sacrificed his family for the sake of his career. Would Edmond be any better if he put off marriage to remain in the force?

He doused thoughts of Lenora. He had enough to worry about with the countryside burning. She was safe for now, and that was all he needed.

"Here she comes," Frank breathed from beside him.

The air caught in Edmond's lungs as the racing flames met the length of earth they had blackened. The thud in his chest almost drowned out all else.

Please stop the fire here, Lord. Please.

The wind lulled, and the fire stood in place, seeking passage but with little success. Still, Edmond couldn't breathe. Not as another gust rose with strength, pushing tendrils of orange over the black soil.

Lord, no.

It was too late. The flames breached the backburn. There was no hope of stopping it now.

"I'm so sorry," came the whispered words beside him.

"Me too." He pulled Ranger's head around, not allowing the devastation of the moment to slow him. He still had a duty to perform—people to protect—a town to warn.

Smoke hung on the night air, and a soft glow of light stretched to the north. Despite the warmth of the day that lingered after the setting of the sun, Lenora hugged her arms as she stood at the edge of the yard waiting for word from Melina or Edmond. Maybe not the safest, to be alone in the dark hardly a day after being confronted by Channing's man, but Porter sat silently at her side, and her own well-being was farthest from her mind.

"Keep them safe, Lord," she murmured, her constant refrain for the past ten or twelve hours. Maybe longer since Melina had returned her to the farm with the promise to come back as soon as she could. Lenora wasn't sure how late it was now. Probably well past midnight. And still no sign of them. Just the constant glow of fire moving northwest. The wind had softened only slightly with evening. "Keep them safe."

The soft creak of a wagon's axle stopped her heart, and she peered toward the road. Minutes passed before the horses and a wagon appeared in the darkness. It was all she could do to remain in place while Edmond and Melina rolled to the barn and began unhitching the team. Having already seen to filling the troughs and manger for them, Lenora forced her feet toward the house. She'd done all she could, and after Edmond's reaction to her earlier, best she keep her distance.

Water sat on the warm stove in a pot so they could wash up, but she dipped her finger into it to check the temperature before pouring it into a basin. Soap and towels were already laid out, but there was surely more she could do to keep her hands busy without being underfoot. She checked the stew she had cooked, cut bread, and laid it out on a plate. Edmond had to be starved after such a day.

The door opened, and she fought the need to glance behind her. Light footsteps neared the basin on the table. "You are an angel," Melina said.

Lenora turned. "How bad is it? The damage?"

"Not as bad as it could have been. The wind shifted, pushing the fire to the north. It's up against the Highwood River and under control."

"So the town is safe?"

Melina nodded and then dipped her head low to splash water across her face.

Lenora passed her a towel.

"A miracle," Melina sighed.

For the town, but what about all the farms in the way? "How

much was lost?"

"Hundreds of acres of grazing and fields," a deeper voice answered from the doorway. "Eight homes, with most of their outbuildings. Countless livestock." Edmond stepped into the room, his boots absent and his shirt removed. He tugged at the top buttons of his sweat-stained undershirt.

Melina took the towel and stepped out of her brother's way.

"A herd of dairy cows wasn't moved in time. They survived the fire, but their udders were badly singed, and they had to be shot to keep them from suffering."

Lenora pressed a hand over her heart. Oh, the poor animals. Poor Edmond. He staggered to the nearest chair, his head tipped forward, his expression grave under layers of soot. He gave the basin of water a passing glance, his blackened hands laid palms up on his knees.

"Was anyone …"

"No. Some burns. But no one was killed." He spoke as though he was trying to convince himself it was a blessing despite all other losses. His eyes closed while a hoarse cough shook his chest.

Lenora lunged for the pitcher of cool water and held a glass out to him. "You should drink something." And eat something, too, but she'd not press him.

His hand trembled as he took the glass. He winced upon contact.

Close enough now to see the red splotches over his hands, Lenora grabbed a washcloth and sank it into the basin of water. "You're burned."

"It's nothing," he muttered before emptying the glass of water down his throat.

Despite his murmured protest, she took his wrist and directed his hand into the light. Hard to see anything under the black, but several blisters oozed moisture from raw patches of skin. He flinched as she wrapped the cloth over his knuckles and across his palm.

"I'll refresh the washbasin." This time with cold water from the pump. She hurried to fetch the water, then made up honey-coated wraps while he soaked his hands.

"You need to eat something," Melina said from across the table, where she sampled some of Lenora's stew. She was either too tired or polite not to condemn its bland flavor or lumpy gravy.

Edmond shook his head, staying just long enough for Lenora to wrap his hands before thumping up the stairs to his bed. Lenora stared after him, unable to move.

"He'll be fine. He just needs rest and time to accept that none of this was his fault." Melina stood and started clearing the table.

Lenora pushed herself into action. "Why would he think for a moment that he's to blame for anything that happened today? He did everything possible to stop that fire. He saved lives."

"Yes. But he's the Mountie over this area. He takes a lot more than just the law upon him. Everyone's well-being. Especially because he thinks the cattle rustler might have been responsible for starting the fire. So in his head, if he'd brought the rustler to justice sooner, this might not have happened."

No wonder he was despondent. How very much for one man to shoulder. What she wouldn't give to lift all that from him or help him to bear up under it. If he'd let her get close enough.

"I'll finish tidying up." Lenora took Melina's arm and directed her from the kitchen. "You go to bed."

Melina halfheartedly nodded on her way into the bedroom.

"Oh, Edmond," Lenora sighed after the door had closed. She tipped her head forward and clasped her hands. Praying for him came as naturally as breathing. "Thank you, Lord, for redirecting the fire, for keeping everyone safe. For keeping Edmond safe. Please grant him peace."

If only she could ask the same for herself.

CHAPTER 25

Hunger slammed Edmond's gut like a cast-iron skillet, followed by a hundred scattered thoughts jerking him awake. The fire. Lenora. All the folks who had lost their homes. The room was still dimly lit, but he had too much weighing upon his mind to linger in the comfort of his bed. He groaned while pushing to his feet. His head throbbed, muscles ached, and sticky wraps clung to his hands.

Having fallen into bed before removing his blackened clothes the night before, Edmond crept down the stairs and paused for a bar of soap. Then straight out to the pump to wash the honey from his hands and the ash from his face. He ducked low and let the chilly water run over his head, lathering his hair well, not caring that his undershirt also became saturated. He was halfway back to the house before realizing his hands no longer hurt but for a general stiffness and some pain where blisters had broken. His burns were hardly noticeable this morning, thanks to Lenora's ministrations.

Back upstairs, Edmond dressed in a clean uniform while making a mental note of everything and everyone he needed to check on. As he straightened his coat, his heart plummeted to his bare feet. He plunged a hand into his breast pocket. Lenora's ruby ring. He had never returned it to her. It was still in the pocket of his other coat, the one he'd beaten the flames with.

Grabbing a pair of socks and detouring for a thick slice of bread to stay his hunger, Edmond hurried to the front of the house where he'd left his boots. He saddled Ranger but stopped himself from racing to where he had dropped his coat. People depended on him. He needed to make sure the fire was still controlled and no one needed him before worrying about a ring, no matter whose it was or what it was worth.

Biting back a curse, Edmond headed north, past Cayley toward the Highwood River. Black expanded over the prairie, the torched ground marking the path of the fire. A haze of smoke wafted from the few trees and the long grass still smoldering along the bank of the river.

Frank and his boys waited at the edge of the burn, their clothes and faces blackened from yesterday's fight. "You look a lot better than last time I saw you," Frank said, moving to meet him.

Edmond dismounted. "You look worse." A pang of guilt hit hard. "You've been out here all night?"

"Wanted to make sure we had her beaten. Sent the others home a few hours ago." He took off his hat to wipe a smutty hand over his graying hair. "Not much left of the fire now. She ain't going anywhere."

"I should have stayed." He mumbled under his breath, but Frank gripped his sleeve.

"What for? You'd done your part, and you have plenty to do today while the rest of us go home and sleep. Folks will be looking to you for help with deciding their futures. You'll have a busy day looking in on everyone and making sure their needs are met. How could you do that without taking a few hours to rest? You're only human." He patted Edmond's shoulder. "Like the rest of us."

The truth of the sentiment sank deep despite the urge to resist it. Edmond knew better than anyone his weaknesses, but when he put on this uniform, he had no choice but to set all that aside. He couldn't let people see what might otherwise drive him to his knees.

Frank took out his pocket watch and flipped open the cover. "The morning is calm, and men from the Bar L will be along by seven o'clock to finish putting out the fire, so I'll stick around here for another half hour. You go take care of that mile-long list I'm sure you have."

Edmond's instinct nudged him to argue and stay put until the other men arrived, but the thought of Lenora's ring forced him to nod. "I appreciate that more than I can say, Frank."

His friend nodded and gave his back a clap. "Back to duty, Constable."

Edmond's mouth turned up a little. "Yes, sir." He swung into the saddle and saluted. Even retired from the North-West Mounted Police, Frank was a man he had to respect.

"And don't forget the duty you have to your family. Nothing is more important than that."

Ranger started to move, but Edmond pulled him short. Family? Sure, he had a duty to his parents and to look after Melina, but how did that supersede his role as an officer?

"I wasn't sure whether or not to offer congratulations."

"For …?"

"Rumor was flying almost as fast as that fire yesterday that you'd married the lady who's been staying with you and Melina. Seemed to explain why she never did leave."

"But how …?" Unless Anderson had gone into town and started asking questions about their wedding. Just what a small community like theirs needed to start a ripple of suppositions.

"Is it true, then?"

Edmond shook his head, too busy in his own thoughts to form a reply. Anderson probably knew the truth now, whether or not he'd stayed in the area. He needed to ride home and warn Lenora, but was there any point to it now? She'd likely still be in bed, and Melina was there with her. Besides, he couldn't go back until he'd found her ring.

Edmond rode over the charred earth, retracing the fire's path to the west. With the pressure of yesterday's wind, the fire had not spread wide where it had started. Just enough to have left his coat blackened where he'd dropped it. The wool fibers clung together, and he dug into what remained of the front breast pocket. His finger hooked a small, circular band.

"Thank you, God."

Though smudged with soot, the gold appeared solid, and the ruby remained intact. He wet his handkerchief in the stream and polished the gem until it shone. Why had he taken so long returning it to Lenora? He should have simply handed it to her weeks ago, and yet here he sat, staring at it, attempting not to contemplate that once he gave it to her, she would have the means to step out of his life and never look back.

Is that what made him hesitate, the thought of her leaving? And yet, all the while, he'd kept himself at arm's length? What sort of coward was he?

Another thing he'd rather not contemplate at the moment.

Edmond shoved the ring into his pocket and led Ranger through the stream to where the fire had started. Yesterday, there had been no time for an investigation or to prove his suspicions. The ring and Lenora would have to wait a little while longer.

Trampled grass and broken underbrush marked the area around the first burn marks. He followed the trail through the grove to the remains of a Hereford steer wearing the Mackenzie brand. The steer was dead but otherwise untouched.

He circled the steer and the growing swarm of flies, searching the area for any other clues. A broken leather rein peeked out of the taller grass, and he gathered it up, wrapping it around his fingers. Old leather. Beside the dead bovine lay a long-bladed knife hilt pressed into the earth. Edmond knelt and dusted off the handle, familiar to him, but he couldn't place it. Must have fallen in the rustler's haste and been trod on by one of the horses. One more piece of evidence. The hoof sizes were about the same, and both were now shod, the only notable marking the small notch on the left front shoe. He followed the tracks for several miles, the indentions deep and spaced due to the speed. Then they plunged into the Highwood River and vanished. Again.

With the sun's steady progress into the sky and much weighing on Edmond's mind, he saw little choice but to let the trail remain lost. He patted the ring in his pocket and headed toward home. The

time for procrastination was passed.

Oh, bless me now, my Savior, I come to Thee.

The line of the old hymn followed Lenora as she plucked one egg after another from the nest boxes mounted along the side of the chicken coop. The words of the hymn were never far, and she'd awakened with the tune in her head the past two mornings, ever since singing it in church.

"Music can preach the most powerful sermons, Lenora," her father had once told her. He used to encourage her singing, saying her voice sounded like an angel praising, bold with its declaration of faith.

Why, then, hadn't he supported her dream? What had turned him against her?

She rubbed the tip of her finger over the pale brown shell of the egg she held, already knowing the answer but not wanting to admit it to herself. Her father wasn't the one who had changed or turned against her. She had.

"You know better than that, Lenora."

She'd known better than to chase after the admiration of men, to forsake her upbringing of faith for a life of fame and ease. But instead, she'd told herself that she knew better than *him*, that Papa was the one who hadn't understood.

Lenora placed the egg in the pail and laid her hand over her stomach. Look where all her great wisdom and vanities had gotten her, despite all the warnings. She ducked her head and stepped into the sunshine. A gentle breeze teased the air with an assortment of aromas. The wild roses blooming along the road. The more potent scent of chickens. The sweat of a dun horse tied near the barn.

"Hard to carry on a private conversation under the watchful eye of the local constabulary."

She twisted to Fred Anderson, who leaned against a nearby tree, smirk in place under his mustache.

"I imagine Constable Bryce will have plenty to keep him busy today. Even if he'd rather be here with the Lovely Lenora."

"No." She stepped away from him, glimpsing the house from the corner of her eye. Melina was nowhere in sight. "That's not who I am anymore."

"Really? Because no one else in the area seems to know the constable took a wife." Fred stalked her retreat.

Her breath came in short bursts. "Lenora. Just plain Lenora. That's who I am." Though when Edmond said her name, it felt anything but plain. Wholesome. Good. Everything she wanted to be now.

"You expect me to believe this is what you want? A crude life on the Canadian frontier? Lenora Perry, the star of the stage. What happened to Boston and New York? What about all that talk of Europe?" He laughed and shook his head. "Mr. Doyle will get a good laugh. We both know you better."

His horse tugged at its lead and stole Fred's attention. The sound of hooves pounded the road in a steady approach.

"Think on what you really want, Lenora. Channing's patience won't last forever." He strode to his horse and mounted, disappearing behind the barn just before Edmond appeared. Dust churned under Ranger's hooves.

Lenora pressed her hand over her heart with the hopes of calming the thunderous drumming. The eggs rattled in the pail, and she set it aside. Her hands were less than steady.

What do you really want?

Edmond reined in her direction, and the question fell away. Answered in full.

"Anderson?" It was more of a statement than a question.

She nodded. "He didn't try to do anything. Just talk. Seems I shouldn't have bothered making up stories. He doesn't believe it, anyway."

"Unlike the rest of Cayley." Edmond dropped to the ground a couple of feet away. Though weariness darkened under his eyes and showed in their depths, he appeared a new man from the one who had stumbled into the house last night.

It was hard to keep her focus on the subject at hand. "What?"

"Seems he sparked some rumors about us being married."

"Edmond, I'm so sorry." Though that wasn't quite what she felt. Lingering regret, perhaps, that it couldn't be real.

He waved her apology aside. "Where's Melina? You shouldn't be alone out here."

"I …" Lenora dried her clammy palms on the sides of her skirt and picked up the pail. "I only meant to be a minute. We needed eggs."

"Well, don't come out here again. Not until that man is gone for good." His voice was edged. Leaving Ranger to stare after them, reins hanging loose over his neck, Edmond took her elbow and led her toward the house.

"What about …"

He kept walking, his expression severe. "How can I leave if I can't trust you two?"

"Can't trust us?"

"I have work to do. I can't sit around all day making sure you aren't putting yourself in harm's way. I told Melina not to leave you alone."

"Before the fire. Then you told her to get rid of me."

He pushed the door open and directed her inside. "You both should have stayed put, to begin with. The path of a wildfire is no place for women."

It wasn't a place for anyone, but she'd save her breath. Edmond seemed to have a different focus, and it had little to do with yesterday's fire.

"Where is Melina?"

Lenora faced him. "In the garden. That's where I saw her last."

He grunted but didn't move. Neither did he look her in the eye. Instead, his hand rose to his chest, and his jaw tightened as though he were in pain, like a man on the brink of having a heart attack.

"Should I fetch her?"

Edmond shook his head and slipped two fingers into his pocket. "I need to return this to you."

"What …?" At the sight of the small ruby, her heart leapt to her throat. "Where …?"

Edmond shifted on his feet. "McRae sent it. Bought it back from Greer for you."

She opened her palm, and he dropped the band into the center. Tears obscured her view, so she clasped it to her heart. "I thought I'd lost it forever. My grandmother passed this ring to my mother, and she to me. It's all I have …" A sob rose in her throat. One last tie to home and family, like a lifeline tossed to a drowning soul. Maybe someday she would be able to return, after all. Maybe that was what she wanted … since a life with Edmond would never be an option. All she had to do was work up enough courage to tell her parents the truth and beg their forgiveness.

CHAPTER 26

Edmond dropped the thin slip of paper to his desk and slumped into his chair. The high back groaned in protest, and he had half a mind to do the same. One of the inquiries he'd sent out the morning of the fire had gained a reply. A telegram from south of the border supplied enough information to link George Bates, alleged cattle rustler and thief, with George Cornwell, homesteader, husband, and father.

Though he was not yet wanted in Canada, the connection urged further investigation. The cattle rustling began about the time George arrived. Edmond would ride past the Cornwell place on his way to pick up Matt. He was supposed to help pack what was left from the Bagley farm. Mrs. Bagley planned to travel to Lethbridge in the morning to live with her eldest daughter. Too much was required to restore the old homestead or the life she had shared with her late husband.

There would be no more warm cookies, apple pie, or grandmotherly hugs to get him through a rough day.

Edmond swallowed past the tightness in his throat and the emotion he couldn't afford to acknowledge. He grabbed his hat and headed out the door. Wednesday already. The last twenty-four hours had been a blur of activity with little time for extra thought. Two and a half days remained to decide about his career. And about Lenora.

He released a stale breath as he mounted Ranger. What was he supposed to do about Lenora? Or his feelings for her? Or about the man pursuing her? They'd seen nothing more of Anderson, but Edmond didn't like leaving her alone for too long. A man didn't spend all that time and money hunting someone to let go without a fight. And he'd get one if he ever came near Lenora again. The mere thought of what Channing Doyle had done to her was enough to drive Edmond over the edge. He was almost of a mind to ride down to Wyoming and give the man a piece of what he deserved.

Edmond raced Ranger across the prairie, giving vent to an anger he was unfamiliar with. One that frightened him for the lack of control he felt over it.

He slowed a mile out from the Cornwell spread, trying to refocus his thoughts. Why would a man risk a new start, his family, everything, by breaking the law? George's hard work was visible in the sturdy corrals and the small house he'd constructed for his family.

"Morning, Constable Bryce." Mrs. Cornwell greeted Edmond with a hesitant smile from where she beat a small rug hanging from a rope line. She set the stick aside and wiped her hands on her apron. "Can I help you with something?"

Before he could speak, the children raced around the corner of the house, hair flopping, braids flying, and grins stretching their young faces. The last thing he wanted to do was take away their father. But if George was behind the rustling, Edmond had no choice.

"My husband went into town this morning for some supplies. Hasn't returned yet."

"That's fine. I only wanted to make sure things were coming along. See if you needed anything."

"Would have thought you'd be busy, what with all them folks who lost their homes. We're … we're well enough off."

Edmond glanced around the yard. "And your husband? How is he?"

She glanced at her hands.

"Is there something that worries you about your husband?"

After a quick look at the children, she shook her head. "George is fine." But the tightness in her voice told another story. "We appreciate you checking in on us, Constable. Let me know if anyone who lost their homes to the fire needs something. We don't have a lot, but we could probably spare a blanket or two and some canned food."

"I'll pass that on to my sister. She's organizing some of the women from church to do a drive for supplies. They'll appreciate anything you can spare."

Mrs. Cornwell nodded, then picked up her stick and moved back to the rug.

Edmond reined his horse away. The short ride to the Lawsons' heightened his suspicions. Not everything was as it seemed at the Cornwell homestead.

No good news met him at the Lawsons' either.

"Matt ain't here," one of his sisters reported.

"He's not?"

"Nope. Said he had some business to attend to, talking all grown-up like. Took Pa's horse."

"Thank you." Edmond again rode off with more questions brewing than when he'd arrived. This close to home, he went that direction to check on the women before going after Matt. He tied Ranger near the water trough, but Molasses wasn't waiting with her usual greeting. Porter followed him to the house at a happy trot.

Lenora shot to her feet when he stepped inside, her hand already halfway to her derringer resting beside the chess table. The black and white pieces were scattered across the board, several tipped and off to the side.

"Is Melina gone?"

"Yes. A boy came for her just after lunch. Someone's in labor."

Probably Mrs. Jensen. Melina had been waiting for word, and last night he'd agreed that she could go if needed—so long as Lenora stayed to the house. He cast a glance around the room. All looked as it should, and lingering alone with Lenora would likely lead to uncharted territory he wasn't yet ready to map out.

You only have two days.

But Mrs. Bagley was waiting. "I guess I'll be on my way, then."

Lenora relaxed in the chair and studied her game. Her black

rook slid across the board to intercept a white knight.

"You have a preference for black, don't you?"

Her shoulder raised in a shrug. "I used to play the white against my father. Seemed wrong to let him lose just because he isn't here."

"Did he win a lot back then?"

"No." A sad smile touched her lips. "He played at my level. Pushing me, challenging me, but always giving me reasonable hope." Her gaze flickered to Edmond and then back to the game. She pushed a white pawn across its one square and into the path of the black bishop.

"Where is your hope now?"

The black bishop made its killing move. "You assume that I have given myself the whites."

"You haven't?"

She shook her head, lips pursing. "Nope. Now, I'm playing against you. I am more a *black sheep* type." Her grin broke free as she moved the white queen into the center of the board, an easy target for most of her pieces.

"That's not fair. You're not giving me a fighting chance."

"Are you asking for one?" She lifted her rook and hovered it over his queen.

"Let's just say that if you take my queen—" He stepped across the room and plucked the black queen from beside the black king. "Then I'm taking yours."

"You can't do that!"

No, he couldn't. Not by the rules of the game, at least, but he was getting mighty tired of playing by the rules. He dropped the black queen into his chest pocket where her ring had once resided. "I'm just not supposed to." He gave the bulge a pat for good measure.

She sprang to her feet. "You aren't seriously taking my queen?"

He shuffled back one step, suppressing the urge to smile at the widening of her blue eyes. "I am. That should give me a fighting chance."

Gaze narrowing, she matched his step and held out her hand.

"Who says you deserve a fighting chance?"

"I think everyone deserves that much, don't you?"

She took another step, and this time he matched her, but forward, bringing them only inches apart. Her outstretched fingers brushed his chest as she lowered her hand to her side. "I ..." Her gaze lowered from his eyes to his mouth and then away. "I do still need that piece."

She reached for his pocket, but he caught her hand, holding it in place over the pocket, over his heart. Could she feel its thunderous applause? Did she know that she was the cause? She was right. He didn't deserve a chance with her. Not after all his crude assumptions, not so long as he couldn't put her before his duty to the uniform he wore.

Edmond released her hand and turned away before he did or said anything he'd regret. Not that he'd regret what came to mind at the memory of her lips against his. Maybe it was time to throw caution to the wind and stop thinking so much.

"Where are you going?"

What a question. He knew exactly what was expected of him for the remainder of the day. His path was well laid out. But what about after today, after this week? What direction did his future take? Would he keep walking away from the desire urging him to turn around or allow his heart some say in his course?

"Edmond?" Lenora sounded concerned. And a little confused.

He cleared his throat. Now was not the time for romantic declarations or decisions of such magnitude. "I should be home in a few hours, but don't feel you need to wait dinner on me if Melina isn't home either." He wanted to reiterate to stay in the house while she was alone, but he'd already stressed that enough over the past couple of days. He would trust her to remember his instructions in case of Anderson's return.

Walking back to his horse, Edmond took the black queen from his pocket and turned it over in his hand. Dare he risk his heart and career on the woman she represented?

A smile tugged at his mouth. Not really a question anymore.

A yawn stretched Edmond's mouth, and his eyes watered. As exhausted as he was, and as much as he wanted to get home before dark, the Lawson farm was on the way. Might as well pause one last time and see if Matt had come in for dinner.

Where was that boy?

Edmond was almost ready to give up on Matt. He'd loaded Mrs. Bagley's wagon and driven her to the boardinghouse to await tomorrow's train on his own. He'd also looked in on the Shaws, who had already returned to their home to save whatever the fire hadn't devoured. Despite black-stained walls, their house remained standing. The barn had not been so fortunate.

Taking the trail at a gentle canter, Edmond scanned the scenery. The gentle sway of hills, rising higher toward the mountains, and groupings of trees that were the surest sign of a homestead and the only protection from the west wind. The Lawsons' was no exception. As he passed the line of cottonwoods and entered the yard, a tall shadow darted into the barn. Edmond followed. No sign of the other children as he swung from Ranger and sprinted into the darkness. Light flashed at the far side as a smaller door opened and closed.

"Hold up!" Edmond broke into a run. He shoved through the door and slid to a stop.

Matt scrambled to get to his feet, shattered glass on the whiskey-soaked ground beside him. The bottle hadn't stood a chance with how many rocks littered the pasture.

"So that's what you were doing all day instead of being here when I told you to be?" Edmond grabbed the back of Matt's soiled shirt and yanked him up. The boy's breath bore final witness.

"Lemme go." He tried to yank away, but Edmond held him fast, gripping both shoulders.

"Why, so you can fall flat on your face again?"

Matt's fist flew with a sharpness Edmond hadn't expected. Knuckles caught his jaw, knocking his head to the side.

Edmond gritted his teeth. He should have been ready. Anger emanated from the boy, but now there was fear too.

"Does that make you feel any better?" Edmond tossed his hat aside. Walking forward, he compelled the boy to continue back-stepping. "I thought your pa taught you better than that. Taught you to respect the law. Respect yourself. He was a good man."

The anger returned in abundance. Matt stopped his retreat. "Don't talk about him."

Edmond started unbuttoning his coat. "I think not talking about him isn't doing you any favors. I considered Henry Lawson my friend. It's for his sake I'm taking off this uniform." He pulled his arms from the sleeves and stepped aside to lay it over the rail fence. "He's the reason I'll give you one more chance. I had a lot of respect for your pa. What must he be thinking, seeing what his son's making of himself?"

"He's not thinking anything. He's dead." The venom in the boy's voice snagged Edmond mid-motion, rolling up a sleeve. That was the nerve he'd been looking for. There was something brewing in the boy, and until he found a way to let it out …

Please, God, give me the right words.

"Yes, he is, isn't he?" Edmond spoke slowly, watching for Matt's reactions. "He died in that blizzard."

"I don't want to talk about it." Matt's face glowed red, his nostrils flared. Almost there.

"Went out to bring some heifers in from the hills, if I remember."

"No."

"Yes, I remember. Couldn't risk losing the calves, so he went out there."

"No."

"And he never made it back."

"Stop!"

Edmond was ready for the blow this time and dodged it. "I can understand how that could make a man angry. Feels kind of pointless, doesn't it?" The next two punches came in fast, and one brushed his ear. "But we don't get to choose when death takes someone we love. And their life, your pa's life, was full of purpose."

"Stop. I told you to stop!" Matt gripped Edmond's shoulder and aimed his next assault.

Edmond blocked but was unprepared for the force or the curve of the swing. Knuckles smashed into his jaw. He grabbed the boy's arms, ready to end the attack but not the conversation. If he let him go now, he might never get through.

"Not until you tell me what's really gnawing at you. Men die, Matt. People we care about die. It's hard, but you have to learn to live with it."

"No!" The full force of the word and the young man's weight slammed against Edmond's body, taking him to the rocky ground. A jolt of pain stabbed the back of his head, and all went dark.

CHAPTER 27

Lenora tossed another log on the fire. The day had been warm, and the fire wasn't required, but the light offered a sense of security. She sat in the rocker and patted her knee for Porter to join her. Wet nose. Silky coat behind the ears. A little comfort as the evening stretched on. Even with every lamp in the house lit, the darkness surrounded her. No wonder Melina hated being alone out here in this wilderness without another soul within shouting distance.

Lamp close, Lenora made another attempt at reading the Charles Dickens novel Melina had lent her. *Little Dorrit*. Such a bleak tale, in her opinion. One could only hope it improved before the end. Fiction should prove happier than real life.

Porter lifted his head and looked toward the door.

"What is it, boy?"

A low growl rumbled in the back of his throat. He trotted across the room, ears perked.

Lenora stood but followed slower, taking her pistol with her. What if Anderson had returned for her? Why wasn't Edmond home yet? Or Melina?

The thud of boots mounted the steps outside, and Porter barked. A hurried rapping on the door.

Lenora set her hand on the latch. "Who is it?"

"Open up! The constable's hurt."

"Edmond?" She swung the door wide.

The young man twisted away and hurried to Ranger. A body draped over the saddle, arms dangling in white sleeves. Coat and hat absent. "What happened?"

"Hit a rock," the boy panted, unfastening the rope that had held Edmond in place. "His head. I didn't know where else to take him."

"Careful." She helped the boy ease Edmond off the horse and then haul, half drag, him into the house. He was by no means a small man, and his unconscious weight was almost more than they could carry together. "To the back." She directed him toward the bedroom. The stairs were more than she dared.

With Edmond's body draped across the quilt, Lenora perched on the edge of the bed to examine his injuries. His breathing was strong, but blood soaked the side of his head, staining and matting his hair. His face also showed damage, but nothing compared to the seeping wound behind his ear.

"Can you warm me some water?"

The front door slammed. Help was gone.

"Water. Bandages." She had to focus on Edmond. She was all he had until Melina returned. "Water and bandages." Heart racing, Lenora hurried through the house, finding what she could. The kettle had cooled from when she had heated it for coffee, but the water was warm enough to wash the blood from the deep gash and Edmond's hair. Fresh scarlet oozed, the skin gaping too wide to be left open. Melina's sewing kit was close at hand, but Lenora's fingers were not at all steady when she neared his scalp with the thin needle.

"Good thing you're not awake for this," she whispered, finding it impossible not to grimace.

She froze before the needle pricked his skin. "I can't do this." She wasn't trained as he was. He'd seemed to have little reservation sewing her foot that first night, but everything was different now. The thought of causing him any extra pain inflicted the same on her. She wanted him safe and happy. Not broken on this bed, unconscious and bleeding. "Oh, God, please help me. Help me help him." Surely, God cared about Edmond, shared her love for him. He was as good a man as they came.

Two stitches. Just enough to pull the gash together, to stunt the blood flow and aid his healing. She had to hurt him to heal him.

It was hard not to squeeze her eyes closed as she pressed the tip of the needle into his scalp. He groaned and tried to shift, so she pinned his head with her elbow. Through and a gentle tug before tying off the thread. The second attempt was only slightly easier, and then the deed was done. A deep breath did nothing for the swooshing inside her. She raced out the front door and spewed over the side of the porch.

Lenora returned slowly, allowing time for a drink and few seconds to breathe. Edmond hadn't moved an inch, but less scarlet showed at the wound. She bound his head and washed his face before worrying about his comfort. His boots protested being removed, but she set them aside and loosened the top two buttons of his shirt. Her fingers lingered on his chest, rising and falling with his breath.

"Please be all right, Edmond." She touched his cheek, then ran the tips of her fingers down his jaw. "I need you to wake up."

He sighed but didn't move.

"Edmond?"

He shifted.

"Edmond."

A groan and a flutter of lashes, and his eyes opened. He peered at her. Then he moaned and closed them again.

Probably for the best. Rest was usually a powerful remedy.

After tucking a blanket over him, Lenora pulled a chair close. She pressed her lips to his brow and closed her eyes. Prayer came easily. As though she'd never stopped.

Pain radiated from the back of Edmond's skull forward, a tight band across his forehead. He blinked against the darkness, fighting the fog from his mind. A dim light cast a flickering glow across the ceiling. The lamp resided on the small table at his side. The master bedroom. How did he get there?

"Please, God, heal him."

The whisper was distinctly feminine, coming from nearby.

"Please."

Edmond tried to push up but groaned at the pulsating stab through his skull. His body felt a little bruised but otherwise whole. Still, he couldn't remember what happened. He tried to mentally retrace his steps. The telegram about George Bates. Riding out to the Cornwell spread.

"Don't try to move." Lenora appeared over him, a halo of gold around her face, eyes wide and moist.

"What ..." He coughed to clear the thickness from his throat. "What happened?"

"I don't know." Her fingers brushed the side of his face before lowering to his chest. "Is there anything I can get you? Water?"

He almost nodded, but the muscles at the back of his neck protested. "Please."

She slipped from the room, and he closed his eyes. What had happened after he'd left the Cornwells'? Trying to remember hurt his brain. He was so tired ...

"Edmond? Edmond?"

The voice called from beyond his dreams. No, nightmares. Blood covered the rocks where his little brother lay, not moving. He scrambled down the steep ledge of the coulee to where Auguste had fallen and dragged him into his arms. All the way home, the weight of his brother's life pressed over Edmond, but no help or relief awaited him there.

"Edmond?"

"I can't ..." Though he wasn't sure what he couldn't do. The image of his brother's bleeding body slipped away, and Edmond felt himself lift from the dark to the glow of light. An angel peered down on him, her hand cool at the side of his face. He leaned into her touch. He wasn't alone. He didn't have to do this by himself.

"You should try to drink something." Her arm slipped behind him, helping him rise enough to take a drink. Wondrous water washed down his throat, crashing against a thirst he hadn't been aware of.

She eased him back down. "Try to sleep."

He put up no argument but found her hand before letting himself succumb—something to hold onto, an anchor to keep him from slipping too far away. Gentle music met him, easing his descent, a melody of peace.

"Let me hide myself in Thee …"

When Edmond woke again, it was to the hushed voice of his sister and Lenora. Something about a baby, Ranger, and a sewing kit. He couldn't make heads or tails of it, so he didn't try.

Brilliant light pierced his eyes though they were still closed. Edmond tested the brightness, and it wasn't as bad as he'd imagined. From the light in the window, it appeared to be full day, but his eyes adjusted. The pain in his head had subsided, but only slightly. It still felt as though someone had hit him with a sledgehammer. He reached up and massaged the muscles in his neck, almost as sore though less acute.

"How's your head?"

Edmond rotated just enough to see the woman beside him. Her hair hung freely over her shoulders, and her cheeks held more color than usual. It was hard not to stare despite the discomfort. Especially as a smile bloomed on her face and lit her eyes. The pressure in his hand was the only thing that could draw his attention away. He brought her hand, fingers entangled with his, to his chest. "How long have I been sleeping?"

"Off and on since last night."

"What happened to my head?"

"The young man who brought you home said something about you hitting it on a rock."

"Young man? Not Matt?" He hadn't found the boy. Had he?

"I think so. That's what Melina guessed. I think I recognized him, but I don't know from where."

Edmond reached up with his free hand to rub his temples. "That first day. He was the one I had locked up. Went home with his mother."

"Yes, I remember now."

"So I did find him." And as soon as he remembered what happened, he'd probably have to go looking again.

Gritting his teeth against the pain threatening to burst his skull, Edmond pushed into a sitting position. Releasing her hand was even more unpleasant.

"Are you sure you're ready to get up?"

He wasn't, but neither could he lay around all day. Two days until his appointment in Fort Macleod, and there were still families who needed help relocating or cleaning up from the fire and a cattle rustler to be apprehended. He had no time for a head injury.

Edmond made it all of three steps before the blotches across his vision threatened to drop him to his knees. He reached out and found Lenora already slipping under his arm. She braced him up, but they were backward steps she took. A moment later, he was again flat on his back.

"I think you are going to have to slow up for a few days, Constable."

Edmond found her hand again before going back to massaging his temples. Anything to release some of the pressure in his head. Maybe staying off his feet for one day wouldn't hurt—two at the most. And then, whether he was ready or not, he had to be on his way south with his answer for the commissioner.

CHAPTER 28

Two days after Edmond's accident, Lenora dropped onto the edge of the bed, head shaking. "I can't go. Not only have I nothing appropriate to wear at a ball, but …" If Edmond truly wanted her along, wouldn't he have asked himself instead of conveying the invitation through his sister? It wasn't as though he hadn't had plenty of time or opportunity in the past two days of laying around the house nursing his headache. This morning, he'd ridden into town early to finish some reports and check on a few things, but before that, he'd sat across from her at the breakfast table without mention of his desires to have her accompany him.

"You have to go. Get out of the house. Enjoy yourself." Melina brushed by on her way to the chest, holding an assortment of never-used quilts. "And don't worry about a gown. We have three hours before you need to leave for the train station." She dug through the chest, setting her works of art aside. She paused longer as she drew a red coat out, hugging it to her before placing it on top of the quilts. Moments passed before she cleared her voice and continued. "Mother left a couple of gowns to choose from. She's attended more than a few balls with Father. Especially after he became an officer. She's little shorter than you, but we have time for a few adjustments."

"If you are doing them." Lenora's sewing skills were rustier than her cooking.

"Here we are," Melina announced as folds of lavender fabric unfolded from the chest. She shook out the gown and laid it across the bed. "This is my favorite, but this other one would also go well with your coloring." The next gown she withdrew was the color of the wild roses Lenora had seen spread across the prairie.

"That is a beautiful pink."

"Yes, and much like that fabric we bought in Calgary." Melina laid the gown beside the first and sprinted from the room, returning moments later with the unused bolt of pink. Possibly a shade darker, but otherwise, a close match.

"If we bring the hem up an inch, we can add a three-inch ruffle with the darker pink." Melina bunched the hem to demonstrate. "And then we'll add something on the bodice with the same fabric—a sash, perhaps—and it will tie everything together."

Ideas sparked in Lenora's head, too, but why go through the hassle of changing the gown when it would make little difference to Edmond? He'd probably be just as happy taking his sister. "Or I can just stay here." And make an actual plan for her future because remaining in this house while haunted by her feelings for Edmond did her heart no favors.

Melina lowered the fabric and gown to the bed. "Why? I thought you would be excited to go. To spend time with Edmond."

Oh, Melina and her dreams of romance. She'd been beaming like the noonday sun since walking in on them holding hands. She considered it a sure sign of her brother's affection. Lenora suspected it was a result of his concussion and nothing more, but the intimacy of those moments had bruised her heart.

"I think we've spent plenty of time together these past couple days," Lenora mumbled. Him silent and brooding or trying to sleep off his headache.

"But he's not been himself. He has so much on his mind. A lot could change for him after his meeting with the commissioner. Rank. Location. He might even decide to resign."

"Resign?" Being a Mountie meant everything to Edmond. He lived and breathed duty and was following in his father's footsteps.

Melina gathered up a gown. "He's mentioned it before, though I don't agree completely with his reasoning."

"I can't imagine him doing anything else. What could make him consider giving it all up?"

Melina sighed. "My father is a good man, a loving husband and father, and a dedicated Mountie. But he made some choices that were hard on our family. Edmond bore the brunt of a lot of responsibility at a young age because of that." She took up the bolt of fabric and gave an apologetic smile. "I need to lay this out on the table and get started on this dress, or it won't be ready. Edmond's not sure how much time you will have once you arrive, so we have to do your hair as well."

"I can manage that much." Lenora's only concern was balancing attractive and demure.

"Perfect." The twinkle returned to Melina's eyes.

Lenora waited until Melina left before letting out a long breath. Her thoughts clung to Edmond. She could not imagine him giving up his career. Not if it was what he loved.

What about what you love?

As though that mattered. Probably the only reason Edmond wanted her along was as an arm ornament to show off to his friends in uniform. No, Edmond wasn't like that. Was he? He could have invited Melina to accompany him if he wasn't worried about the opinion of his peers.

Lenora moved to follow Melina to the kitchen but paused as she caught her reflection in the wall mirror. She hardly resembled the woman who had once drawn men to her like seagulls to breadcrumbs. What if she stepped back in time for one night? As stalwart and above reproach as Edmond was, he was still a warm-blooded man.

"I reached the farm. I must have reached the farm." Head in hands, Edmond leaned his elbows into his desk. "I must have found Matt and talked to him." But then, what? He was not much closer to figuring that out than when he'd first awoken. Not with Matt missing along with the memory.

The train announced its approach, and Edmond glanced at

his pocket watch. Where were those women? Melina and Lenora were supposed to have met him twenty minutes ago. He pushed up from his desk and picked up his hat. He needed it to hide the bandage wrapping his head. Unfortunately, nothing would disguise the purple bruise coloring his jaw. There would be questions, and he had no answers.

He'd rather stay home and forgo the whole trip. The only thing he looked forward to was holding Lenora in his arms for a dance or two. He smiled. *Or all of them.*

If she comes. He should have asked her himself before this morning, but forming complete thoughts had been hard enough with the pain in his skull and buzz in his brain, never mind coherent sentences with all that he wanted to say to her. All of which hinged on an overwhelming feeling—and three simple words he'd taken for granted far too long.

Edmond tugged at his dress coat, anticipation and nervousness knotting his intestines. After locking his office, he turned to see a wagon rolling toward him, two women high on the seat.

She came.

He raised his hand in greeting and stepped from the boardwalk to meet them, his heart taking on a new rhythm as they neared. His feet momentarily faltered, but he pulled his gaze from Lenora before he could make a fool of himself. Now wasn't the time to gawk like a recruit fresh out of the academy.

Melina scooted over to give him the reins, and he climbed up beside her. Not daring more than a glance at Lenora, he encouraged Molasses forward. "I already have the tickets, so we should have plenty of time to board. Ranger's at the livery. Hal will help you hitch him for your ride home. I do hate leaving you alone overnight."

Melina chuckled. "You used to all the time. I can still handle it."

Yes, but he'd felt better lately knowing Lenora was there with her.

"I plan to spend my quiet evening working on that baby blanket for Mrs. Jenson's new little boy. I used to always have a quilt ready to give."

A lot of things had changed since Lenora had come, and Edmond couldn't imagine going back to life before her. He had no desire to try.

He pulled the wagon behind the station and hurried around to assist Lenora. She waited patiently, regal with the pale skin of her bare shoulders visible through the light weave of a lace shawl. Most of her waves were caught up on the back of her head, but several perfect ringlets brushed her long neck. He lifted her down and ripples of pale pink cascaded from her waist.

"Thank you." Her red lips pursed with a coy smile.

He raised his hand with the need to touch the softness of her face, to hold her in place while he closed the distance between them with the kiss he needed to return, but the train blared behind him. He dropped his hand. "We should go."

Edmond turned, but not too quickly as to miss the subtle tightening of Lenora's jaw. He'd been too hasty, too detached, not greeting her properly or complimenting her appearance as Melina had instructed. The role of a suitor was not one he had much experience in, but he'd make amends once they were settled on the train. They would have almost two hours for conversation while traveling.

After grabbing Lenora's travel bag from the back of the wagon, he led the way to the passenger car. If it had been only him and he didn't still fight with waves of dizziness, he would have ridden Ranger. The journey might have taken him quite a bit longer, but he preferred the fresh air and quiet to the smelly, contained train ride. Though with Lenora at his side, there was no room for complaint. Before the end of the evening, he hoped to have the details of his future—their future—fully agreed upon.

Down the aisle, he chose a seat with no other occupants. He stood aside while she sat next to the window, and then he sat beside her. Their luggage was small and easily stowed at their feet.

"There," he murmured.

An awkward silence loitered between them while other passengers hastened to find seats, adding to the steady din of conversation, farewells, and foot treads. Finally, they settled, and the engineer released a final blare. The wheels squealed against the iron rails. The train reached full speed before the noise eased to a volume one did not have to fight against to be heard.

"Thank you for agreeing to come." He should apologize for the lateness of his invitation and the way it was conveyed, but the throb in his head had risen to an unrelenting blade of pain from temple to temple. He needed to save his energy for more important discussions. He looked to her hands, but Lenora had weaved the ends of the shawl between her fingers and nestled them on her lap, making them off-limits.

"It'll be fun escaping the house for once." She looked straight ahead, a slight curve to the corner of her mouth. "A night dancing with men in uniform."

He shifted on the seat. "You should find most Mounties to be quite the gentlemen."

"Won't that be a fine change?" She angled a glance at him, looking him up and down.

Edmond frowned. Had he offended her? Or was this an example of who she'd been, the woman from the front of the Pot O' Gold bulletin? Looking at her now, with gold ringlets piled elegantly on her head and gown fitting to her feminine curves, it was too easy to picture the *Lovely Lenora* on the stage, breaking the heart of every man who listened to her angelic voice.

He closed his eyes against the drumming in his head and the unease breaching his confidence. Anderson's warning rang in his ears.

And when the curtain closes, and she's gotten everything she can from you, she'll be on her way to the next stage.

Was that all he was to her? Someone to perform for, to wrap around her finger?

No. He knew her better.

Didn't he?

It was hard to think straight with the pain in his head. Now wasn't the time for declaring his heart. He would wait to discuss a future between them until they were away from the racket of this iron monster. But what did that mean for his meeting with the commissioner?

CHAPTER 29

L enora stared at her image in the full-length mirror hoarding the corner of her hotel room. She hardly recognized herself—the woman she had been. While the gown Melina had altered for the event was more modest than the ones she'd worn on stage at the Pot O' Gold, it was far from the day dresses, skirts, and blouses she'd become accustomed to. She wanted to look beautiful for Edmond … unless this was all he saw. Why draw his gaze if he didn't see who she was on the inside?

A knock sounded on her hotel room door. Edmond was finally here to rescue her from herself. He had insisted she freshen up at the hotel during his meeting with the commissioner, and so here she'd remained for most of an hour, unable to sit still while she sent prayers heavenward for Edmond's sake, that all would go well. At the same time, trying not to consider what that meeting could mean for the future.

"One night," she whispered. One night to be in Edmond's arms and pretend he cared for her. Even if it were make-believe, she would enjoy the few hours of dreaming and stave off reality until tomorrow. Who knew, maybe if God really could work miracles, one night would be enough to make Edmond fall in love.

Shoulders squared, Lenora opened the door.

Hat tucked under his arm Edmond stood resolute in scarlet. Proper and perfect in every way. Oh, how would she make it through the night when she was ready to melt at his feet at the sight of him?

She struggled to find her voice. "What did he say? The commissioner?"

Edmond shook his head, a swift action followed by a wince. "We can talk of it later. We don't want to be too late to the ball."

"Of course." She set her hand on his waiting arm and walked beside him down the long stairs and into the pleasant evening air. He had a buggy waiting, but it wasn't a long ride to the tall log walls of the fort with open gates beckoning them inside. Walking through them was like stepping back in time, the rustic fortifications whispering secrets about the early years when the area had been untamed, no bustling town or railroad just outside, and the first Mounties had stepped in to bring law and peace.

The center of the compound boasted hundreds of lamps hanging from the fronts of surrounding buildings and poles erected around a floor apparently constructed for the purpose of dancing. The band, made up of uniformed men, already played a gay melody with their broad assortment of instruments. The tune, she knew well, having sung it frequently enough in the past.

"You like dancing?" Edmond asked, his voice tight. Pain pinched the corners of his eyes.

"Very much," she replied, unable to hide the anticipation bubbling through her. Her greater concern was for him, though. Lenora was about to say something more when she heard a mumbled remark aimed at her that would make a proper lady blush. She glanced at the group of uniformed men and forced an indulgent smile, the easiest way to keep her dignity intact. "Good evening, gentlemen." Thankfully, this was no longer a part of her daily existence.

Lenora returned her attention to Edmond to find him frowning. She shrugged and resumed their conversation. "You don't have to dance with me if your head hurts too much."

"No, I suppose not." His gaze traveled the length of her. "I don't imagine it will be hard for you to find eager partners."

What? She hadn't meant *that*. He was the only partner she wanted, whether they danced or not.

"You look very beautiful tonight." He spoke the words she had been waiting for, but his voice held no warmth. He looked away.

Lenora stiffened her jaw against the swell of heat behind her eyes and forced her most beguiling smile to her lips. She'd not let him see the depth of hurt, instead looking over the sea of red surrounding them, mingled with a speckling of colors worn by the ladies.

"Why, thank you, Edmond. I do hope you're correct that I'll easily find willing partners."

A muscle ticked in his cheek as he led her deeper into the compound. Two men called out to him and hurried over. They both slowed their approach as soon as their gazes fell on her.

"I was about to ask how you are doing out there by yourself in Cayley, but it seems you are managing quite well," the dark-haired one said. "Very well, indeed."

"Are you providing introductions?" the sandy-haired constable asked, smiling at her.

"Constables, this is the *Lovely* Lenora Perry." Edmond's voice was tight, but no one else seemed to notice. Neither had they the consideration to inquire after his obvious injuries. No, their attention was riveted on her, and it made her ill. But not as ill as hearing the way Edmond said her name—as though announcing her to the stage.

"No relation to Commissioner Perry, I hope?"

"None," Edmond replied.

"Of course not." Sandie laughed. "She's much prettier." He extended a hand. "Has your first dance been spoken for, Miss Perry?"

Edmond released her arm before she had a chance to speak. "Just as you hoped."

Legs stiff with protest, Lenora took the offered hand and allowed herself to be led through the waltz. Her partner peppered her with compliments and questions, but she was too numb to do more than mumble the odd reply. She smiled from habit, and because they expected it, while she broke inside.

As soon as the number ended, the dark-haired Mountie was at her side, begging for the next dance. Then after him, another. And another. And another. She caught a brief glance of Edmond standing on the sidelines in conversation with an older couple, but he didn't look her way. Too busy to rescue her. Couldn't even spare the time or desire to dance with her once. Not even a trace of jealousy. She'd come all this way … just to be thrown to the wolves.

"May I have your next dance, ma'am?" The sentiment was spoken by three at once, all young, probably unattached, and obviously hungry for female companionship. Lenora shook her head and tried to back away, only to run into a fourth uniform, brass buttons down the front glinting with lamplight.

"I'm afraid I must sit this one out, gentlemen. I am quite exhausted."

"I'll accompany you to the refreshment table." An eager one stepped forward to claim her arm.

"That isn't necessary. I must find my companion." She weaseled through the barricade they had erected and hurried to the large gates at the front of the fort. She again searched the crowd for Edmond, but he'd moved from his previous location. What did it matter? He had abandoned her and apparently had little concern for what she did for the remainder of the evening. She would see herself to the hotel and her room.

Edmond kept his back to the dance floor, for the little good it did. He could picture Lenora easy enough as she floated from one partner to the next, smile on her face, soaking up their attention. A long drink of punch did nothing to douse the flames charring his insides.

"Is your father enjoying his new position up north?"

Edmond lowered his glass and tried to give Superintendent Williams his full attention. A longtime family friend, the man was almost an uncle. "I have yet to hear him complain." In truth, Edmond had never heard his father complain. Not when it came to duty. It was simply what he did. What would Father say if he knew Edmond had asked the commissioner to wait for his answer on the offered promotion? A corporal. Father would expect him to take it. And most likely, he would.

He stole a glance at the dancers swirling across the platform in an array of colors. The belle of the ball, Lenora shouldn't be so hard to locate. All he had to do was seek out a large group of constables, gathered like schoolboys to a cake in pink frosting. Edmond would do well to hunt out the commissioner instead and accept his offer, a much more generous one than Edmond had anticipated. More than he deserved.

"We've lost you again, haven't we?" Mrs. Williams squeezed his arm. "Looking for that lovely lady you arrived with?"

"Good luck getting her back," Superintendent Williams said. "Not unless you make her Mrs. Bryce. That's the only way to keep back the swarms of hopeful bachelors." He patted his wife's hand.

"I'm sure she is enjoying herself." Edmond again dragged his attention away from the dance floor. "I'm not much use to her tonight." Not with the competition so rigorous and his head ready to bust in two.

"Oh, is that her there?" Mrs. Williams pointed toward the gate.

Edmond turned in time to see a flash of pink vanish past the roughhewn pickets. The color seemed right, but any reason for her sudden departure only stoked the fire in his gut. "I should check. Excuse me."

He weaved around ongoing conversations and couples on their way to the center of the compound. By the time he reached the street, there was no sign of Lenora. For all he knew, he was chasing a shadow.

He looked back to the crowd, and the thought of returning fell away. Not for a little while, at least. Lenora would get along fine without him with so many eager partners, and he needed some peace and quiet to settle his mind.

And if she had left?

The hotel seemed a sharp contrast to the noise down the street, its rust-colored brick walls shielding them from much of the merriment. A single electric lamp lit the stairs, with two in the corridor leading to Lenora's room. He paused outside, feeling a fool. But what harm would come from knocking to make sure she wasn't there? The rap of his knuckles resounded down the hall.

Footsteps shuffled on the other side of the door. "Did you need something?"

"Lenora?"

"What do you want?" The question was followed by what sounded like a sniffle.

His guard dropped like a stone. "I wanted to make sure you were all right. Can you open the door?"

"I'm preparing for bed." Her voice sounded pinched and resonated a little higher than usual.

"I'd really like to see you. Just for a moment." Concern rode over the jealousy that had consumed him for the past hour. "I'll wait while you dress."

Silence gave no clues, so he leaned his head against the wall and let his eyes close while he could. Minutes passed before the door cracked open just enough to make out a sliver of her face and the sunshiny yellow robe with all its silly ruffles. All it took to turn his thought to sweeping her into his arms as he had that day by the well after Porter had tried to make her acquaintance. Except this time, Edmond probably wouldn't be able to let go before stealing a taste of those shapely lips.

"I'm quite fine—and *alone*, if that is what you were worried about."

The terseness of her words and the insinuation dropped him back on his heels. "I wasn't. I just worried when I saw you leave so early. You seemed to be enjoying yourself." Hard to keep his voice even.

She said nothing for a moment, peering at him through the crack in the doorway. Her eyes glistened in the light of the lamp behind him. "Of course. Why wouldn't I be having the time of my life? It's all I ever wanted, the undivided attention of my audience."

The door snapped closed.

Edmond stared at the cream-colored paint only inches from his nose, mind slogging forward and the temptation growing to plow his forehead into the solid wood. No wonder he couldn't track a single cattle rustler. He couldn't see what was sitting right in front of him. He'd allowed his personal uncertainties to blind him. Didn't he know Lenora well enough by now? Hadn't he prided himself in knowing the difference between her fake smiles and the ones that reached her eyes?

He moaned and wiped a hand down his face. "I'm so sorry, Lenora," he whispered to the closed door. Sorry that he continued to misjudge her. Sorry he'd wasted what could have been a wonderful evening together. He'd ruined everything.

CHAPTER 30

Edmond awoke to tapping on his door and lurched into action. Perhaps his opportunity to apologize had come earlier than expected. Though his brain ached from lack of sleep, having spent the wee hours of the morning trying to work out what he wanted to say to Lenora, he hurried to pull on his pants and button his shirt.

A young man stood outside his room with a missive in hand. "Constable Bryce?"

"Yes." Edmond took the slip of paper. "Thank you."

A message from the local superintendent. The Canadian Pacific Railway Company was sending a large payroll through the area and had requested two Mounties to assist the regular guards in securing its transportation. Edmond had been assigned the duty from Fort Macleod to Calgary this afternoon. He'd be on the same train as Lenora, just not sitting with her.

Edmond sank onto the firm edge of the mattress. He had all morning to make amends before reporting for duty, but he'd looked forward to that time together. Yet another reason to walk away from the force if they were to be together.

He donned the rest of his uniform, slipping each brass button into its corresponding hole, his motions slowing. It would be hard to give up his uniform and that sense of purpose that came every time he put it on. He tucked his hat under his arm and squared off to the mirror. Lenora would be worth the sacrifice. Heart in his hands, he went to her room and knocked on the door.

No answer. Perhaps she still slept.

He paced the hall for a half hour before trying again.

Nothing.

"Lenora?" He leaned his head against the door.

Silence.

Maybe he'd somehow missed her, and she'd already gone down for breakfast.

Downstairs, he searched the dining room from the doorway, but there was no sign of her.

A waiter beckoned him into the room. "Would you like to be seated for breakfast, Constable?"

"No. Not yet. Thank you." Edmond retreated to the hotel's main entrance as a dull headache pounded his temples. The town surrounding the fort was not too large. Perhaps she'd taken a walk and would be easy enough to find.

No such luck. He returned to the hotel almost two hours later and again checked her room. His knock went unanswered. He sagged against the wall, frustration and concern battling within. So much for making amends. What choice remained but to finish packing? He only had an hour remaining before reporting for guard duty.

Where is she, Lord? What would he do if he couldn't find her in time? She wouldn't have left without him. Or would she have? Had he ruined his chance with her?

His satchel slung over his shoulder, Edmond returned a final time to the door he had haunted most of the morning and raised his knuckles to the solid wood.

Footfalls from within bolstered his confidence. "Lenora?"

The door opened, and she appeared fully dressed in her blue skirt and a blouse. The lace shawl hung from her shoulders. "Good morning, Edmond," she said with a flat tone.

"Where have you been?"

One fine eyebrow rose. "Were you looking for me?"

"Of course. I had hoped to talk." He glanced up and down the hall, gauging the timing. One other person was visible, locking their room, about to depart.

"I woke early and went for a walk." Her gaze lowered to her

hands, again tangled in the ends of her shawl, but a small smile teased her lips. "There is a fine little church just down the street, so I joined them for their service."

Edmond had walked by that church two times and hadn't considered looking inside for her. "How was it?"

The tightness around her eyes softened. "Good. Folks were very welcoming."

"I'm glad." Edmond nudged the smooth floor with the toe of his boot. Now what? "Um … about last night, I hadn't—"

A door slammed and a child squealed. Some children had joined them in the hall, pushing and teasing each other as they waited for their parents.

His rehearsed speech fell aside, leaving little more than, "I'm sorry."

Her gaze flickered to his. "You don't owe me an apology."

"Yes. I do." He looked at her hands, wishing to take one, but her fingers were still tangled. "You came all this way at my request. The least I owed you was a dance. Lenora, I—"

Another shout from one of the youngsters. Their mother stepped into the hall to quiet them.

"I wish we had more time to talk, but I need to leave earlier to the station than planned. And I'll be riding the line all the way to Calgary."

She made a little sound in the back of her throat he wasn't sure how to interpret. "On Mountie business?"

"Yes." He switched his hat to the other hand, feeling more like an adolescent than a grown man. "I want to see you safely to the train, though. And Melina should be waiting in Cayley."

"Of course. I'll gather my things."

She closed the door before he could say anything more.

Blowing out his breath, Edmond paced the floor, nodding to the two young boys as he passed. Their mother again absent, they took up the trail behind him. There had to be a better way to go about winning Lenora's favor, but romance would have to wait until he returned from Calgary. There simply wasn't time for everything he needed to say.

Five minutes later, the door opened, and Lenora came out with her bag. One of Melina's hats, blue to match her eyes, perched on her head.

He saluted the boys behind him and stepped into action, extending his hand toward her bag. "Let me carry that for you."

Lenora passed it to him without a word before turning down the hall. She waited at the front of the hotel while he settled their bill with the attendant at the front desk and then took the lead, three steps ahead. Not that he minded a chance to watch her, to admire her grace and the loose strands of hair dancing on her neck. She was a beautiful woman, but she was so much more than he had given her credit for. He'd misjudged her on so many accounts he didn't dare tally them. And all because he was a coward, afraid to risk his heart, afraid to acknowledge that God wanted control of his life. To bless him.

At the station, Lenora turned and extended her hand. "You'd best give me back my bag in case I don't see you in Cayley."

Edmond complied, very conscious of how carefully she took the handle so that their hands didn't brush. He opened his mouth to tell her how much he regretted that they couldn't ride together, but a man in a suit and a uniformed officer were almost to them. Probably to brief him on his assignment. He surrendered her ticket.

"Thank you." Something in her tone suggested a deeper meaning than gratitude for his assistance with her bag. It almost rang with goodbye.

"I'll see you tomorrow. In Cayley. Can you let Mel know?"

"Of course. I'll tell her." Lenora turned and hurried aboard the waiting passenger car.

He watched until she'd found a seat on the far side and vanished from his sight.

"Constable Bryce?"

He nodded and forced his attention to the task at hand and the men who waited for a proper reply. The ride to Calgary and back home would be one of the longest he'd ever taken.

Lenora didn't see Edmond disembark at the Cayley station but hadn't expected him to. Had only hoped to see him one last time.

Melina met her with the wagon, and Lenora explained Edmond's absence, feeling it more with each minute. Not that seeing him and saying goodbye would change anything. She'd had plenty of time to consider every alternative, and her mind was made up. She'd overstayed and could no longer put off the inevitable.

"You must tell me everything about the ball," Melina said as soon as they passed the last home marking the edge of town.

"There isn't much to tell."

Melina gave the horses their head, turning her full attention to Lenora. "Oh, no. What happened?"

"I didn't say anything happened."

"You didn't have to. It's written all over your face. You sound miserable."

I am. Lenora looked toward the mountains so Melina couldn't see the moisture building in her eyes. "It wasn't so bad. Lots of dancing."

"What did Edmond do?"

"You assume he did something." She pretended to laugh. "Your brother wasn't the problem." *I was.* She couldn't blame him for how he felt. It was perfectly natural for a man not to wish to tie himself to a used woman. "I just wasn't feeling well."

"I'm sorry. I'd hoped you'd be over the worst of your morning sickness by now."

Though it might be a sin, Lenora didn't correct her assumption.

When they reached the farm, Porter greeted them with excited yaps, and Lenora crouched to scratch behind his ears. She would miss the happy dog and his eager companionship.

"Why don't you lie down for a little while?" Melina said when they reached the house. "I'll fix some tea."

"That would be nice." Lenora managed a smile, but as soon as she closed the door to the room, she emptied the travel bag on the bed and set about repacking. The rose-pink gown was Melina's mother's, and Lenora had no use for one so fine. Not once she left here. She packed the green dress she had arrived in. How many times she'd suppressed the urge to stoke the fire with the awful thing, but having the extra gown was useful as was the reminder of where she'd been. Into its folds, she tucked her derringer. The train would come back through tomorrow afternoon with Edmond on it. She almost hoped she could avoid seeing him, but she planned to be on that train when it left Cayley.

With her few belongings packed away, Lenora pulled the pins from her hair, relieving her aching scalp. She laid down just as Melina slipped in with a tray carrying a teapot, two cups, cheese, and sweet rolls. She laid a large napkin out like a picnic blanket. "I see no reason to make you get up."

Lenora squeezed her hand. "You're too good to me." Like a sister. *If only.*

"Nonsense." Melina climbed onto the bed beside her and stuck a pinch of roll into her mouth. "It's myself I'm spoiling. My feet are tired, and I am hungry for company. I don't know how I survived before you came."

She offered Lenora the tray, but she couldn't lift her hand to accept anything. "I need to tell you something. And I need you to accept my decision. Please don't argue with me or try to change my mind. This is already so hard to—"

"No, Lenora." Melina lowered the platter to the bed and gripped her hand. "You can't be thinking that."

"I'm not thinking it anymore. My mind is made up. I would stay if I could but ... but I can't."

"But why?"

"Mel ..."

Her eyes widened. "Because of Edmond."

Not the direction Lenora wanted the conversation to go, but it seemed inevitable now. "Some things aren't meant to be."

"He chose the promotion?"

"I—I don't know. We never talked about his meeting."

Melina slumped back against the headboard, arms crossing. "My brother's a fool if he's willing to give you up to further his career."

"I'm sure I have nothing to do with it. Why shouldn't he continue on as a Mountie? Why not pursue what he loves?"

"Because I think he does love you."

Lenora bit her tongue to keep her expression neutral. She cleared the sudden constriction from her throat. "I don't think so." Friendship, perhaps. A little attraction. But not love. "No, he should stay as he is. While I have no doubt he would be successful at anything he put his hand to, I can't imagine him as anything other than a Mountie. And the law needs men like him. Brave, honorable, and true." Lenora grabbed a roll and took a big bite to stop her mouth from spilling her heart.

Melina already looked at her with far too much discernment. "At least, wait to leave until Edmond returns."

"He can say what he wants to say at the train station." She unfolded the handkerchief that hid her last possession of any worth, one that shouldn't belong to her anymore. "I don't have money for the ticket or to repay you for everything, so I want you to have this." She held out the small ruby ring.

Melina stared but shook her head. "You don't owe us anything."

Other than room and board for almost two months, train tickets, the cost of fabric, friendship ... and helping to restore her faith. Lenora owed them more than a simple ring could ever compensate.

CHAPTER 31

Edmond counted the miles. Although Commissioner Perry's offer had been generous, a very different Perry held his thoughts and heart. But the distance between them was driving him mad. He would get off the train in Cayley, write the commissioner his resignation, give Lenora his full apology, and then ask for another chance to kiss her like a man in love ought.

He stared out the smoke-stained glass in the second passenger car, watching the hills roll by. The funds he needed for a new start were hidden under a floorboard at the jail. Not the most conventional hiding place, but practical since the nearest banks were in Calgary. He had the means to buy some fine quarter horse bloodlines for a breeding operation. The farm was a perfect place to raise children, starting with the little one already on the way. He'd always be close at hand in case they needed him and be there to watch them grow. And to hold their mother every night.

Edmond perched on the edge of his seat when the train pulled alongside the Cayley station. He'd grin like a fool if not for the uncertainty of Lenora's answer. He hadn't felt this nervous since his first day at the academy. How hard he had prayed that day not to mess up.

Dropping deeper into his seat, Edmond looked at his hands. When was the last time he'd prayed like that, the last time he'd truly trusted his life's course to God?

The answer wasn't one he was proud of.

Ignoring the squeal of breaks and the bustle of the other passengers, Edmond tipped his head forward. *Please, Lord, guide me through this. I am right in giving up my career for Lenora, aren't I?*

His choice of words struck him with foreboding. Give up. Sacrifice. But that's what you did for the people you loved. It would be worth it in the end, even if it smarted a bit now.

Not liking the downward spiral of his thoughts, Edmond looked out the window. Lenora stood with Melina on the platform, waiting for him. Every other thought flew away.

Any passengers disembarking had already done so, leaving no obstruction in his path off the train. His feet met the platform at a jog but slowed at the sight of the old travel bag clutched in Lenora's hands. She ducked her head when he drew near.

"What—what are you doing?"

"I'm getting ready to board that train."

His chest deflated and his head spun. "What? Why?"

"It's time for me to move on. I spoke with a lady at that church in Fort Macleod. She said they are always in need of more laundresses with so many single men posted at the fort. I should have no difficulty finding suitable employment and a new home."

"But—"

"I am so very grateful for everything you and Melina have done for me." Her voice wavered. "Thank you, Edmond." She took a step as to maneuver around him.

He grabbed her arm. "Lenora, I can't—"

"Edmond!" The call came from the side of the station. Frank swung from his horse, whose black coat dripped with sweat as it heaved each breath. The look of the man's face portrayed a fear Edmond had never seen on him. "Come quick."

"What's happened?" He released Lenora and darted across the platform.

"Greer and his group caught the Lawson boy on Mackenzie land. They think he's the rustler."

"They'll bring him in?"

The shake of Frank's head spoke more than Edmond wanted to hear. He twisted to where Lenora and Melina stood watching.

"Don't leave yet." But he couldn't wait for her answer. Duty called, and a life might be on the line. He raced to Frank's horse. "Where were they headed?"

"They were near the creek up about a half mile from where the fire started."

Edmond whipped his reins against the saddle, driving the horse past town and over the prairie. Behind him, the train whistle blew. All he could pray was Lenora would wait for him, but the look in her eyes didn't lend much hope.

The horse churned dust in its wake, taking Edmond away with so much left unsaid. But it was for the best. No matter how it hurt.

Biting the inside of her cheek to keep the tears at bay, Lenora held tight to the travel bag and started toward the train. A whistle signaled time was short. She might have missed this one if Edmond hadn't been forced to leave. She might have been compelled to stay a little longer. Or forever.

Oh, foolish dreams.

A tear slipped free, and she swiped it away.

"Why not stay one more day?" Melina touched her arm. "That wasn't a proper goodbye. He never had a chance to say anything."

"He didn't need to." Lenora tried to smile for her friend, but it was easier to bury her doubts in an embrace. "I will miss you so much."

Melina had tears on her cheek by the time they drew apart. "Don't leave."

"I have to. Please try to understand that." As much an admonition to herself. "I'll write when I'm settled. I promise."

"Then I'll come and visit soon."

Lenora managed a nod. "I still need to get my ticket." The perfect excuse to turn away before she lost all composure. She hurried to the ticket window. "Um, one ticket to Fort Macleod." She wasn't sure if she would remain there, but at least it gave her a direction.

"One way?"

"Yes." The word tightened in her throat, begging to be kept back. She passed him the coins Melina had lent her.

"There you go, miss." He slid the ticket to her, but it took her two tries to pick it up.

The train's call almost deafened her, and she hurried across the platform. The second passenger car appeared crowded, so she climbed aboard the first with one final wave to Melina. She found the last empty bench and slid against the wall, but not so she could look out the dirt-coated window. The train jerked then eased forward, a rattle and clang announcing their departure. She would miss this little town and all she found here. The laughter. Late-night talks. The look in Edmond's eyes when he drew her near. The security of his arms around her. The smell of his neck. His callused hands. The rumble of his voice in her ear. Safety. Love. Home.

Straw bonnet pulled low over her eyes, she tried to control the ache spreading through her with such exquisite agony. The realization of loss. The slow hemorrhaging of any hopes.

But mostly ... utter and complete loneliness.

Don't leave me, Lord. I can't do this on my own. Not this time.

She would give her life to Him and try her best to trust what He wanted for her. Even if it wasn't what she had wanted for herself.

A pair of polished black boots approached, and Lenora looked out the window at the rolling prairie bathed in green with patches of pink. The last of the wild rose blossoms. After a summer of ornamenting the prairies, Melina said they would soon be finished flowering. She wasn't the only one fading away.

The owner of the black boots sat on the seat beside her, close enough that their arms brushed. She tried to pull away, but his voice froze her mid-motion.

"Hello, Lenora."

Her heart mounted in her throat. She swiped the moisture from her face before daring a glance at the man she had never expected to see again. He wore a half smile that broke with a dimple in his cheek, the one that had once tugged at her heart.

"What are you doing here, Channing?"

"I meant to ask the same thing." His green eyes glinted. She'd forgotten how smooth he spoke, a hint of Irish to add to his draw. "I had planned to get off the train at Cayley. That was quite the touching display back at the station. Was that your supposed husband riding off like the devil was on his tail?"

"I ..."

"Did you really think Anderson would be deterred by your little ruse? A couple questions to some neighbors, and the truth was easy enough to discern."

She straightened and faced him fully. "Why did you come? I'm not going back with you."

He leaned back as though unaffected. "You say so, and yet here we are on the same train, headed south."

The irony. "I can't go back to that life. I won't go back on the stage. I won't work in the Pot O' Gold again."

A muscle twitched beside his eye. "Have I asked you to?"

"I ..." She'd not expected that reply.

"A man doesn't want his wife out on display for other men to gawk at."

"Wife?"

That smile crept up again. "I plan on marrying you, Lenora. Return with me to Wyoming and become my wife."

Lenora leaned back to catch her breath. His wife? Was this what the Lord had in mind for her despite how far she'd run? Channing Doyle was the father of her child. What could be more proper? Once upon a time, she had been swayed by his handsome face and easy ways. Maybe someday she could learn to love him—if she could somehow get Edmond out of her heart.

CHAPTER 32

Edmond pushed the horse as hard as he dared, ripping over the burnt prairie with the prayer that they wouldn't snag a hoof in a prairie dog hole or arrive too late. He only slowed to drop down into the coulee and splash across the stream. A cluster of horses came into view, tied at the edge of the trees. One horse stood apart, Lawson's Morgan, under a large willow, the boy on its back. A rope hung taut from one of the branches high overhead. A noose wrapped Matthew's throat.

What have you done, Matt?

"Easy." Edmond slowed his approach. The last thing he wanted was to ride in hard and startle the horse under Matt. He advanced head on, his revolver buckled in its holster. Father had made sure he knew from a young age about the most important rule Mounties were given. Guns were a last resort.

"No closer, Constable Bryce." Greer stepped away from the others, rifle in hand. "We caught him red-handed. If you won't do your job, we will."

"Not today, you won't." Edmond rested his hands on the pommel of the saddle so everyone could see them. He glanced toward Matt, whose red face dripped with sweat. Large eyes pleaded as the horse shifted under him. "Turn the boy over to me, and I'll see that justice is done."

"What justice? You've had more than enough time to find the rustler. But no, we keep losing stock, and nothing gets done."

"I'll get it done."

"When?" Greer bellowed, startling Matt's horse back a step. The boy gulped, then gagged. "We lost another two head last Wednesday, strung up and cut like the others. And one more today. Those losses are adding up fast, Constable. Besides, you don't look in much of a position to be ordering us about." Greer nodded toward Edmond's holster. "Do you even know how to use that thing?"

"I do. But I don't see why I would need to demonstrate that to a group of civilized men who don't want trouble with the law. Now go cut the boy down, and hand me the reins to his horse."

Greer didn't move, jaw flexing.

"Either you cut him down, and I take him to town, or I lock you up. If you try to go through with a hanging in my territory, that constitutes murder, and you will be tried for such." Edmond held the man's gaze, waiting for him to bend, praying he would.

Greer spun and grumbled a command to his men. "Get him down."

The end of the rope loosened, and Matt gasped for air. Edmond had to stop himself from following suit—now was not the time to show weakness. He held out his hand for the lead to Matt's horse, and one of the men grudgingly handed it over.

"Now, I know you all have work to do, so I'll ride out to the ranch sometime in the next day or two to hear your story in full detail. Either that or you are more than welcome to stop by my office." Edmond touched the brim of his hat and turned toward town. Only once they had crossed over the next stream and climbed out of the coulee did he breathe easy and cast a glance back at Matt, hands still tied behind him.

"You want to explain what happened?"

The boy blinked hard to maintain composure, but he wasn't far from crumbling. His voice quivered. "You saved me."

"That's my job. The law is on your side. For the time being. You want to tell me why they suspect you of cattle rustling?"

"I was camping out. After what happened, I—I got scared. But I didn't do anything to their cows. Came upon their missing steer like he said, but I didn't kill it. I was just trying to salvage a little of the meat that had been left."

That explained the lynch mob.

"Ain't the only carcass I've found. There's another one a ways up the creek, stinking up the area something fierce."

Edmond had gotten a whiff on his ride past. "Near where the fire broke out?"

Matt nodded.

"Yeah, I've seen that one." Simply hadn't had time to do anything about it between the fire, his head, and business in Fort Macleod—which reminded him of where he should be right now. On his knees, asking for more than just Lenora's forgiveness.

"Then you know I didn't have anything to do with it or the fire. I know I was wrong to hit you, but I'm not the rustler." Matt craned his neck to see behind them, probably double-checking that the lynch mob hadn't changed their minds and were coming after him again.

"I know that." And now Edmond had a better idea about what happened to his head.

"Then who is?" The boy asked as though fully expecting Edmond to have the answer.

"I have a couple of suspects." One, at least. But he'd never had his conversation with George. They'd be passing the Cornwell place. As much as Edmond wanted to race home and make certain Lenora hadn't left on the train, he hadn't resigned from this posting yet and wouldn't feel good about stepping down before this case was solved. Hopefully, Frank could do without his horse a little while longer.

Edmond stopped the horses long enough to untie Matt's hands. "Just don't get any idea about being in the clear. I still have some questions for you." And some gaps in his memory to fill.

They rode for another mile before Matt spoke. "You were right, Constable."

Edmond glanced back.

"I'm the reason my pa's gone. He told me to bring in those heifers before the storm. He trusted me to do it. And instead, I went and spent the day down at the creek. He shouldn't have been out in that blizzard—he wouldn't have been if I'd have done as I was told."

Fragments of conversation returned. They'd been standing behind the Lawson barn. Edmond trying to get him to talk about his pa. The tussle.

"I killed my pa. I deserve to be locked away."

"Do you think that's what your pa wants?"

Matt stared down, sun-bleached hair hanging over his glistening eyes. His jaw clamped tight.

"One thing I know for certain is your pa loved you. Neither of us can go back and change the past or foolish mistakes. If you love him, though, you'll honor him and what he left you. You're his son. You carry his name. You can drive your life into a hole or decide to be the man your pa raised you to be—give him something to be proud of."

Silence stretched over the last several miles to the Cornwell homestead. The crack of an ax called from beyond the shanty. George straddled a pine log, splitting it down the center. A wagon load of logs sat nearby, suggesting he'd hauled them down from the foothills.

"What do you want?"

Edmond dismounted. The other man's gun lay against a tree out of reach, so he didn't have to worry about his own. Not yet. "I have a few questions for you."

George's fists tightened around the ax handle. "What about? I haven't done anything wrong."

"Then maybe you'll tell me where you were last Monday morning and again on Wednesday. And if anyone can vouch for you."

His Adam's apple dipped low. "The wife said you came by, but why should my whereabouts matter? Isn't no law saying a man can't leave his land."

"No, but there is a law against killing another man's cattle."

Color sank from his face. "I'm not a cattle rustler."

"Not anymore, don't you mean? Perhaps you'd like to explain why you changed your name when crossing the border."

He staggered back a step, almost tripping over the log. "What do you know?"

"I know you used to go by George Bates, and you got yourself in trouble more than once south of the border. I also know cattle have been poached off two of the large ranches near your spread since your arrival. More than once, I've tracked the rustler as far as your land."

"Why ..." George was breathing hard, wiping sweat from his face. "Why would I ruin any chance I had of starting fresh with my family for a few measly cows? I promised Cassandra a better life after I got out of prison. She waited for me. I couldn't ask her to do that again."

Edmond hooked the reins over a nearby branch, noticing for the first time that one was slightly thicker and much newer than the other. "How long did you spend in prison?"

"Ten years. She gave up most of her life. For me. You've got to believe me that I didn't go anywhere near anyone else's cattle. I swore I'd do it right this time. But there just wasn't any way I could do it down south. Too many folks already knew about my past. Wouldn't give me a chance."

Edmond could feel for the man's plight, but he had a job to do, and George Bates was still his most likely suspect. "I won't hold your past against you if you can prove you didn't kill those cattle. Where were you Wednesday morning?"

His hold loosened on the ax, and his head dropped forward. "I took the train to Calgary the afternoon before. All morning I spent going from one bank to another, trying for a loan."

A loan? "You have your ticket stubs?"

He nodded.

"Good. Let's go see them." Edmond waited for George to drop the ax and move before mounting Frank's horse again. The crazy animal had no patience and had already gnawed the thin branch in half. He gave Matt back his reins with the order to ride close, then skirt around the corrals between them and the house.

George met them outside, wife at his side, and receipts for his train tickets in hand. Edmond wrote down the banks he had visited to verify his story, but it appeared George had the perfect alibi, and there was no reason to keep him from his work.

"Did you get your loan?"

George glanced at his wife, and he could see the answer before it was spoken. "No. Not enough to see us through."

"What'll you do?"

A look of defeat crossed his face, but his spine remained resolute. "May be selling my bull to Mackenzie if he still wants it. Might go away for the winter and try to find work for myself. I don't know."

"I wish you luck." And for a way to help the family stay together and make a go of this farm.

"Who do you have left as a suspect?" Matt asked as they rode toward town.

Edmond frowned. Matt and George had been his only suspects, and two lines now crossed out their names. Who was left? As much as he needed to solve this case before Greer took the law into his own hands, Edmond couldn't think about that until he'd spoken with Lenora. Until he'd set things right between them.

Back in town, he rode straight to his office, where Frank leaned against the outside wall beside the door, likely waiting for news and his horse. Edmond dismounted and handed him the reins. "Thanks for the help."

"I couldn't stand by and let an innocent kid get hurt." He gave a tight smile and turned.

Edmond stared at the tracks leading away in the dry dust, and his world began to tip. "How did you figure his innocence, Frank?" He started after him, his mind churning with each facet falling into place. No wonder he recognized the knife he'd found. He'd seen it before on Frank's belt. "Why were you out there?"

Frank turned back, expression grim. "Been keeping my eyes wide since the trouble started."

"Your horse is quite the cribber. Near gnawed through a branch I had him tied to. And his left front shoe has a notch in it." Edmond stepped over to his friend, numbness spreading through his limbs.

"Why did you do it, Frank? Why?"

A muscle ticked in Frank's jaw, and he shook his head. "You're too much like your old man. Would never understand."

"Frank ..." Edmond could only look at the man he'd known and respected for as long as he remembered. The burn behind his eyes almost went unnoticed next to the throb in his chest.

"Mackenzie stole my land. Everything I'd worked for."

"And the fire, Frank? That was you too?"

The older man's face blanched under his tan, and the creases deepened around his eyes. "I didn't mean for that to happen, didn't mean for it to get out of control. It was just supposed to keep you busy for a few minutes."

"So you could get away. A dozen homes and buildings. Some folks lost everything."

"No one was supposed to get hurt." Sweat glistened on his forehead. "I just needed a little more time, a little more money. I could have given my family a new life away from here. We were almost ready."

Edmond's gut hurt as though he'd been gored. Frank had broken the law, but for the sake of his family—to give them something better. Justice would never see that side of it, though. Only the crime. And Edmond had a role to play. "I can't let this go, Frank." He swallowed the lump in his throat and cleared his voice. "You're under arrest."

Frank shook his head, stepping back.

"I can't let you go."

Frank reached for his revolver.

Edmond left his in the holster, raising his hands shoulder high. "You going to shoot me now, Frank? You know that won't solve anything. And you know I have no choice." He stepped to his friend and held out his hand. "I guess I am too much like my father."

The breeze stirred the dust at their feet and the horse's black mane.

Frank's eyes misted. "Don't let my boys follow me." He released his revolver and then the reins into Edmond's hands.

"I'll do everything I can for them." With a motion to the jail, Edmond allowed Frank to lead the way inside, pausing long enough to hoop the reins over the hitching post. Frank was already seated on the cot in the small cell when he entered the dimly lit office.

God, I can't do this. The man was like a father to me, and his family needs him.

"I quit," Edmond whispered. He couldn't continue on. Couldn't sacrifice the people he cared about for the uniform he wore.

CHAPTER 33

"Our train leaves in an hour." Channing's terse voice penetrated the door and Lenora's peace, stealing it from her.

Lenora hugged herself and pictured him standing just outside, the same scowl on his face that had been there yesterday when she'd insisted on a pause in their journey, when she'd asked for time. Just one day to give him his answer.

Would he accept a no?

"I'll be down."

"Good." His footsteps faded away.

Lenora moved away from the door, her stomach more volatile than it had been in weeks. Every time she thought of Channing in the room next door, waiting on her answer, offering her and her baby a future, bile climbed her throat. Lenora groaned and looked heavenward. She still hadn't told him about the child growing within—wasn't sure she wanted to. But what choice did she have? She had no way of supporting herself once the baby was born, and the child needed a father.

But Channing Doyle?

Swallowing the bitterness on the back of her tongue, Lenora crossed to the hotel window. Though she could see no more than a corner of the fort's tall log walls, a pair of Mounties strolled down the street, probably toward the diner at the end of the block. It was too easy to picture Edmond hidden under one of the flat brims, and she longed for him to look up and see her. A fantasy. Channing was her reality.

"Lord, what should I do?" As taken as she'd once been with

Channing, as handsome his smile, there was no affection behind it. She would only ever be a possession to him—something he could control. Surely, a loving God, the one who would grant forgiveness to someone as fallen as she, would want better for her.

And what of her baby?

Lenora laid a hand over her abdomen, no longer completely flat. Channing had spoken of his own da often enough, and not a single positive word had left his lips. What would it be like raised by a saloon owner? They might never want for anything … except God. Would Channing allow her to take their child to church every Sabbath? Would they even be welcomed into the building by the *good* Christians in Cheyenne?

Minutes passed with no sure resolution.

"What choice have I, Lord?"

Another knock shook the door. "Lenora, it's time." Channing's voice held an edge. She'd inconvenienced him, and he wasn't hesitant to let her know.

She gathered her things and opened the door to her potential groom. A stylish black trilby covered his dark hair, always immaculately groomed. The trim cut of his coat fit to perfection, just as Edmond's always did, but one boasted self-importance while the other spoke of service. Her heart squeezed, but not with the pleasant sensation Edmond evoked. This was more akin to indigestion.

"Good. Let us be off. I have a business to run." His words were clipped, their meaning evident. *You have already wasted enough of my time.*

He extended an arm, and she obediently took it, letting him lead her down the stair.

There is always a choice, a voice whispered to her heart. Some choices simply required more faith.

Channing hurried her down the stairs to where Fred loitered, several bags—probably Channing's—in hand. "A buggy is waiting," he said and then followed them out the door.

Lenora allowed herself to be boosted into the back of an open buggy and slid over for Channing to climb up beside her. All as though a ritual, done with no actual thought behind her actions. Fred joined the driver, and with a jostle and lurch, the buggy moved down the street toward the train station. Peace settled into her heart along with the words of her song.

Nothing in my hand I bring, Simply to Thy cross I cling ...

Somehow, Channing would have to accept her answer, and she would put her fate in her true savior's hands.

As the buggy turned onto the next street, a Mountie passed them on a large bay. She jolted upright. The animal she knew well. As she did the Mountie's face, despite the trail dust and two days' growth of whiskers.

"Stop the buggy!"

The abrupt drop in momentum flung her forward, but she caught herself on the side before grabbing for the handle of the door and lunging out. Her skirt snagged under her boot, and she stumbled in an attempt to run.

"Edmond!"

He spun in the street and kicked Ranger into a run back toward her.

"Edmond." He'd come for her. What other explanation could there be? By the look of him, he'd probably ridden most of the night.

He swung down and met her with an embrace, lifting her feet of the ground. Or was that just the sensation of being in his arms?

"I was so afraid I'd lost you," he murmured in her ear. He pulled back enough to capture her mouth ... and suddenly, nothing else in the world existed. He kissed her with such sweet longing, answering every plea of her heart. He loved her! Wanted her despite all her faults and mistakes.

She slid her hands to the nape of his neck and sank her fingers into his trimmed hair, breathing him in as she tasted his lips and replied with her own. This was all she wanted. *He* was her dream. To stay here with him. Forever.

"What is this?" The grind of Channing's voice cut through the perfectness of the moment. "Is this the Mountie you claimed to be married to? And this is the show you put on?"

Edmond relaxed his hold to look past her. His eyes became thin slits. "Who are you?"

"Lenora's fiancé." Channing huffed out a laugh. "Or has she not made that clear?"

Edmond's expression of confidence faltered when he glanced down. "Lenora?"

Oh, to bury her head in Edmond's shoulder and wish the nightmare over. But he deserved the truth. "I never agreed. I never—"

"But you know him. Who is he?"

"Channing Doyle. The—"

"The man who forced himself on you?" Edmond braced her shoulders, his clenched teeth making the words he spoke a whisper. "He should be in jail, not—" His nostrils flared as he pushed her to the side and lunged toward Channing.

"No, Edmond!" She grabbed his arm already cocked with a balled fist. "Please, Edmond, listen to me."

He turned back, but only to move her out of the way. His dark eyes flamed with a rage she'd never seen in him before.

"Edmond, no. You can't hurt him. It wasn't like that."

"You told me what he did to you." He pulled away.

"No, I didn't. He didn't hurt me. Not like you think he did."

He looked back at her, and she hurried to finish, lowering her voice so only he could hear her confession. "I know what you thought, but I couldn't say anything, couldn't bear for you to think worse of me again." She touched his cheek, the bristle of his stubble sending tingles through her palm.

"No, Lenora …"

"I'm so sorry. But the mistake was mine. It was myself I was running from, the person I had become."

"You gave yourself to him?" His words were hardly more than air.

She nodded, the answer clogging her throat.

Edmond pulled away. His hands fell to his sides.

"I'm so sorry." That she hadn't been honest with him from the beginning. That she hadn't been the woman her father had tried to raise her to be—one worthy of a man like Edmond.

Channing's arm slipped around her waist, tugging her firmly to his side. "Thanks for taking care of my girl, Bryce."

The world swam, and Edmond vanished behind a sheen of tears. Yet she was still very aware of his hasty departure and that there was nothing she could do or say to bring him back.

Beside her, Channing laughed tightly. "Imagine that, the Lovely Lenora in love with a Mountie who won't have her. The woman who was too good for the Pot O' Gold ready to spend her life in the wastelands of the Canadian prairies. Admit you were never better than me. You are just like any of the silly girls who come through the Pot O' Gold looking for a little attention." He sneered. "To think I tried to prove myself to you."

He pulled his arm away. "I have a train to catch. If you come back with me, you'll have to work like before. You don't warrant a ring."

Channing strode back to the buggy, leaving Lenora at a crossroads with nowhere to go. He was right—she wasn't worth marrying.

Edmond rode hard out of town, his head foggy from lack of sleep and trying to process what had just happened. Lenora had lied to him. Again. She'd freely given herself to that man—who was not at all like the image she had painted. Or at least, not the one he had imagined. Fiancé? She would return to her old life most likely, the stage and the gawking men. And what did it matter to him? Other than that, he'd made a complete fool of himself.

Better to ignore the burn across his sinuses, the pain growing in his head from trying to hold a mountain of emotion at bay. Better to not think about how good she had felt in his arms for that brief minute or how she had kissed him in return. Better to not dwell on the hunger she had planted within him, along with a thirst that he had no hope of quenching.

"Such a fool."

To believe, even now, that she might care for him. That she might have stayed if he asked her and if he'd been able to overlook what she'd done.

The road took a turn to the east toward Lethbridge, and he pulled Ranger to a stop. He was riding in the wrong direction. Setting his jaw, he turned back toward Fort Macleod. He was exhausted but longed for the open road. Longed to go home. Ranger needed a rest, though, so he returned to the fort, ignoring the sound of a departing train. Or at least, trying to—to not feel like he was being ripped in two.

What if he had ridden away too quickly? What if he was making a mistake leaving her?

A young constable met him and took Ranger's bridle.

"You want me to brush him down? Looks as though you've come a far piece."

Because he hadn't stopped since arriving on the train in Cayley yesterday. The almost lynching, locking Frank behind bars, and then learning from Melina that Lenora had left even after he'd asked her to wait for him … a blur of hours.

"Feed and water him, too, please."

Edmond almost lost his footing when he met the ground but managed to stay upright and make his way across the compound to the office. Commissioner Perry had said he'd be in the area for most of the week, so Edmond would give his response in person as he should have in the first place.

"*It was myself I was running from, the person I had become.*" Lenora's voice invaded his thoughts, making his steps falter. What if she had changed? What if she truly was the woman he had come to love?

You love her. Why are you leaving her?

Hadn't she left first? And now she was in the arms of her fiancé and the father of her child. Jealousy burned through him and stole his strength, but he pushed forward.

Two desks took up most of the small office. As he entered, the man behind the closest glanced up. "Yes?"

"Where is Commissioner Perry?"

"In an officers' meeting. Is he expecting you?"

"No, just a message." Edmond snatched a blank paper from the empty desk and a pen. "Can you see that he gets this note?"

"Of course. As soon as he's available."

Edmond scrawled his answer on the paper, not caring for sloppy penmanship. He was too tired to care.

I accept the promotion and posting and await instruction.

Not allowing himself to think further on his choice, he signed his name and folded the paper. Too late to turn back—for him or Lenora Perry.

"Thank you." He passed the note across the desk and pivoted on his heel. He would find something to eat before he collapsed and then start for home. No second-guessing. He'd accept the role God had given him and not let himself wonder what might have been if Lenora had never left.

CHAPTER 34

The wind howled, but from the north, bringing a chill through the walls of the house and suggesting winter might not be far off. Halfway through October, it was only a matter of time before snow spilled across the foothills and over the prairie, but Edmond had too much to do to think about anything but dressing for the cold before he started his rounds.

He opened the top drawer of his bureau and reached for a pair of wool socks. Instead, his fingers snagged the black queen. She belonged on the chess board downstairs, not hidden away, but he still couldn't bring himself to part with her. Beside the chess piece sat the small ruby ring Melina had found after Lenora left. Repayment for all they had done for her, her note read. One day, he might convince Melina to take the ring or pawn it. But, like the queen, he tucked it out of sight for now, allowing it to feed the ache that never quite went away despite the passing of days and weeks.

Edmond's hand tightened around the black queen. He should have tried to convince Lenora to stay. As dark as the moment of truth had been, he saw clearly now. She wasn't the same woman he'd brought home that first day. She'd turned from her errors—she'd sought God.

"It was myself I was running from, the person I had become."

He tucked her words away and returned the queen to her place. What was the sense in dwelling on things he couldn't change? He hurried with his final preparations for the day.

Melina had breakfast waiting. "I'll probably be away again tonight," she said after grace. "Mrs. Walker asked me to look in on

Mrs. Yorst and stay with her if she's started showing signs of labor. With Mr. Yorst out of town, we don't want her to be left alone for very long. I guess she delivered her last baby two hours after the start of the first contraction."

Edmond nodded to assure her he was listening while forking eggs into his mouth, but it was Lenora and her baby pestering his thoughts.

"I don't think I care as much anymore if I marry or not," Melina said between bites. "I have a purpose now, something to give the community. Like you and Auguste."

"I don't think there's much question as to whether or not you'll marry, Mel."

"Why do you say that?"

He grabbed a biscuit for the road and pushed away from the table. "Because there are too many men around here with their eyes set on you." Even Constable Benton, the reinforcement Edmond had been sent, constantly fixed his uniform when Melina was in the same room as him. Though Edmond liked the young man and appreciated his help overseeing the ever-growing population of the Cayley area, he hoped his sister would find happiness with a farmer or rancher or even the livery owner. Mounties didn't make good husbands.

He passed through the parlor, pausing to pull his boots on while admiring the quilt Melina had laid over the back of the rocker. Another baby quilt splashed with a dozen colors of fabric. Only part of the edge remained to be stitched. Everything had settled back into its usual ebb and flow.

Edmond blew out his breath, trying to dislodge the thought. For all he knew, she was already married to that saloon owner from Cheyenne.

Hat tugged low to keep the wind from snatching it, Edmond strode out to saddle Ranger. He headed toward town but with a slight detour. He found George chopping wood and piling it high along the side of the house. Smoke poured out the chimney, a reminder of the wind's bite and the possibility of an early start to winter.

George sank his ax in the log and came over. "Morning, Constable."

Edmond returned the greeting. He never bothered correcting anyone on his rank, so only Constable Benton ever called him Corporal Bryce. "Have you considered my proposition?"

The man gave a long, slow nod. "I have. If you're sure I'm the man you want to go into business with."

"You have an eye for both horses and cattle and time to work with animals that I don't." The man had a good work ethic, too, judging from the progress he'd made on his farm, and now that they'd looked past any suspicions between them, a mutual respect had settled into place.

Besides, even if everything went awry and he lost his savings, he still had at least five years left with the North-West Mounted Police. Enough time to put a little more away. And if they did succeed, he'd have a line of stock already producing by the time he considered retiring from the force.

"We have a deal, then." George extended his hand.

Edmond held his grip. "I already spoke with Mackenzie. We'll pay for the five broodmares now and then bring them over once they've foaled in the spring and are rebred. The cattle, I'll leave up to you. Pick out your bloodlines and breeder, and we'll pick them up when you're ready. Until then, let me know what you need."

Edmond rode away feeling better than he had in a long while. He met Constable Benton at the office, and they discussed who should be checked on and what needed to be done before Edmond left to testify at Frank's trial in Calgary next week.

The thought, like a cold pail of water, doused any anticipation Edmond had enjoyed. He'd tried to help at the Walsh place, but for the most part, the family didn't want him around, and he couldn't blame them. The oldest two boys had taken jobs at the Bar L to make up for their pa's absence—the absence Edmond was responsible for.

"You all right, Corporal?"

Edmond nodded, though he didn't feel it. He had to remind himself that Frank had made his own choices. He knew he was breaking the law, knew there would be consequences if he were caught, but not being able to let go of his grudge against Lawrence Mackenzie had been the start of his downfall. No wonder Christ had spoken so emphatically to His disciples of forgiving your enemy.

Constable Benton was still talking, and Edmond worked to focus. Something about mail already on his desk. He picked up the envelopes, a mix of personal and business. One from Calgary headquarters, the official request of his presence at the Walsh trial as the arresting officer. Another from his mother that he would leave for Melina to open. The last also bore Melina's name, from an L. Perry. Edmond dropped his gaze to the return address, and his heart missed a beat.

Fort Macleod, Alberta.

Lenora?

He couldn't think of another L. Perry, but if she was writing from Fort Macleod, did that mean she'd never left, that she had been so close these past two months? Or had she returned?

"Morning." Matt's chipper voice preceded the door slapping closed, and Edmond folded the letter into his pocket with the one from his mother.

"Good." Edmond startled, facing the other men in the room. He forgot what he was going to say, so he straightened his coat and clapped Matt's shoulder on the way out the door. "You're with me."

He didn't worry whether or not the young man followed. He often trailed Edmond around when he'd finished his chores on the farm. His siblings still called him Edmond's deputy, and he had even begun asking about joining the force when he turned eighteen. Edmond wasn't sure how Mrs. Lawson would get along without him, but didn't discourage the boy.

"Where are we off to?"

A cold blast of wind met them on the street. "Constable Benton is riding out to look in on the settlers up in the foothills—make sure they are set for winter, so we'll make some calls closer to home." Starting with the smaller homesteads and those still recovering from the fire.

He pulled out his notebook and flipped through the pages, seeking the name of one of the newest families to the area. Names sketched in lead jumped from the page as he skimmed down. Jim Greer. George and Cassandra Cornwell with little Heather and Lindon. Lyman McRae. No mention of Lenora Wells or Lenora Perry. As though she'd never existed.

"You okay, Constable Bryce?" Matt waited for him, already mounted.

"Fine." He found the sought-for name and put his notebook away. "I'm fine."

After a busy day, darkness had settled over the farm by the time he rode down the trail toward home, and the first snowflakes dusted him. No lights showed from the house, which meant Melina wasn't home and probably hadn't been for hours. The letter from Lenora burned in his pocket, begging to be opened.

With the house empty and no dinner waiting, Edmond took his time with Ranger, brushing him down and picking his hooves. Still, the letter beckoned.

Inside the house, he left the mail on the table and went in search of something to eat. A can of beans sat on the shelf, and a couple biscuits were left over from breakfast, so he grabbed those and plopped down at the table. Since he was alone, there was no reason to bother with a plate. He ate the beans cold from the can. A warm dinner would have been nicer after riding around the chilly countryside all day, but dirtying a pot didn't seem worth the trouble. Not with two letters staring at him the duration of his meal.

Edmond pushed the empty can away and sagged into his chair. How late would Melina be? Or would she come home at all? More likely, she'd stay at the Yorsts' for the night whether or not the baby came. Should he ride out and check?

With a groan, Edmond extended his hand across the table and

snagged the letter from his mother. He stoked the fire and put the kettle on the stove before tearing the end of the envelope.

A short letter, letting them know all was well, though winter had dropped on them already and probably had no plans of letting up until spring. A note about Auguste, that he was doing well at the academy but was excited to get his first posting in the new year. He had some time off for Christmas and planned to come to the homestead. She hoped to come as well, whether or not Father could get away.

Edmond slipped the letter back in its cocoon and poured hot water into his mug. He hadn't thought to add coffee beans, so he dropped in some of Melina's peppermint tea instead. Lenora had seemed to really like it, and not just because it took the edge off her nausea.

Lenora. He wiped a hand down his face. Until he knew the contents of her letter, he'd not be able to rest. Melina would laugh at him if she were here. She'd question why he would torture himself. He set a finger on the corner of the envelope and drew it across the table. Maybe if he read what Lenora had written, he'd finally be able to let her go and not think about her at every turn.

He carefully slit the envelope, working his finger along the side like a knife. A single paper waited inside.

Dearest Melina,

How I miss you and the farm. Everything about that place.

What about *him?* Did she miss him at all? Nothing was mentioned.

I am sorry I took so long to write as promised. I wanted to settle in first, figure out what I'm doing. The town of Fort Macleod has been good to me. I attend a small church here regularly and work as a laundress near the fort.

Edmond straightened in his chair. She hadn't left. She hadn't gone back with Doyle.

We never lack in business.

So you don't worry, know that I am feeling fine now and am careful not to do anything too strenuous. The matron I work for has been very accommodating, seeing that the other women do most of the lifting. The baby seems to have no complaints, though he is proving to be a rambunctious one.

Instead of the anger he had once felt at the thought of the child and its mother's choices, tenderness was all that remained. And concern. He didn't want her having to work. He wanted her here so she could be taken care of.

Now, another reason for this letter. I finally worked up my courage to write to my parents. I told them everything. Yesterday, I received a letter in return. They have offered me and my child a place to stay. I'm finally going home.

The words knocked the wind from his chest. He leaned his elbows into the table, trying to get a breath. She was leaving. Might be gone even now.

He dropped the letter onto the table and paced the floor. This was good. She was returning to where she belonged, back where she could be cared for by people who loved her and who would love her baby.

But what about me?

He laughed out loud, and it echoed off the walls that surrounded him, that were closing in on him. He was in no position to take a wife and raise a child. Sure, other Mounties did, but he wanted better for his family.

Would he simply not have a family? Would he give up the woman he loved? Or would he give her the best he could? Was it possible to do his duty to both his country and his family without sacrificing one or the other?

He looked to the ceiling, wishing he could see beyond, maybe even to the heavens. "What do you want of me, Lord?"

Silence surrounded him except for the crackling of the fire and Porter's panting at his feet. He took the lamp up the stairs to the loft, where he slid open the top drawer of his bureau. The black queen stared back at him, challenging him to choose his next move with care.

CHAPTER 35

Last night's snow covered the town in a downy blanket. Lenora wouldn't have minded but for the hole in the bottom of her right boot that let in more than just cold air. A good thing she would soon be on her way to a warmer climate. All the money she had put away the past two months would provide for little more than the journey home.

Home.

She had taken to repeating the word since receiving the letter from her parents telling her to come. She tried to imagine what it would be like, how grown her sisters would be, and how good it would feel when surrounded by people she loved ... but somehow, Edmond always commandeered her thoughts. And Melina, another sister she would always cherish. Even if from a distance.

"That's all your luggage?" Pastor Keeler reached for her single bag. He'd been kind and volunteered to deliver her to the train station—or rather, his wife had volunteered him.

"This is all." Not much, but so much more than she had arrived with in the spring. The skirts Melina had made for her, a Bible the pastor's wife had given, and a heart full of hope. A gift from God himself.

The pastor set the bag on the floor of the carriage and offered her an arm. With the growing expanse of her stomach, even the smallest maneuvers were becoming awkward and uncomfortable. Five months along—how much larger would she get in the next four?

The carriage pulled forward, and Lenora watched a troop of

scarlet-clad Mounties ride past. Despite the impossibility of it, she searched for Edmond's face, just as she always did. Once on that train, the chance of seeing him again would vanish with the miles.

"Here we are."

Already? She offered a smile of gratitude as he helped her down and wished her all the best in her travels.

"Thank you," Lenora whispered, her voice useless. She took her bag, ticket already in hand. She'd purchased it three days ago, just after mailing her letter to Melina. Hopefully, she would share it with Edmond so that maybe he would think better of her, knowing she hadn't left with Channing, hearing that she'd given her life back to God.

Though the train would not leave for a half hour yet, Lenora climbed aboard the back passenger car and found a place near the middle. She settled into the seat and bowed her head. *Be with me, Lord, and guide me home.*

As she waited, a song rose from her heart, one she had clung to for so long now. *Rock of Ages, cleft for me, let me hide myself in Thee.* She sang the words in her head, the faintest hum on her lips as she continued on through the second verse. *Could my zeal no respite know, could my tears forever flow, all for sin could not atone; Thou must save, and Thou alone.*

The babe moved within her, and she laid her hand over the simple miracle. Yes, she had sinned, but Christ had saved her, had redeemed her. Purified her. Forgiven her.

If only Edmond could.

Other passengers began filing into the car, finding their seats, their chatter incessant and snatching at her peace.

The child twisted with enough force as to draw a gasp.

Hush, my love, all is well. We're on our way home.

Why then did it feel as though she was headed in the wrong direction?

Edmond tried to wipe the ache from his eyes, but the burn remained, a result of another sleepless night racing across the prairie, this time as the temperatures plummeted below freezing. He hadn't dared wait for the morning, though. Not once his mind was made up.

"Whoa." His leg was dead weight as he swung it over Ranger's back and dropped to the ground. He stomped his feet against the hard-packed earth to move some blood back into his muscles. According to a friend at the fort, three laundries stood within easy walking distance. This was the second he'd visited, the first lending no clues.

A stout woman was on her way out as he reached the door. He held it for her, standing out of the way. "Thank you, Corporal." She looked him up and down. "You know we can't wash the clothes you're still wearing, though they appear to need it badly."

He chuckled, unable to disagree. "I'm looking for someone. Do you work here?"

One of her fair brows rose. "This is my shop. Mine and the husband's. Who are you hunting?"

"A woman. About this tall,"—he held a hand at his shoulder— "with light hair and the prettiest blue eyes. Her name's—"

"Miss Perry?"

"Is she here?"

The woman's mouth pressed into a frown. "She left on today's train. Heading back to her family's place down in Oregon."

The whistle sounded from the station at the other side of town.

"Or, I should say, about to leave."

Edmond sprinted away, tugging Ranger free of the hitching post while swinging onto his back. "Come on, boy."

Weaving through traffic, Edmond raced toward the station. He had to catch Lenora before she left, even if to just say goodbye. Though he wasn't sure a goodbye was possible for him. Not when he yearned to hold her and to have another chance at that last kiss— before he'd spurned her and walked away.

Would she even want to see him? He deserved a good slap in the face.

The train whistle again pierced the air, three small bursts announcing its departure. Steam rolled from the stacks at the front before blending with the already white sky. The rumble of wheels pulled forward down the track.

"Please, Lord, no." He drove Ranger past the station, asking him for everything he could offer. If they didn't catch the train before it gained speed, they'd never catch her.

Hooves struck the loose gravel nestling each railroad tie. Just a little closer. He pulled alongside the caboose and reached for the bar. His fingers brushed it.

"Come on!" He grabbed hold of frozen steel and hoisted his body aboard as Ranger veered left off the track. Edmond shoved through the caboose and into the next car. Luggage was piled high, but a narrow path allowed for a man to slip through the center. Next was a stock car that gave no other option but up the steel ladder that seeped freezing cold through his gloves. The wind caught him with an icy blast as he crawled along the roof, the train trembling as it gained speed beneath him. Two cars later, he dropped low again and into the last of the passenger cars. He slowed his pace, searching faces that turned to him in curiosity and fascination. No sign of Lenora. He pressed on. The next car bore no trace of her either. And neither did the first. He leaned into the door and tried to catch his breath. Where was she if not on this train?

He reversed his course. He must have missed something.

But no, another thorough search revealed the futility of his attempt to find her. His heart crumbled inside his chest as he made his way to the engine to request a full stop of the train. He had a horse to catch or a long walk back to Fort Macleod.

CHAPTER 36

Lenora slipped onto the lone bench, grateful someone had already swept the snow away. She stared after the disappearing train and the Mountie who had raced past only minutes ago. Bag beside her, she clasped her hands on her lap. It couldn't have been him. Edmond was in Cayley, not here, not running down the train she was supposed to have been on. Just because this Mountie rode a horse similar in coloring to Ranger and had about the same build and color of hair as Edmond. It was impossible.

No, most likely, a bandit or some other unsavory character had boarded the train, and one of the local Mounties was chasing down the man.

And yet, despite logic, she remained in place as the crowds dispersed. The next train, the one back to Cayley, was not due until tomorrow afternoon. She looked down at the new ticket in her hand—a detour she couldn't afford.

Minutes ticked away on the large clock hanging under the eaves of the station.

"Do you need a ride, ma'am?"

Lenora smiled at the man who asked but shook her head. "I'm waiting for someone." Not quite the truth, as much as she wished it, but she couldn't find it within herself to move. "Thank you."

He nodded and headed to his wagon, a heavy load under an oiled canvas.

Lenora looked down the tracks. She was being foolish just sitting here. She needed to return to town and secure a place to spend the night. She'd given up the apartment she'd shared with another woman from the laundry, but if need be, she could ask the pastor and his wife if they had a place she could sleep. And tomorrow, she'd be on her way back to Cayley. One last time.

A form appeared on the horizon along the track, dark against the snow. Gradually, it grew closer, and she rose to her feet, leaving her bag behind. The Mountie's horse was returning. Without his rider. She stepped down from the station platform and extended her hand to the animal as it came near. She caught the reins and rubbed the familiar face, her heart picking up pace. "Ranger? What are you doing here?"

She stared down the tracks until her eyes hurt. No sign of Edmond, but he might be long gone. Or he might be hurt somewhere along the tracks. Not that she didn't think him perfectly capable of mounting a moving train. But what if something had gone wrong?

Eyeing the horse, Lenora considered her options—continue to wait, walk Ranger back to the fort and try to explain what she thought happened, or ride out and see for herself. She cringed at the last one. It had been years since she'd ridden on her own.

But what if Edmond was out there somewhere?

"He's fine," she reassured Ranger. "He's a Mountie and knows how to take care of himself."

The horse nudged her with his nose. Maybe he sensed her deeper feelings, that she wanted to be the one to take care of Edmond.

"I'm being foolish, aren't I, boy? He's probably halfway to the next town by now." Comfortable on the train she should have been on. What if she hadn't changed her plans? Would he have found her and asked her to stay? Or did he pursue someone else?

"Come on, boy." She led him back to the platform, climbing the stairs while leading the horse at the edge. Getting on him seemed far less daunting from above. All she had to do was slip her leg over his back.

Ranger shifted, and Lenora grabbed the horn. It wasn't as though she hadn't ridden him before, but now she had the reins. What she didn't have was Edmond's strong arms protectively around her.

"Nice and slow." She jiggled the reins, hoping that would be enough to induce a forward motion.

Ranger gave her a look out of the corner of his eye but took the desired step. He set out along the rails, following the indents his hooves had left in the snow. Lenora's legs hung loose, the stirrups out of reach. She clung to the horn and pulled back on the reins when the horse tracks veered to a sharp left and then circled back. It appeared Edmond had made it onto the train after all.

Lenora sat, starring down the tracks. All that remained of the train was a hint of smoke on the horizon.

Edmond was gone.

Then a spec of red appeared, moving along the track toward her. Gradually, the speck grew into the form of a man, brilliant against the backdrop of white. Her heart leapt.

Edmond.

She nudged Ranger forward, wanting to get down but not trusting she wouldn't fall, closing the distance between them. Edmond watched her approach, eyes squinted against the brightness of the snow-covered terrain. His cheeks were red either from exertion or the cold, and his chin wore yesterday's shadow giving him a haggard look that was all too attractive on him.

"Lenora?"

The emotion conveyed in that one word misted her vision. She brought up the reins to slow Ranger, but Edmond grabbed hold of the bridle before she succeeded.

"Lenora." He wiped his free hand over his eyes. Relief and something she didn't recognize mingled on his face. "I thought I was too late."

"Too late?"

He motioned up the track. "You were supposed to be on that train."

She wanted to throw herself into his arms and tell him she hadn't been able to leave without seeing him again, but she gripped the saddle horn to hold her heart at bay. "You make it sound like a crime that I'm not."

His head gave an almost indiscernible shake, his deep brown gaze never leaving her. "Might have saved me some effort if you'd been more specific about your travel plans in your letter."

"I didn't think it would matter."

Edmond set his hands at her waist and lowered her to the thick gravel. "It does. You do." His palm touched her cheek, and she leaned into its strength. "You matter to me."

"But after …"

His mouth covered hers. Long and slow, he drew her in, encircling her with his arms, bracing her against him. Warm lips caressed hers, speaking to her soul. Forgiveness. Love. And desire.

With her hands trapped against his chest, she hooked a finger around one of the brass buttons adorning his uniform, anything to keep him in place.

"Don't leave," he whispered against her skin. "Don't leave me."

"I couldn't."

"Then forgive me." His mouth smiled against hers. "Please be my wife."

Lenora drew back enough to see his face, to be certain he meant the words, that she wasn't imagining this, but she could hardly see him through tears.

"Tell me I'm not too late. That I haven't lost you." Edmond held tighter. "I shouldn't have left you that day. I should have listened. Not assumed you'd already chosen him."

She tried to shake her head, but he held her too close. "It's my fault. I shouldn't have let you believe me innocent."

"It doesn't matter anymore. None of that does."

"What about the baby?"

Edmond's hand slipped to her curved abdomen, and he leaned back enough to meet her gaze. "He needs a father. I can't guarantee I'll be a good one, but I'll try my best."

"He?"

With a chuckle, Edmond pulled her close again. His breath warmed her neck. "Or she. Hopefully, someday, we'll have a few of each."

Lenora pressed a kiss to his mouth and strong arms encircled her, cocooning her in more than just his warmth and protection. A dream come true.

Edmond dusted off the front of his coat—for the little good it did after the abuse he'd put it through in the past twenty-four hours. Maybe he should have accepted Lenora's suggestion that they take a few hours and dress for the occasion or even wait until they arrived home tomorrow on the afternoon train before marrying. Melina might never forgive him, but he was done waiting. Besides, this marriage was between him, Lenora, and the Lord, not a gawking community. In the end, Lenora hadn't resisted. And so here he stood, in the parlor of a parsonage waiting for his bride.

The door cracked open, and the young parson Lenora had introduced him to twenty minutes earlier walked in, a subtle smile on his face. "They will be along in a minute. I must admit, this was the last thing I expected after dropping Miss Perry off at the train station this morning."

"I might have been here sooner if I'd known where to come." Edmond lowered his gaze to the hat in his hands, guilt sitting heavy in his chest. He shouldn't have waited on her letter. He should have come earlier and tried to find her, even with the chance she had already left.

Soft footsteps led to the door before it opened again. The parson's dark-haired wife, who also appeared to be in the family way, smiled and moved to stand with her husband. Edmond glanced back to the door. Surely, it shouldn't take so long for Lenora to slip out of her winter garb and freshen up enough to join them …

His breath slipped from him as she stepped into the room, dressed in a light shade of pink similar to the gown she had worn to the NWMP ball, but with a simpler cut that hung loosely over her middle. Her hair was pulled up in a loose bun, allowing for several strands to fall loose against her neck. Roses bloomed in her cheeks to match the gown. This was his bride, the woman he was giving his life to.

The blood drained from his face.

"What's wrong?" She stepped near and searched his face.

"In the rush, with everything, I forgot to tell you." Edmond pressed his lips thin, searching for the best way to explain the life that awaited her if she tied herself to him. "I have another five years in the force. Right now, I'm posted in Cayley, but I have little control over how long that will last or what I will be asked to do. But I can't wait five years to be with you."

Lenora released her breath in a gust of what sounded like relief. "I fell in love with a Mountie, Edmond. Five years, or ten, even twenty, won't change how I feel about you or that I want to be with you. No matter what happens." Her smile twinkled in her eyes. "I trust you. And that this, serving as a North-West Mounted Police, is what God wants for you. For us."

Edmond tightened his jaw against a wave of emotion he'd not braced for. He barely had a chance to blink before a droplet of moisture trickled down his cheek. His wrist disposed of the evidence, but Lenora had already seen the effect of her words and her faith in him.

Lord, never let her faith in me be in vain.

To be a good husband. A good father. Only his duty to God could come before his family. And with God's help, he would find a way to keep all his promises. Both those to his country and to the woman gripping his hand.

"Are we ready?" Parson Keeler asked from the front of the room.

"I know I am," Lenora whispered, though only he would hear her.

Edmond cupped her cheek and planted a kiss on her mouth. As simple as kisses came, but he hoped she felt his unspoken gratitude. With her hand gripped in his, they stepped forward with hope and love … into forever.

AUTHOR'S NOTE

Through my writing, I have had the privilege of taking readers back in time to Colonial America, through the American Revolution, along on the Oregon Trail, and even into the heart of the American Civil War. But to finally bring you home with me to Alberta, Canada, has been an incredibly special pleasure. Thank you for joining me on this adventure. Please come visit me on my website, www.angelakcouch.com, where you will find links to connect on social media and my newsletter. Also, if you enjoyed this story or wish to warn others away, please consider leaving a review.

If you enjoyed this book, will you consider sharing the message with others?

Let us know your thoughts. You can let the author know by visiting or sharing a photo of the cover on our social media pages or leaving a review at a retailer's site. All of it helps us get the message out!

Email: info@ironstreammedia.com

   @ironstreammedia

Brookstone Publishing Group, Harambee Press, Iron Stream, Iron Stream Fiction, Iron Stream Kids, and Life Bible Study are imprints of Iron Stream Media, which derives its name from Proverbs 27:17, "As iron sharpens iron, so one person sharpens another." This sharpening describes the process of discipleship, one to another. With this in mind, Iron Stream Media provides a variety of solutions for churches, ministry leaders, and nonprofits ranging om in-depth Bible study curriculum and Christian book publishing to custom publishing and consultative services.

For more information on ISM and its imprints, please visit
IronStreamMedia.com